T0028359

THE EX AGREEMENT

REGINA BROWNELL

www.bloodhoundbooks.com

Print ISBN: 978-1-5040-8879-4

To anyone who has followed me on this journey. For the ones who have been there since the beginning and the ones who have come along the way. I appreciate all of you.

PROLOGUE

JUNE

"You're later than you said you'd be. I tried calling." The slight harshness in my tone was out of pure frustration. I immediately regretted it.

My husband Bryan tossed the blue shirt of his police uniform into the white wicker hamper beside our bedroom door.

I held a sick, sobbing preschooler in my arms. It was our son Hunter's second virus in two months, and my patience had wound down to nothing.

"Do you not understand how demanding my job is?" Bryan ran a hand over the fuzz on his head. The purple under his eyes, and the way his shoulders sagged, told me it was another rough day. It was easy to see, yet I still ignored it.

"I do." I attempted to speak over Hunter's sobs. "But you could at least give me an update. I've been worried that something happened to you."

"God damn it, Charlotte." Bryan threw his hands in the air. "My job is fucking hard. My life is on the line and all you care about is nagging me. I don't get a break. You get to sit home all day and play house, while I'm out there protecting people."

I tried to stop my lip from quivering, but it was hard to control it when we got into a screaming match. Did he mean those words? Was my role in this life, in this marriage, not important? "I get that," I whispered. "My job is hard too, not in the way that yours is. But I don't get a break. I don't get to sleep. No days off."

"It's not the same, Char," he grumbled.

"I'm sorry," I said. "I get worried."

"Believe me, I'd give you an update if I could. But how can I when I'm dealing with a shooting victim? Stop being so selfish."

His words stung. It wasn't the first time we'd fought over his lack of texts. Was I being selfish? Maybe a little. If I could go back in time, I'd yell at myself for arguing over it.

"Fine. I'm being selfish. But you can take less hours. I do the bills. I've seen the bank account. We can handle—"

"I don't want to just handle it! I want to provide the best life for you and Hunter. When my mom took a few years off to care for my sisters and I, my dad worked his ass off every day and Mom never complained."

I stopped mid-stride and gawked at him. He didn't look my way. Instead, he continued to take off his clothes.

"Newsflash, Bryan, I'm not your mother." I was running on fumes. Hunter had been waking every twenty minutes with the croup cough and nothing soothed him. During the day he slept on me and at night I laid him on the wedge. But thirty minutes had been the most he'd slept without choking on the mucus in his throat.

"I fucking know you're not. I'm just saying that you can handle it on your own."

My gaze flashed to his, and regret swelled heavy in his eyes.

"I thought we were in this together?" My voice broke.

He crossed the room, determination on his features. Bryan wasn't a big guy but had lots of muscle from his workouts and running. He had to stay in shape for his job. He took wide strides towards me, closing the space between us in seconds.

I let my gaze drift to the floor. I hated fighting with him.

"Char, we are in this together." He touched my hand, but it was brief. "And this is why you have to understand that I'm doing this for us. I'm doing it to provide a better life. To allow us to have money to do things outside this house."

"You always use the same excuse. I already have an amazing life. What would make it better is having you here with us. I want you to work. I'm not asking you to quit. But maybe take on less hours. I also want to go out and do things outside this house, but when was the last time we did that, huh?"

He crossed his arms at his chest. "We did, before Christmas."

"It's June. The last event we did together as a family was our short trip to Hershey Park. You've missed everything else. And what about us?"

"What about us?" he echoed. The muscles in his arm tensed as he tightened his fists.

"When was the last time we made love? Or had crazy wild sex? Went on a date?"

"Making money is the most important thing right now. It's not all about sex." His lips pulled into a straight line.

"I never said it was just about the sex!" I stomped my foot like a child. The impact jostled Hunter in my arms. "I'm saying— You know what? Forget it."

I didn't know where we'd gone wrong or how it had ended up getting this bad. If I could go back and tell the past me to let it go, I would have.

Hunter's silence was short lived as a cough brought him to the verge of hysterics, and he cried once more.

Bryan held out his arms. "Give him to me." He held his son, skin to skin, while rocking him.

My lips trembled as my husband took charge. My brain raged with stupid thoughts. One of them being that maybe I wasn't cut out to be a mother. I could help other people's children, but not my own. Hunter's crying stopped almost immediately and within minutes he settled him down in our bed.

"We need you, Bryan." My voice was softer. "Not only to make money, but to be here and present."

"I am here! I'm here right now, right?"

I hug myself to keep grounded. "It feels like we are roommates and not spouses."

"Well, if that's the way you feel, then maybe it's all we are now."

A knot the size of a golf ball formed in my throat. It hurt to swallow. My mind was in a panic, and I wish I could have predicted what was going to happen next. It was stupid to egg him on, but exhaustion had worn us down into this.

"I'm going to go to Connor's tonight. I have to be up in a few hours for my next shift. I signed up for over-time. I need some sleep." Bryan's voice was softer, but the annoyance was clear as day.

"You can sleep in our bed, Bryan."

"I think I'm going to stay there for a while." He stepped away from me and crossed the room to the closet. Bryan grabbed his suitcase and rolled it over to the dresser. My chest tightened and pain shot through my heart. I had words I needed to say, but the only thing out of my mouth was a squeak.

Bryan packed half his drawer, then stood. "We both need to cool off, but Char, I don't think this is working anymore."

I still had no words. They were on the tip of my tongue, and I willed them to come out, to beg him to stay, but I couldn't. He got dressed in casual clothes and pulled some work clothes from the closet. I watched in silence as he wheeled the suitcase to the door.

"Bye, Char," he whispered.

My eyes stung, but no tears fell. Nausea swelled in the pit of my stomach, but nothing reached the surface. The door closed and I waited.

The house shook from him shutting the front door. His car started up. I kept thinking it was a dream, praying it was a nightmare I'd wake from.

I heard the gear shift, and the sound of him backing out of the driveway, but nothing, not even the noise made me move.

CHAPTER 1

DECEMBER

Thwack!

"Shit," I say, rubbing my head.

I'm brought back from my own painful thoughts by a blow to the head from a yellow plastic ball. My son Hunter giggles while my brother encourages the behavior with a high five. Shit, again. I said it out loud in front of him. I wait for him to repeat it, but he's too busy to notice.

"It wasn't me." My brother Logan points directly at Hunter. You'd think he was a child himself, but no, he's thirty-one, getting married later next year. Still a child at heart, though. It's what I love about him.

"Not me. Not me. Not me." Hunter picks the ball up and checks it out.

"Real cool, Logan. Blame the four-year-old."

He grins sheepishly, flashing his warm brown eyes in my direction and then turns to his soon-to-be wife, my best friend, Ellie. He doesn't just look at her though. Those eyes light up and twinkle at the sight of her even in yoga pants and her soft brown hair tied up loosely in a bun with static making the ends stick up.

He truly loves her. I hate the pang of sorrow in my chest as I watch their interaction.

Ellie lifts a purple ball from the spiderman blow-up ball pit they bought for Hunter and throws it at Logan. He's so busy laughing at his childish behavior that he doesn't even notice until it hits him.

Rubbing at the spot he glares at Ellie, not in an evil way, more of a look that says, *Later you'll pay for this in bed.*

I roll my eyes, not because I'm trying to be a bitch, but my best friend and brother and their happy banter are killing me. I had everything they did and more. Bryan and I were... God, we were something special. He brought happiness back into my life after my dad passed. Up until six months ago things were perfect, but all the little things from over the last few years led to one huge argument that ended everything. Now on the verge of divorce I'm holding on to a little bitterness in my heart.

My eyes land on the overturned photos beside the chair where my soon-to-be ex-husband used to sit. I don't have it in me to remove the photos of our wedding, and of our life yet, but even after six months, I still don't have the courage to look at them.

"Are you sure it's okay that you watch him today? I know it's last-minute and you both had to run from work—"

"Charlotte." Ellie scoots herself closer on the couch and rests her hand over mine. There's not an ounce of pity in her beautiful brown eyes. "Of course, we'll watch Hunter for you. It's not a problem."

I've got an interview today. When Hunter was born, Bryan and I thought it would be best for me to stay home. The cost of daycare would eat up one of our paychecks, and it wasn't worth it. I went from teaching full-time to being a stay-at-home mom. While I'd love to continue this beautiful journey, I can't allow Bryan's paycheck to keep me home if we aren't together. Out of the kindness of his heart he offered it to me until our son was in school full-time. Hunter already goes four hours a day to a local school free of cost from early intervention, and I've stayed home in case of an emergency, but I think it's time.

Standing, I brush off my black dress pants and straighten them so the bell at the bottom covers my dress shoes. Logan watches me carefully, waiting for me to break. His big brother protective side has been more extra lately, and while I appreciate it, it makes me feel worse.

"BAM! Unca Logo," Hunter shouts as he releases another ball, this time knocking Logan in the head.

He's got quite the aim. It narrowly misses Logan's eye. For a second the room grows silent, minus the possessed talking bear from the small wooden toy chest in the corner. We all break out in bubbling laughter. I cross my legs and attempt not to pee. Hunter keeps a straight face the whole time, which makes the whole thing ten times funnier.

"On that note..." I wipe the tears of laughter from my eyes. My stomach hurts from laughing. "I'll let Uncle Logan take over. But first I think I should pee."

Ellie giggles. "See, now that is why having kids scares me. I don't want it to wreck my bladder. I already have to pee every two minutes."

"Oh, you mean having mini-Logans around doesn't scare you more?" I ask her. My heart suddenly feels lighter. Logan and Ellie have been there for me since the night I called a little past one in the morning, when Bryan left after our heated argument. Ellie and Logan drove over here in the middle of the night to comfort me.

"Well, that is probably number one on the list."

"Hey. My kids—" Logan pauses. "Our kids," he corrects and gives Ellie a loving smile, "will be awesome. In fact, Logan junior will bring a girl ice cream from all the way across town one day out of the kindness of his heart. Because he secretly loves her."

He once again stares at Ellie. Logan was the one who trekked all the way across town one summer when I was away at camp, because Ellie was sad and missed me. He brought her ice cream, but before he could get there it melted. She still fell head over heels for him, but hid it from me, because of one ridiculous rule we made as kids.

"Number one, we are not naming a child Logan junior. Sorry, not sorry," Ellie says.

"I agree. I mean it's weird for the parents and in bed when…"

"Okay, point taken." Logan laughs. "Donald…"

"Donald is a duck." Ellie crosses her arms at her chest. "And why are we naming our kids already? We still have a year until our wedding. Let's work on one thing at a time, shall we?"

"Right, babe," he says.

Ellie cringes, she hates when he calls her baby or babe, but he does it to annoy her. All in good fun though.

"Well, I really need to go, or I'll be late. They were kind enough to give me a four-thirty interview after school hours so I could find a sitter." I would have asked my mom, but she's off gallivanting on her honeymoon. She recently eloped with her boyfriend, Tommy, and the two of them went off to Jamaica for some fun. I'm grateful Ellie and Logan were available. I need to get my life back together. It's been a struggle, but I'm stronger than I give myself credit for.

"Go. But don't forget to pee."

"Thanks for the reminder, El." I cross the room and pat Logan on the head. "Behave yourself." He stares up at me and winks. I turn to Ellie. "I'm sorry you have to babysit both of them."

She bats her hand. "Hunter is easy, Logan on the other hand… He might need to be punished when we get home."

"La, la, la." I hold my hands to my ears. "If he wasn't my sibling, I'd be okay hearing you talk about your sex life, but he is so…"

Ellie chuckles. "Good luck. You're gonna kill it!"

"Thanks." I lean down and scoop Hunter up into my arms. He

squirms and squiggles struggling to be released. I let him down and he goes back to playing with the balls. He stares at the yellow one intently, rolling his hand to get a view of the whole thing.

Being a special education teacher, I can't help but over-analyze everything he does. He has decent vocabulary and has gotten there through the help of early intervention, but we finally have an appointment for autism testing. I'm ninety-nine percent sure he'll receive a diagnosis. Bryan insisted we wait until he was older in fear of a misdiagnosis—in fact, it was one of our main fights for a while—but I knew. My job prior to being a mom was working with children on the spectrum, and my son clearly is autistic. All I want is for him to get the proper education for his needs. I've seen how proper schooling does wonders for children.

I give one last wave before heading to the bathroom and leaving. The school I'm interviewing at is one of several local elementary schools. It's for a maternity cover position in one of their special education classrooms.

My phone buzzes on the passenger seat. As I stop at a red light, I peer over at it. A picture of Bryan and me from our Hawaii honeymoon flickers on the screen, catching me off guard. The air in my lungs deflates, like it does every time he calls. I didn't tell him about the interview, and I probably won't until I know for sure.

Instead of answering the call, I allow it to ring until it eventually goes to voicemail. Someone honks at me from behind. The light has changed, and the two cars in front of me have already gone. I get myself together and drive the rest of the way to school without incident.

Only when the phone chimes notifying me of a voicemail does my heart ache again. I won't let it stop me from nailing this interview. I've got this, I can live life without him. I've done it before, and I can do it again. The only difference is back then, I didn't know he existed, and now I do.

CHAPTER 2

"She's over here!" My co-worker Anne called over as the cop car pulled up to the school.

The day I slipped on ice outside the first school I worked at was embarrassing, but it was also the day I met Bryan. It was out front and happened during drop-off. Parents saw it, and the principal too. I was student teaching and on the verge of graduating college. I hit my head hard enough that the first aider assumed it was concussion.

Bryan nearly slipped on the same ice I had as he exited the police car and briskly walked over. He caught himself unlike me, and I giggled.

"Don't need you going down too, officer," I said.

Bryan's grin was what had me crushing from the second he arrived. He kneeled in front of me. His sparkling blue eyes caught me off guard, and at first, I thought I was woozy from the fall; but no, they really were that blue, and right then and there I was smitten.

"I'm okay, ma'am, but what about you?"

"Ma'am." I giggled again. "People call my mom ma'am. You can call me Charlotte."

His cheeks dimpled, and I couldn't stop staring.

"Charlotte." His velvety voice struck me, and a thousand tiny butterflies danced in my stomach.

Bryan was caught up in me as much as I was with him. He didn't even hear the paramedics behind him as they took over. He stayed by my side while they lifted me onto the stretcher, and I swore I heard him ask which hospital, but at the time, I thought it was the concussion making me hear things.

I was admitted for overnight observation, and the following day a few hours before my release, he showed up with flowers and hot chocolate. I fell for him right then.

"Did you get permission to bring me something from the outside?"

His laughter was a low rumble coming from deep in his chest. "Ma'am—Charlotte, I have some pull around here." The light in his eyes shone so bright.

"What's this?" I asked, as I eyed the cup from a local coffee shop.

"You're not allergic to chocolate or peppermint, are you?"

"No."

"Good. Try it. It's like Christmas in a cup." He placed the cup on the tray attached to the bed and rested the flowers beside it.

"That line is from a movie…" The tug on my lips was strong.

He watched me closely as I put my hand around the steaming cup. "Try it."

"Okay, fine!" I put the hot chocolate to my lips and couldn't help the tingling in my lower abdomen at his intense gaze. A moan louder than I intended left my mouth, and his devious grin did me in. I had to know him. The man who came to my rescue.

Before he left, he put his number in my phone and a week later we went on our first date. I fell for him fast. Sometimes I wonder if it was maybe a little too fast and we were blinded by lust.

❄

Logan and Ellie have worn Hunter out. I made us both pasta and butter. It's now become a staple in the house since I haven't felt much like cooking. It hasn't done any good to my midsection. We eat together, which mostly consists of him throwing half of his portion on the floor. I'm tempted to join him but hold back.

The interview went well. They have a few other candidates they are considering. Part of me hopes they never call. The other part is excited to get out there again and be with other adults. Some of the issues between me and Bryan stemmed from the loss of who I was before I became a mom.

He'd come home from a day out with other adults, and I was covered in spit-up and stunk from my showerless day. He'd shower, sit in his chair, and pass out.

Then there were the nights he'd work, and I'd be alone with a crying baby, then need to be up the next day to tend to household chores and the baby.

Bryan's job isn't easy, and I respect that. I understand he needs his time to chill on the couch and unwind from a hard day. Being a police officer comes with risks, but we managed before. Only once there was a little life in the picture and he took on extra hours, there wasn't room for romance anymore.

The woman who was full of life became depressed and isolated. She looked for love and affection but with a tired husband she wasn't getting any of it. It wore her down—wore me down.

I wipe the tears in my eyes. My gaze wanders to the baby monitor as I soak myself in a nice steaming hot bubble bath. Lavender fills the room, my favorite scent. It's supposed to calm me, but tonight it's only partially working.

After dinner, Hunter threw a tantrum and with his lack of communication skills, I couldn't figure out what he needed, but assumed it was something sensory by his behavior. I gave him a quick bath, we read our nighttime books in the rocker in his room, and minutes later he passed out.

While I had time, I drew this bath, and I've been here ever since. The scalding water is now down to a mild temperature. I'm sure my toes are wrinkling, but I don't care. I've left my phone in the other room and opted for a book. A spicy one. One where I can dive into the fakeness of a fictional romance and not feel any sadness for my situation. In fact, no high lord would ever consider me for their mate, so it doesn't feel as heartbreaking.

With one hand on the book, and the other under the water I release the tension of the day, while chapter fifty-five— my favorite part—sits open on the bath tray. I read it over and let my imagination fly wild.

It took me a while to get back into the swing of things, to be able to read books with spice, but now, even with a broken heart, I enjoy some of my favorites while indulging in some self-care.

The fictional world fades away and I slip into the past. My imagination allows me to remember Bryan and his hands being the ones to make me flow over the edge. I don't know why I'm still thinking about him. It hurts but feels so good at the same damn time.

Satisfied and dried off, I lie in my bed in my favorite comfortable pink sweats and matching sweatshirt. Really, it's a blast from the past outfit, but it still fits and I'm not complaining. Not like I have anyone to impress.

I scroll through my phone, trying to distract myself on social media, but my gaze keeps flickering towards the voicemail notification. Swiping down I click on it. My heart has a lot to say and beats wildly in my chest.

"Please enter your password. Then press pound."

With trembling hands, I type in the password, which is our wedding date. The automated voice goes through the date, the time, and the phone number, before Bryan's smooth voice takes over. "Hey, Char."

I suck in a breath and hold it.

"I'm meeting with a lawyer on Monday. Um—just to see what we have to do to move forward with our plan. I'll let you know how it goes." There's a long pause, and as I press the phone closer to my ear, I can hear him taking several breaths. "I'll swing by afterwards to pick up Hunter. Probably around two or three. I'll bring him back on Wednesday night when I go in for the night shift. Umm… yeah. Talk to you then. Bye."

"To save this message…"

I let the automated voice go on and on. It repeats but I'm too caught up in his voicemail to move. I don't know why, but I expected to hear his usual *Love you, bye.* Every time I get a voicemail or every time, we hang up the phone or say goodbye, I wait for the words, but they never come.

I grant myself permission to have a good cry. I'm allowed. Then turn off the lights and hide under the covers until sleep eventually finds me.

CHAPTER 3

Bryan called around noon and he's coming in ten minutes to pick up Hunter. I spent the weekend cleaning the house and playing with my son.

Ellie had to work at the mall, so we didn't have time to hang out. She has a part-time position at a clothing store, and on the weekdays, she spends her days at a local radio station either filling in on-air or working at sales. She called me and texted, so we spoke, but I was mostly on my own.

The doorbell echoes through the house. I've already told Bryan numerous times he can walk in. It is still technically his house too. The door creaks open.

Hunter sits at the kitchen table. Both him and my table are covered in vanilla yogurt with a ton of blueberries smushed into the surface. From his hands to his beautiful blonde locks, there is white goop everywhere. I gasp. This kid loves sensory-seeking activities. If he wanted a sensory box, I would have made one.

"Oh, Hunter! Now I have to bathe you." I rush to him and try to clean up what I can. There's only a small distance between the entrance at the front of the house and the kitchen. When Bryan's footsteps stop, I turn as a wad of yogurt hits me in the eye. My shoulders fall and I want to be mad, mostly at Logan for teaching the little man it's okay to throw things, but when my non-yogurt filled eye meets Bryan's piercing blue eyes all the anger fades as he snickers at the scene before him.

My hair is probably a train wreck, and I've realized the V-neck of my white T-shirt is now stained with blueberries. It hangs so low he catches a glimpse of my sagging breasts. Clearing his throat, he studies my face.

"Oh, so you save all the food fights for when Daddy's gone. Huh?" There's a playful gleam in his eye.

Lifting a non-squished blueberry I chuck it at him, hitting him on the head.

"Oh, so we are now, are we? Don't forget I'm the champion food fighter." He steps forward and grabs the only other intact blueberry and fights back, completely missing me. My heart swells, but my brain tells it to calm down. Things are over between us, and this is digging up too much pain.

"Champion, huh? We're not even two feet apart and you can't even hit me with a blueberry." My lips turn upward.

There's this strange flicker of hope in Bryan's eyes. They widen like he's waiting for everything to be normal again. When I slink back realizing I can't do this, his shoulders fall and his lids draw closed with heaviness.

He throws me another grin, but it falls flat. "Hey, Hunter," he says, bending down. "Did you go to school today?"

"Daddy, boo-berry is messy. Like?" Hunter leans his head to the left, and fidgets with his hands.

"Yes. You made quite a mess for Mommy. Daddy loves blueberries."

For a few seconds I watch him talk to Hunter. As usual, asking him a question and getting him to focus on the answer is hard, but it doesn't stop him from lighting up at the sight of his dad.

I can't help my wandering eyes. I'm drawn to Bryan like always. Since we've been married Bryan has grown his hair out significantly. Today there are dark blonde pieces sticking up in all different directions. I hate the way my heart tears into two as he leans down and tickles Hunter. His body is so close that his cedarwood shampoo infiltrates my nose making it itch.

"I'm sorry. I'll go run him a bath. I know you need to get going."

"Oh, no. I've got time. I'll give him one. No problem. Come on, buddy."

He lifts Hunter from his seat, and places him on the floor. They race off to the bathroom together, leaving me to clean up the mess and the broken pieces of my heart.

I am wiping up the spilled yogurt when my phone goes off. The name of the school where I interviewed pops up on my screen. Taking a loud deep breath, I pick it up. "Hello?"

"Hello, Mrs. Holmes?" A man asks.

"This is she."

I attempt to keep my voice steady. I'm full of nerves from the call, and then hearing him call me Mrs. Holmes breaks me some more.

"Hi. I'm calling because I regret to inform you that we have gone with another candidate. You were more than qualified for the job, but we decided to hire from within instead. But please, don't hesitate to apply for future openings."

I grab hold of the table. "Oh. Okay. Thank you for your time." Blinking back the tears I hang up and hold the phone to my chest, closing my eyes to center myself. I can't let Bryan know, and I can't let him see the disappointment on my face. I smell the flowers and blow out the candles five times, like I used to tell my students, and then get back to cleaning.

I type a quick text to Ellie.

Me: I didn't get the job.

Before I even put my phone down, she already sent me a reply.

> Ellie: We have an opening in the women's department at the store. I can get you an interview. It's part-time and a few days a week. Maybe my mom or yours can watch Hunter or get him from school? It's not teaching, but it's something.

Something. I need something before I lose my mind. I sent her a quick message back telling her to set it up, then place my phone on the counter.

I wipe away the remaining tears and square my shoulders. I'm taking my life back, one step at a time. Whether it's with Bryan or not, living like this is not healthy.

By the time Bryan is done bathing Hunter, I've already straightened up the kitchen, and have calmed down.

"Well, he's all clean now. Where is his overnight bag?"

"Oh. It's by the door on the porch. Everything is packed and ready to go."

"Great. Um, so I spoke to the lawyer today and he said we can draw up the papers ASAP. I told him I'd call him back, but if you're good, I'd like to start the process." Bryan's face is stone cold, lips pulled into a straight line. I can't read him like I was always able to.

I bite down on my bottom lip and nod. "Yeah." It comes out as a squeak. "Yeah. Start the process."

"Alright then." He turns to leave, Hunter tucked in his arms with his head on his shoulder. Hunter's eyes are heavy with sleep. "Say bye to Mommy."

Hunter stares down at the pop-it toy in his hand, a blank expression on his tired face. I make my way over and run a hand through his blonde hair and press a kiss on his forehead. When I lift my chin, I come face to face with Bryan. I silently gasp at the intense gaze in his eyes. I should look away, but I can't.

"Oh—uh will you be able to go to his appointment? It's Thursday. I think it's important for you to be there."

Hunter's testing is this week. We'll find out if he falls on the spectrum or not. Bryan has known about the date for a while, but with everything going on I wanted to make sure he remembered.

"This Thursday?"

"Yeah. At three."

"I think I can. I get out a bit before it, so I might be late."

"That's okay. I just—" I pause and stare down at my fingers, flicking something out from under my nail. "I think it's important and I'd really like it if you could support... I—" My eyes flutter. "I just think you should be there."

We stand close, but I swear his body moves closer. I can feel the heat as he leans in, his woodsy sweet scent mixed with the lavender of Hunter's shampoo.

"I'll do my best," he whispers, attention drifting between my eyes and my lips.

"Okay. Perfect."

He grimaces as if he's in pain. His tense body is almost touching mine. I fight the urge to reach out. His mouth twitches like there's more he wants to say. I've learned a lot about his facial expressions over the years. Sometimes I think I know him better than I do myself. I hate how he has more to say but can't find the words. He'd do this a lot when we'd get into an argument.

"Bye, Char." He turns away. His light tone catches me off guard. My brain understands he has to leave, but my heart wants him to hang on.

"Bye."

The tension and weakness in my response stops him in his tracks. He faces me and licks his lips. His mouth opens but again the words fail him. He then walks away with our son in his arms.

When the door shuts, I fight the tears and immediately call Ellie. I don't sob or ugly cry, only ask her to put on our favorite show so we can watch it together while talking on the phone. It's the only thing that keeps me from breaking.

CHAPTER 4

My stomach has been in knots all day. Not because this is going to be a bad thing, but because I'm nervous Bryan won't show up. This diagnosis could mean more services and better opportunities for our son. While he's a smart boy and progressing well in his speech and other therapies, there's still more we can do to help him, especially once he gets into elementary school.

Hunter and I are in the waiting area in a beautiful newly renovated building. The wooden floors shine, and the large windows allow plenty of light to make it bright and welcoming.

Hunter is engaged in the wheels on a dump truck, while I pace back and forth in front of the window. "Where are you, Bryan?" I mutter.

He said he'd be late, but the appointment itself should have started thirty minutes ago. I expected a long wait, but to be stuck without someone to calm my nerves is terrifying. I didn't want to drag Ellie and Logan along, plus Logan had an awards thing after school for his soccer team.

"Hunter Holmes." A woman in green scrubs stands beside the large reception desk, a clipboard in her hand.

"Hunter, come on, buddy."

He doesn't respond, so I go to grab him. When I attempt to take away the toy, he squeals.

"He can bring the toy in."

I give her a polite nod, and kneel in front of him.

"Hunter, baby, the nice nurse said you can bring the truck."

His arms flap as a smile grows across his face. He happily picks the toy up and follows me. We're escorted back to get his weight, height, and blood pressure, then into a room where I spend the next fifteen minutes checking my phone.

After another fifteen the doctor finally shows up, apologizing. She introduces herself as Doctor Nicole Hanson. She's nice and so good with Hunter. While he doesn't give her any eye contact, he still cooperates. The toys she brings out spark some interest, but when she starts asking questions, he gets a little fidgety.

"Okay, Hunter. Here are four blocks." She pushes over four different colored cubes. "And I've got four too." She watches him while she speaks. "I want you to build this train."

Hunter is somewhat focused on what she is doing, but his attention flutters elsewhere too.

"Have two hands," he says to her.

"Yes, you have two hands. Do you think you can use them to build the train with me?"

"Five fingers. Five fingers."

"Does he do this often?" she asks.

"Yeah. The teachers use a lot of visual prompts to keep him on track."

She nods. The evaluation continues and Hunter has a hard time responding to what she says, and he does talk and say little things, but it's mostly gibberish.

"Hey, Hunter, what is something you use to drink water?"

He answers her, but they aren't real answers at first. After a few tries, he tells her it's a cup. When she finishes all the proper steps, she goes through and calculates what she's learned from him.

I can't keep my eyes off the way her hands move between each section of her paper, as she checks things off, adds them up. My heart races in my chest. I want this for him, I want him to thrive, and while I could do it on my own, I know kids sometimes act and behave differently when they learn from others.

"Well, Mrs. Holmes, I'm sure you're aware with your experience that your son is on the spectrum. I'm going to forward the results to his school so they can prepare it for his IEP meeting. Will you be having one soon?"

Every year since he started his services we meet with the school to determine placement for the following year. He has been going part-time since he was two, and with my experience of sitting in on other meetings during my career, I know what I'm in for.

"Yes. I think April or May for kindergarten."

"Perfect."

When the meeting is over, she stands, shakes my hand, and says goodbye to Hunter. We have everything we need, but for some reason I want to cry. Maybe it's because we did it, but maybe it's because Bryan still hasn't shown up.

In the car, I dial Ellie's number through the car stereo. It's after five now, but the darkness makes it feel much later.

"Hello?" Her voice echoes.

"Ann El, Ann El," Hunter says.

"Hi, Buddy. Hey, Char, how'd it go?"

"We got the diagnosis and I'm really happy we can move forward. Bryan didn't show."

"What? I thought you said—"

"He said he was going to be late. He didn't say he wouldn't show. I want to be pissed at him. I know it's wrong of me." I breathe in a sharp inhale. "Do you think something is wrong? Like maybe something happened to him?"

The thought, even though we are separated, makes my stomach churn. There has never been a day since I've met him that I don't worry about his safety. No matter how angry I was at him, my deepest fears always made me uneasy.

"I'm sure he's okay. Ugh. I'm sorry, Char. Do you want me to come over? We can watch some trash TV when Hunter goes to bed."

I chuckle. "What, like reruns of *Teen Mom*?" I ask.

"Well, duh."

"I think I'm going to go home and relax. Thanks for the offer though. It's been a fucking week," I say.

"It sure has." She releases a long-winded breath. "Oh, I almost forgot. Two things. I got you the interview for Monday morning. Is that okay?"

"Yeah. I think. I have to find someone to drop Hunter off at school, but it's not a problem. Thank you, El."

"Of course. Also, the DJ called today, and we're going to meet with him the first week in January to discuss the wedding. It's real."

I squeal for her. I'm so excited for her and Logan's wedding. My best friend and brother are perfect for each other. "Ah. Did you get the guy you wanted?"

Logan and Ellie have taken their time with getting married. They got engaged when I was pregnant with Hunter. They didn't want to rush it and I agreed. Logan's heart was in the right place in regard to Ellie, but when they first started their secret relationship Logan was not prepared for anything more. He had a lot of growing up to do.

He fled right after Dad passed away and then barely talked to us for years. I think being with Ellie, getting his own house, and finding a stable place to call home helped. It figures their wedding is coming at a time when my marriage is ending.

"We did," she squeals. "Logan talked to his friend from work and he hooked us up."

"Wow, El. That's great news."

"I'm so nervous," she says. "I mean for this whole thing. Am I really doing this? Am I marrying Logan Fields?"

I chuckle. "Yes, you are. And now you'll be officially family."

Her laughter carries through the car, calming me. Ellie is my best friend in the whole world, and no one will ever come as close to being my sister as she is. Sure, she snuck around behind my back for two weeks with my brother, but in all honesty, I was happy for her, and she helped my brother overcome a lot.

I turn the corner, under the motion light in my driveway is Bryan's Kia. My heart skips several beats and I gasp.

"Char, are you okay?"

My mouth goes dry, and my lips seal shut. *He's here. Why is he here when he should have been there with us?* I grip the steering wheel with every ounce of energy I can. "Holy shit." The words roll from my mouth. I cringe and check on Hunter in the rearview. He doesn't notice. "Yeah. I uh— Bryan is here."

"Do you need backup?" she asks.

I let go of a light laugh. "No. I'll be okay. I'll call you later. Love you."

"Love you more." There's a click and then silence fills the car.

Hunter is passed out cold. He endured a lot in the almost two hours we spent at the evaluation.

As I get closer Bryan's outline becomes clearer. He's leaning against the passenger side of his car. I pull into the driveway beside him, and he pushes himself off the car. There's a small part of me relieved that he's okay, but then the other part wants me to tear him a new one. This was our main problem when we were married. I'd pace the floors at three in the morning and pray he wasn't hurt or worse off—dead.

Stepping out of the car I try to keep my composure. "Where were you?" I ask, evenly.

"I—" His eyes shimmer and part of me wants to reach out and

27

apologize for being so short with him, but the other, the one still hanging on by a thread won't have it.

"There was a situation. I almost got—" He pauses. There's plenty more he has to say, but he's holding back. Like always.

"There will always be a situation, Bryan. Always. Why do you never tell me what goes on? Not knowing drives me crazy."

"I don't bring my work home with me, you know that. I said from the beginning: what happens on the job... The things I see would only give you nightmares."

"Fine." I cross my arms. "But today was important." I take a breath and shake my head. "I'm sorry. I guess I expected some support from you today. I know this isn't ideal, but our son..."

"Is the most amazing person on this planet," he finishes for me.

I nod. A knot forms in my throat, preventing me from speaking further.

"I'm sorry. I was stuck at work an hour longer than I had to be, and then things g-got... g-got..." He shakes his head to try and mask the stutter. "They got bad. I told you I'm not explaining it."

I hug myself tighter. My gaze falls to the space between us. I want to look him in the eye, needing the comfort of his gaze, but know these are no longer eyes I can stare at. They will soon be someone else's. So instead, I stare at the old oil stain on the concrete driveway.

"So, what did she say?"

"He's autistic." Saying it, the realness of it hits me, and the tears start. "But he's Hunter and he's going to take the world by storm."

"I know he will." Bryan swallows hard, and I find myself staring at his Adam's apple, but still not at his face. "Our son will be a spectacular adult, because he's got you as his mom."

My chest aches for him, for our life together, but it's not what Bryan wants. He steps forward, reaching out, but halfway through the motion he decides not to go through with it, crumbling whatever else is left of my heart.

"I should get him inside. We've had a long day."

"Char, can we please talk about this?" There's a strain in his pleading voice that catches me off guard, and almost makes me cave.

"Talk about what, Bryan? There's nothing to discuss. You missed the evaluation and there's nothing we can do to fix it and talking will only lead to fighting—"

"Because you make it a fight," he spits back.

"Because I'm angry. You could have just—"

"NO, CHARLOTTE! That's the thing." He's so loud it feels like he stepped closer, but he hasn't. The sound makes me jump and my heart beats erratically. "I couldn't have just texted you. I can't always text you. I wish you'd understand."

"I do, but I told you two months ago about this appointment and how important it was to me, to us, as a family." My throat hurts from straining, and I don't want to argue anymore.

"I'm sorry there was nothing I could do. My hands were tied. You'll never get it. I tried, Charlotte. I really did. Tell Hunter, Daddy said goodnight." He spins on his heels and starts for the driver's side of his car.

My body is aching for me to reach out, to stop him, but I'm planted into place. I can't watch him drive away again, can't listen to it. I drown it out by pulling Hunter from his seat and trying my best to ignore the hurt inside my chest. It's hard, but I do it. I do it because I have to. It's just Hunter and me now. The family I pictured is a faded memory.

I'm tempted to call Ellie, but instead I spend my evening eating pasta again. This time mac and cheese. I bask in the one thing that still brings me joy, my son. My Hunter. My everything.

CHAPTER 5

I pour myself a glass of wine. Sure, it's only four in the afternoon, but so far today I've already cleaned the bathroom, kitchen, and the living room. While Hunter was in school, I purged some unused toys and outgrown clothes to donate. I think I deserve a glass.

My phone chimes as I throw myself onto the couch beside my sleepy child. He's a quiet sleeper unlike his dad, but as I stare at him and his perfect little round face, he's the spitting image of Bryan.

Ellie: What are your plans for tonight?

I send her a picture of my legs sporting my favorite pink sweatpants, with my feet propped up on the coffee table, and the wine in my hands. A few seconds later the chat bubbles appear. It takes a while for her to type up whatever she's typing.

Ellie: Well, put some real pants on, because Lily got us tickets to something really cool.

Lily is Ellie's friend from Sheer Threads, the store she works at in the mall. After I got back from my honeymoon, we started including her on a lot of our outings. I loved getting to know Lily, and now she and I are friends too.

> Me: Have you forgotten I have a child?

I don't have the freedom like she and Lily do. Lily's been dating a guy named Jett for the last few years. While their relationship can sometimes be rocky, they always find a way back to each other.

> Ellie: Uncle Logan to the rescue.

> Me: No. You two go and have fun. I shouldn't. It's not fair to Logan, and...

I start to type out the words, but before I can finish the doorbell rings. I place my glass of red wine on the coaster on the table and attempt to leave the couch without waking Hunter. The doorbell rings again, and I almost lose it on whoever is out there, because Hunter needed this nap.

Opening the door I come face to face with my brother's wide grin, and Mom's worried brown eyes. She returned from her honeymoon yesterday. I open the screen door and they step inside.

"What are you both doing here?"

"Where's my grandson?" she questions.

As they walk in I take notice of mom's newly dyed black hair. She has completely covered the grays she had a few weeks ago.

"He's napping on the couch. Don't wake him. The teacher said he had a rough day."

After school wasn't any better, he threw his snack on the floor, then screamed for a good twenty minutes, and I had no idea why. Sometimes he holds himself together at school so well that when he comes home he falls apart.

"Looks like you did as well." Mom observes my state. From my dark curls tossed up into a "mom-bun" and the sweats.

"I did. What are you both doing here?"

"Well, Logan said he was watching the little guy tonight, and I missed my grandson, and figured I'd help him."

"I never said I was going out."

"Charlotte, clearly you need it. That and a shower." She waves a hand in front of her nose.

I lift my arm and sniff at my pits. I've been running around all day, but all I smell is my soft powder deodorant I put on this morning during my morning routine. I still try and keep my routine to feel human. Some days it works, others not so much.

"Mom's right," says Logan. "You need a night out."

"You know, Ellie never used to scam me before she started sleeping with you." I point at him and poke at his chest.

Logan presses his lips together, hurt flashing in his eyes. "She's looking out for you, Char. What's going on?"

With their gazes on me I almost lose it, but hold steady. "It's nothing. Really. I'm okay."

They still have all their attention on me. I'm not getting away with comfy pants and wine tonight.

I exhale. "Okay, fine. I'll go shower. But please try not to wake him."

By the time I get out of the shower, Ellie is sitting in my room waiting for me. Lily sits beside her, makeup kit in hand. She's got freshly dyed pink tips in her beautiful blonde hair. On occasion she changes the color, but pink is by far her favorite.

"What are you guys doing?"

"We're giving you a girl's night out. GNO." Ellie beams.

"Now we're quoting *Hannah Montana*?"

Quiet falls upon the room. Downstairs the sound of giggles catches my attention. Hunter's laugh is contagious. And then there's my brother, attempting a terrible Blippi impression. Ellie and I meet gazes and the two of us roll our eyes.

"At least he's good with kids," Lily says. "But I think secretly he wishes he was one."

"Funnily enough I can imagine him sitting on the couch, beer in hand, with Blippi episodes on demand."

Ellie chuckles. "You should have seen him when we babysat last week." Ellie holds her face in her hands, shaking her head. "He lined up all of Hunter's cars and made them race around the living room. Hunter sat there and watched him in awe, not sure what to make of it."

"Ellie, I know you're scared about the whole kid thing, but with my brother you'll never have to worry."

A sweet rosy blush climbs up her cheeks. "He is pretty great, but we're not talking about my baby-loving fiancé. We have a GNO to prepare for."

Lily does an amazing job with my makeup. It's not too over the top, it's perfect and natural. I straighten my hair, which I haven't done in ages. Curls are a thing I live with, but tonight I figured if they were going to help me go all out, I might as well.

"Okay, now for the big reveal."

Ellie jumps up from her spot on the bed and strolls towards me, grabbing a garment bag hanging off the opened white louver doors of my closet.

"What is that?"

She hands me the bag. "Go ahead, open it."

She and Lily stand side by side. Their eyes both wide with excitement. Ellie's hands are pressed together against her chin, like she's waiting for something miraculous to happen. I unveil it, and inside is a beautiful A-line vintage-style dress with a black top and floral skirt that flares outward.

"It has pockets," Lily whispers loudly.

Ellie shoves her playfully. "Shh, she was supposed to figure that out by herself."

"Guys, I can't…"

"Employee discount, and we split the cost. It's all yours."

I want to cry, but my tear ducts have run dry. Thank God because I'm tired of tears. I don't know how I'll ever repay Ellie and Lily for the things they've done for me the last few months, but I'm so overwhelmed with gratitude. I drop the dress onto the bed and hug them both at the same time.

"Hurry, get dressed," Ellie pleads. "Or we are going to be late."

"Late for what?"

"You'll see."

CHAPTER 6

I should have known it was going to be something music oriented. Lily is big into the club scene, and bars, and all things to do with music. We took a five o'clock train out of Babylon. About an hour and a half later we hit Penn Station and are now carefully navigating the hot steamy subways of Manhattan.

We get off somewhere downtown and head out into the nearly darkened streets. The winter chill hangs in the air as we navigate the city sidewalks. We walk a few blocks over to a club. Music bleeds out of the building. We aren't far in line, and quickly get let in.

Inside the venue women are shouting the lyrics to a familiar song. Although it's one Ellie and I danced to at my wedding, I don't feel a sting of sadness as we enter the main floor.

"Jonas Brother night?" I ask.

"Well, I would have gotten us tickets to see them live, but they aren't coming back till the fall, and I wanted to take you out now."

"I love it!" I yell over the crowd.

It's easy joining in with the other singing women. Song after song we yell at the top of our lungs, while drinking some amaretto sours, and taking a ton of selfies. Ellie was right. I needed this.

One of the bartenders offers to take a picture of us. Ellie immediately uploads it to her social media pages and tags me.

I should feel guilty being out, while Logan and Mom watch the baby, and while Bryan is probably working his ass off. I try not to let it get to me, but as the alcohol swirls around in my system the emotions of the past few months come rushing in. I hide it well, sing, and dance.

Feeling a bit flushed I head back to the bar, maybe for some water, maybe alcohol, I'll see what kind of mood I'm in once I sit. Sliding into one of the stools, I find myself next to a man. He's taller than Bryan by a few inches, and his hair is much darker, nearly black. When will I stop comparing other men to him? He has a Joe Jonas vibe to him, and I can't stop peering over.

"Hey," he says, shouting over the music.

He's definitely a man on eye-candy level. He's got those dreamy dark eyes... If I wasn't in the situation I'm in now, I'd probably attempt to flirt right back. That was the old Charlotte though, the new one has no idea how to flirt. Mostly, she doesn't want to.

"Hey. Big Jonas fan?" I ask, grinning.

The man shakes his head, smiling right back at me. "It's my sister's birthday. I couldn't let her down."

I nod, flagging down the bartender walking by. She stops, winks at the man next to me, then turns back to me. "What can I get for you, doll?"

"Tequila sunrise, please."

"Make that two," he says. "Throw this one on my tab, Jeri, would ya?"

She doesn't question him, only turns to go make the drinks.

"Oh, you don't have to."

"Don't worry about it. What about you? Huge fan?"

"The hugest... that's not a word is it. Sorry, I'm a little wasted. I think I'm headed for divorce, and drinking seems to numb the pain. Sorry. It's been a weird six months. I don't even know why I'm here or telling a stranger everything. Sorry."

He chuckles. "You say sorry a lot."

"Sor—" I stop myself and laugh.

The bartender returns with our drinks, and winks at the man again as she walks away. Her hips sway, and she peeks over her shoulder at him with flirty eyes. I wish I had her confidence right now. I've lost more than the little things. I've lost almost a whole part of myself.

"What do you do for a living?" he asks.

"I'm a teacher. Well, was a teacher. Now I'm just a mom. I mean, wow that sounds bad." I giggle and blame the alcohol for it. "I'm a stay-at-home mom. I'm looking to get back into teaching though."

"What do you teach? I work here in the city. I'm a high-school teacher."

I throw back some of the sweet drink. "Elementary, special education for me. The city, huh? Never get any snow days though, do ya?"

He chuckles, and it's friendly and warm, but it doesn't give me that home feeling, not like Bryan's laugh does. There I go again, comparing. It's hard not to. Six months should have been enough time to forget, but it's not.

"I'm Ryan by the way, and you are."

"Ryan?" I ask again to make sure I'm hearing him right. Nausea creeps up my throat, but I swallow it back down.

"Yeah. My name."

My chest squeezes tight. What am I doing? I'm supposed to be out with Ellie and Lily, not sitting at the bar allowing another man to buy me a drink. I'm not ready. I don't know if I ever will be.

"Would you excuse me? I need to use the restroom."

I stand but haven't moved yet. He gives a polite nod. Before I step away, I chug down the rest of my drink. "Thank you," I say, holding up the empty glass.

There's a hint of disappointment in his downcast dark eyes. "Of course. Hope things get better."

Without another word I slip away and head towards the bathroom. I blame the alcohol for the teardrops falling from my eyes. It's not very clean inside the restroom, but I lock myself inside a stall so I can take a few minutes to breathe again.

Resting my head against the tan stall door, I close my eyes. It's just a name. It was similar, but it was a name, that's it.

My phone vibrates in my small black clutch. Digging through, I reach for it and check to make sure everything is okay back home. The name on the screen leaves me winded.

> Bryan: Can we talk tomorrow? Please. It's important.

The text only makes me feel worse. I throw the phone back into my bag and rest my eyes again, hoping to relax. It doesn't stop my brain from rewinding back to the night Bryan finally asked me to be his girlfriend and our first kiss.

"See, now that's how I want to be kissed by someone. I mean look at the way he grabs her face and tilts her head." I pointed to the TV screen. We made a deal to watch each other's favorite movies and used one cold snowy Sunday to do a marathon. We watched three rom-coms and three action movies.

Bryan chuckled beside me. "I'd kiss Julia like that too."

I giggled and snorted at the same time. "I could say the same about Heath, I mean when a man breaks the rules and gets detention for you, now that's love."

"Yeah, but she flashed the teacher, so that's winning right there," he said.

I shoved him playfully.

I was more nervous than usual. I was scared that if we kissed, I'd be terrible at it. I hadn't dated much before him. The first guy I kissed was Ellie's brother. We were young and he broke my heart. Kissed me because he felt bad. I saw him with another girl the same day.

"Have you really never been properly kissed?" Bryan asked.

"What do you consider properly? Is Julia and Heath's kiss not proper?"

His eyes were hungry for what we hadn't done yet. I don't know if he was holding back because I told him my fears about finding love, especially after my dad passed away, I feared the worst, always.

"I'm sure I can do better." He shifted on his old brown couch to face me.

"Is that so?" I asked, moving closer.

He nodded. "So, first, I'd take her head in my hands, like Heath did, but I'd grip right at her jawline."

His deepened rough tone had my insides screaming, and then he played out every word. His hand stretched out and wrapped my jaw and chin in a tight hold. My muscles tightened and I hissed.

"Then," he narrowed his eyes. "I'd lean forward and tease her a bit. Allowing my head to meet hers, our noses rubbing together."

He came closer, rested his head against mine, then slowly allowed his nose to do the same. My breath trembled at his touch.

"Then I'd tease her lips with my finger, tracing them ever so slightly."

The moan I released didn't even sound like it had come from me. It was raw as if I'd had a sore throat.

"Pressing my mouth to hers she'd gasp."

And I did, very much.

"Her lips would open, our tongues would meet, her hands would thread through my hair."

He had a buzz cut then, so his hair was soft and smooth. I enjoyed running my hands through it.

"Want to know what I'd do?" I ask.

"Please tell me, Charlotte. How would you have me kiss you?"

I smirked and got to my feet. Then I stood in front of him.

"I'd continue to run my hands over your hair, then I'd put them to your neck, and lower myself onto your lap, straddling you for a better angle."

He drinks me all in with widened eyes. I felt sexy and powerful under his hooded stare.

There wasn't a day that had gone by when he didn't view me as if I was his world... until everything came crashing down.

"Then I'd press my mouth to yours, because I wouldn't be able to take it anymore." I took charge and his mouth immediately accepted mine.

"Charlotte," he whispered into my mouth.

"Yeah?" I squeaked, still a bit dizzy from the kiss.

"Can we make this official? Will you be my girlfriend? I like where this is going, and I really like you. I think this could be something great."

And it was easy to say yes, especially after the way he kissed. I had no doubt in my mind that I could love him one day. And I did. Loved him so fiercely. Still love him, no matter how much I fight it, I think I always will.

Back out on the dance floor I fall into step with Ellie and Lily. Even when my feet tire, and the buzz turns into a full-blown headache, I allow the memories to fade, and for the moment I'm living to take over.

Ellie reaches out for me, and I do the same for her. My best friend is truly an amazing person.

"So, are we having fun yet?" she yells over the pulsing vibration of the speakers.

A new Jonas Brothers song engulfs the room. Women scream around us as colorful lights bounce all over.

"I know I am! And I only know the big named songs," Lily shouts.

They stare at me. I'm lost in the song.

"Best night I've had in forever!"

And I'm not lying. I may have things on my mind, things that should be taking priority over a night of fun, but I'm too drunk to care, and the girls are right, I needed a night to do something for myself.

Finally, between midnight and one, we rush back to Penn Station in hopes we find a train. Sometimes if it's late and you miss one you have to wait at least two hours, but luckily, we make it just in time.

On the ride back I rest my head on Ellie's shoulders and close my eyes. The world spins and my head throbs from the alcohol. Am I going to regret my decision to drink, in the morning? I sure as hell am. Am I going to regret a night out with the girls? Hell no.

CHAPTER 7

A piercing bell rings in my ears. I moan at the sound, hoping it will stop. Only, it doesn't. Groaning, I throw the covers off me, and stumble down the stairs to answer the door. Logan and Mom took Hunter back to Mom's, and he spent the night. She's planning to drop him off later.

I tug at the door, flinging it open. Standing there, wide eyes staring not at my face but at my body, is Bryan. Glancing down I check myself. I vaguely remember crawling into bed after ripping the dress off, and only sleeping in my bra and underwear.

The guy at the bar, followed by his name, and the text from Bryan all come rolling back in. A strangled gasp escapes my lips as I cover myself. My stomach churns with the consequences from last night. Holding up a hand, I rush away from the door. My goal is to make it to the upstairs bathroom, but it's already in my throat, burning its way up.

I stumble over a crate of toys, and nearly take myself out, but gracefully land on my knees in front of an orange pumpkin bucket from Halloween. Reaching for it I retch into it.

"Oh, Charlotte, the Halloween bucket? At least it's not your shoe again," he says, laughing a little.

"Shut it," I say, unable to hide the half-grin on my face.

Of course, out of all our memories, he'd remember the one time I got drunk at a wedding, felt sick and on the ride home instead of puking on my lap, I grabbed my shoe and puked in it. He will never let me live it down.

The smile doesn't last long as my stomach lurches again, and some more vomit spills inside the bucket.

Emptying the contents of my stomach takes a lot longer than I expected. As the cramping lets up, I sit back, and am wrapped up by Bryan in my favorite fleece blanket. I stare at him, and for a flash I swear there's a twinkle in his eye.

His lip curls, and he shakes his head. "Amaretto, huh?"

I laugh and it's followed by a groan. Of course, he'd know my party drink.

"Come on. Let's get you to bed. I saw the pictures Ellie tagged you in. Is Hunter here?"

I cringe. Of course he saw them. I fight the urge to lean into his warm touch as he helps me to our... no, my room.

"He's at Mom's. They all bombarded me last night and forced me to go out. I'm never going out again." I fake cry.

Bryan chuckles. I haven't heard his laugh in so long. It's light, airy, and the most beautiful thing in the world. *Do it again.*

"You were smiling though. Which is all that really matters. It was nice to see you smile, Charlotte." The way he says my name almost sounds like a term of endearment.

Pain strangles my broken heart, but I have to move on. Bryan and I are done and there's no going back. I crawl into the bed we once shared.

He rummages through the drawers tugging out some sweats and an old T-shirt. He playfully throws the clothing at me. "Troublemaker." He sighs.

"I blame Ellie and Lily." I attempt to put on my shirt, but somehow, I get stuck in the arm hole.

Bryan laughs again; it's the most I've heard of it in a while. His hands are on me before I have a chance to protest. His touch is heated and if I wasn't so hung over, I'd... *no, Charlotte, stop.*

He helps guide the shirt over me.

"I can do my own pants," I say.

His brow lifts and a flash of how we used to be flickers between us.

Luckily, I can get my pants on, because having him put my shirt on was awkward enough. I crawl to the unmade portion of the bed near my pillows and curl up, moaning as my head aches.

Bryan fixes the covers and pulls them over me. "Be right back."

I'm not sure for how long he's gone, but I've definitely nodded off. When I open my eyes again, he's entering the room, concern plaguing his features with a tight knit brow. "I grabbed you some medicine."

"How long did I conk out for?"

He peers down at me. "Bout a half an hour."

"And you stayed?" I blink away the sleep mixed with the unfallen tears and wipe at my eyes.

"Yeah. Your bucket of puke is all cleaned up. Hunter will never have to know." He gives an uneasy smile. "Here." He picks up the small round pill and glass off the bedside table and hands it to me. I slowly sip while downing the meds.

"You don't have to take care of me anymore."

An icy cold glare passes through his blue eyes. I'm not sure what it all means, but I ignore the plea in my heart to grab on to him and tell him I want to try again. Clearly, he doesn't want that, or he would have offered.

The bed shifts as he sits on the end. I was so embarrassed by my own wardrobe malfunction I didn't realize he was in his blue officer uniform. A gasp catches in my throat. I hate that he looks just as handsome as the day we met, when he rescued me from my spill on the ice at work. His muscles flex as he shifts on the bed. What I wouldn't give to tighten my arm around them and lay my head on his broad shoulder.

He runs a hand through his hair and stares at the doorway, like he's plotting his escape. The wanting I felt a few minutes ago vanishes, knowing he doesn't want it.

"You probably don't remember, but I sent you a text last night."

I shake my head, lying. I'm trying to push that part of the night out of my head.

"I-I kn-know you aren't well, but I have-have to ask you something." He's stuttering, as he does when he's anxious. I sit up a little more in bed. The motion makes me dizzy, but thankfully the nausea has subsided. "What's up?"

"Well, my family is still hosting everyone for Christmas this year."

I completely forgot. Last year we planned on going to his family's cabin upstate. They are all spread out around the states. His older sister Morgan lives in Colorado, and his younger sister Sydney goes to school in Florida. While his parents do have a house in upstate New York, they spend their winters in Florida and summers are spent in a small town in Maine. Getting together for the holidays is rare, so last year they all planned a trip for this Christmas, so his younger sister, Sydney could make the trek.

"Oh. You want to take Hunter with you? I'm fine with that. I know how much your parents miss him."

The idea of not having Hunter for Christmas breaks my heart, but I understand Bryan's family doesn't see him much.

He's quiet as he continues to stare outside the room. He's lost in his thoughts and fidgeting with his hands. Crawling to him at the end of the bed, I sit beside him, and lay a hand on his shoulder.

He jumps at the touch and his eyes meet mine. Swallowing

hard, he closes his eyes, attempting to form the words he needs to say. "Actually, Mom, she doesn't… She doesn't know."

I purse my lips. "Doesn't know what?"

"Uh, that we are, uh, separated."

It takes me a second to process what he's said. I tap my hand against my leg. The silence slices through the room. "Say what now?" I want to make sure I've heard him correctly.

Bryan reaches up and scratches at the back of his neck. "I haven't told her about us. She thinks we're still happily married living under one roof. She has no idea I'm staying with Connor."

"It's been six months, Bryan, and you still haven't told her? How does she not realize?"

He nods, unable to meet my gaze. Me on the other hand, I can't keep my eyes off him. Biting down on my lip, I try to get more out of him. "Why not?"

He shrugs and goes back to fidgeting with his hands in his lap. "I-I was holding out. I only call her when he's with me and usually when we're out and… you should come. We could tell her when we get there."

"And ruin Christmas for her. Bryan, what the hell were you thinking? How could you not tell your own mom what was going on?"

He sighs and lowers his head. "I just couldn't, okay?" His voice wavers, and I attempt to ignore it.

"So, you want me to go with you and pretend everything is fine and dandy? That we are happy and everything that happened the past *six* months never actually happened?"

"Yeah."

"No! No! I refuse. I'm not lying to your family. You and Hunter can go. You'll tell your mom the whole story, and everything will be the way it should be."

He winces. Why should he? It was his idea to separate. There's no reason it should affect him in that way. He has no right to ask me to do this, he hasn't made a move to make amends, so why should I? The only thing he did was meet with a lawyer and start the process of serving me with divorce papers.

"Please. One week, and then when we come back, I'll tell her things have been rocky."

"No!"

"Just think about it, please?" His eyes finally meet mine, the crystal blue edges shimmer.

I'm pulled in like I was when we met. "I—" When my heart finally catches up with my brain, the idea of missing Christmas with Hunter hurts more than I can handle. My heart races leaving a tightness in my chest.

"Please. Just think about it."

I suck on my bottom lip. Our eyes dance over each other as we stare, speechless.

He squeezes his eyes shut and pinches the bridge of his nose. "Please."

"Fine. I'll think about it. But I'm not making any guarantees."

"That's all I can ask. I have to go. It's been a long night. Let me know. Okay?"

I walk him out, even though my head is still pounding. Mom and Logan pull up as we reach the doorway. Logan hands Hunter to Bryan, while I lean against the door frame watching their interaction. Hunter tolerates Bryan for only a few seconds before he struggles to get down. Bryan hangs his head low as he retreats to his car. Maybe it's because I know every one of Bryan's tics, but it's so easy to see he's hurt.

"What was that all about? Are you two…" Logan questions as he comes up the walkway.

"No. No we aren't. He came to talk. I really don't want to talk about it right now. Thank you for watching Hunter."

"No problem. We had fun, right, buddy?"

"Fun, Mamay. Had fun, had fun. Unca Logo, look, big eyes." Hunter widens his eyes and fidgets with his hands.

"Yeah, buddy. So awesome!"

I jump at Mom's touch. She places a steady hand on my shoulder. "Sweetie, I think you need to do what's right for your heart. And this thing with Bryan, I think you can fix it."

"Mom, please. I'm a bit hungover and confused. It's not a good time."

She sighs. "Okay. Seeing you like this is breaking my heart."

"Do you want me to take him with us to brunch? Do you need some extra time?" Logan asks.

Shaking my head, I take Hunter into my arms. He snuggles in deep, and I know he's what I need to feel better. "I'm okay, Logan. Thank you."

Logan narrows his eyes at me, knowing full well I'm not okay, but he doesn't push it. "Okay. Come on, Mom," Logan says, taking her by the shoulders. "I'm going to be late for brunch with Ellie's mom."

"Fine. Goodbye, sweetheart." She presses a small kiss to my cheek, then turns to Hunter in my arms. "Bye, my handsome man," she says.

Hunter and I say goodbye to Mom and Logan. While I'd love to get some rest, I know it's not on the cards. I brew myself some caffeine and go about my day with the idea of spending the week with Bryan swirling around in my head.

CHAPTER 8

"Wait, so he asked you to do what?"

It's a warm winter's day one where sweatshirts are enough to keep you warm. It's crazy for this time of year. Hunter and I are hanging out in Logan and Ellie's backyard. After I told Ellie what happened yesterday, she invited me over for lunch.

"The plan is to leave Wednesday morning and come back either New Year's Day or the following day. Tomorrow is already Monday. I have to make my decision soon. I feel bad, they don't get to see Hunter often, and we kind of already RSVPed last year."

"Wow, that's um... that's pretty crazy. Are you thinking about going?"

I tense my shoulders in a sort of shrug/nod, then stare out into the yard where Hunter and Logan are running around. When Ellie and Logan bought the house, it was a shell of itself, but with my brother's love for renovating things, this place went from house to home. The deck is stained with beautiful mahogany that goes nicely with the soft sky-blue siding he recently added.

"I have the interview with Maryann tomorrow. What if she

hires me? I'll have to tell her I can't work until after Christmas. Isn't this like the prime time in retail?"

Ellie shrugs it off. "No worries. Tell her you had plans before the interview. Plus, the real horror is the returns after the holidays. Yeesh." She chuckles.

I keep my eyes over in the distance. A shiver rolls through me. Even with the warmth of the sun, there's a slight chill in the shade. Hunter's cheeks are bright red as Logan pushes him around in the little coupe car. Mom had somehow saved it from our own childhood. How the toy is still in one piece baffles me, but it works, and now my son gets to enjoy it too.

"That's true. I don't know what to do. I feel like I should go. I don't want to upset his parents, and I don't want to lie to them either. It's going to eat away at me. Like, why can't he tell them?"

"The question I want answered is why he *didn't* tell them. Was he expecting you guys to get back together?"

"You know that's the thing—" I pause and turn my attention to my brother and Hunter. The smiles on their faces are priceless. Hunter's screams of joy echo through the yard as Logan chases him.

I resume my conversation with Ellie. "He had this distant look in his eyes when he came to tell me. Maybe I was imagining it."

She rests a hand over mine. "I'll support whatever decision you make. I just want you to be okay."

"Hunter airlines flight number two, coming in for a landing." Logan flies Hunter right into my arms in a fit of giggles.

"What's happening?"

"Bryan asked Charlotte to go spend Christmas at his family's cabin, and pretend they are still together."

Logan sits on one of the soft padded chairs with us. His eyes meet mine from across the small glass table. I hand Hunter his juice box, and he sits quietly on my lap, sipping and reaching for the crackers I've put out for him. He lifts his hands, palms facing in, and giggles happily, then repeats the motion, while rocking back and forth. It's a gesture he does when he's excited, a stim. He's in his own world, oblivious to what is happening around him, but smiling and enjoying life.

Logan scratches the scruff on his face. "So, while he and I haven't spoken much since the separation, I don't hate the guy, but this sounds like an attempt to keep you in his life."

My chest tightens. The organ there that hammers so wildly every time I think about Bryan does a double beat. I raise my hand to rest it over the spot. A sliver of something resembling hope shines through at the thought of Bryan still wanting any part of what we once had.

Ellie grabs one of Hunter's snacks and tosses it at his head.

"Ow! Why does everyone have to toss things at my head?"

Hunter giggles and follows along, giving us all something to laugh at.

"What do you mean, you think he wants to keep me in his life?"

"The guy is clearly still in love with you."

I choke on my spit, and cough to clear my throat. "If he was so in love with me then why is he drawing up divorce papers?" I attempt to blink away the building tears. They sting behind my eyes, making my nose itch like I've snuffed a helping of pepper up my nose. I rub at the bridge of my nose to settle it, but it's not helping.

"He did?" Logan's voice echoes through the yard.

"Logan," Ellie hisses.

"What? I'm in shock. I didn't see that one coming. Why did he wait so long?"

"I don't know." I don't allow sadness to consume me. Neither of us has made any moves towards reconciling our relationship. Maybe Bryan thought I was done too. I only pretend to be okay because he mostly seems like he is.

A tear slips and I toss my head back and scoff at my own dismay. *Emotion's score: one thousand. Charlotte's score: zero.* I wipe the tear away and it somehow stops. "He left me a voicemail and then when he came to pick up Hunter he asked if I thought it would be a good idea. He seemed already set on doing it, so I said yes."

Ellie stands, grabs Hunter, and takes him off my lap. Now it's her turn to go and play with him, and he happily obliges. He may love Logan, but Aunt Ellie is his favorite person.

Logan lifts his chair and brings it closer to mine. "I'm so sorry, Char. I didn't know. I really thought…" My brother leans forward and takes me in his arms. I'm a mess. I've dug myself this hole and I have no idea how to get myself out.

"No. It's not your fault, Logan. I know Bryan isn't a bad guy. I can't hate him because there's nothing to hate. Minus how he walked out on me. I don't know what went wrong. What's wrong with me?"

"Char, there is absolutely nothing wrong with you. People fall out of love all the time. It happens. Dynamics change things. I'm not saying that beautiful son of yours isn't a blessing, but kids put stress on a marriage."

"And you know that because…"

"Because your best friend is terrified of being a mom, and me on the other hand, after working with kids all day, and being with my nephew, I never wanted anything more. We have fought more times over it than I can count."

"Yeah, but the difference is you two make it work, and you don't have children yet."

"I think you should go."

"What, why? That's the most ridiculous thing—"

"Char, the guy hesitated to get in his car yesterday, then stared at you. It can't hurt. It will be you two stuck in a room together."

"Yeah, but we'll be in vacation mode and that can make anyone rethink things, but then you come back to reality, and it gets hard again."

"It doesn't have to."

"Since when did you become a marriage expert?" I ask, chuckling lightly.

"When I snagged your best friend. Loving her from afar was never quite enough. I might get angry that she and I don't see eye to eye sometimes, but it doesn't matter, I won't ever let her slip from my fingers again."

"You're a sap now too," I tease.

"It happens." The blush on his face says it all.

Ellie is sitting in the grass with Hunter, the two of them absently staring up at the sky. Ellie points and we can't hear them from here, but I know she's telling Hunter all about the clouds.

"So, I should go then?"

"Yeah. You should. Do it for Hunter. I'm sure he'd love to have his mom and dad back in the same room for the holidays."

Since he and Ellie have gotten together, I have noticed a significant change in the way my brother views things. When Dad died and Logan disappeared, I thought we'd lost him for good, but Ellie brought him back to life. She gave him all the love he was missing. He turned his life around so he could make her happy. I want that for myself again. I'm not expecting anything to come out of the time away, but to spend one last week as a family of three, I think it might be worth it. But I'm not ready to tell Bryan my decision yet. I want to sit on it for another day, to let the idea sink in.

Logan makes his way over to Ellie and Hunter and lies down on Hunter's left side. I stand, and wait, observing them. Ellie points up. Logan and Hunter are concentrating hard on whatever it is.

I join them, finding a spot beside Ellie on the grass, and she grabs my hand intertwining it with hers. Ellie smiles and somehow, here and now, everything feels right in the world.

CHAPTER 9

Sitting in the parking lot of the mall where Sheer Threads is located is nerve-wracking. It's Monday. I've got a tall cup of joe in my hands, warming me up, and the entire day to myself. Mom is dropping Hunter at school today, and offered to pick him up too, so I can go for my interview and have some me-time. There's guilt building in the back of my mind. Bryan is working, I'm off gallivanting, because he still fills the account in my name with his money. I loathe it now that we aren't together. While this job won't fill my bank or heart fully, it will give me a sense of control over my own finances.

I'm parked in front of Barnes and Noble. I plan on going in after and using up the gift cards I have. Afterwards, it's home and a nice relaxing bath. Today's for me.

Inside the mall it's quiet but will soon be bustling with shoppers prepping for the holiday. There's only four shopping days left, crunch time for most. Sheer Threads is one of my favorite stores. I love the clothing, so working here instead of in the classroom won't be half bad when I get the associate discount.

I stroll into the women's department, the scent of lavender

hitting my nose. Everything is lit up in here with bright lighting, making the fixtures and clothing pop with a clean feel. Lily is the first person I see. She's already helping a customer but notices me right away. Ellie is working her job at the radio station this morning, but she's been texting, waiting for updates.

"Hey, Charlotte, be right there," Lily says.

"Take your time." I sip from my coffee. My phone beeps in my bag. Bryan started texting and attempting to FaceTime with me last night. He wants to know what my plans are, and while I've decided going is the best course of action, I'm still not ready to tell him. The thought alone sends my heart into a frenzy. Checking the message, I see it's another one from him.

> Bryan: Good morning. Let me know soon. K?
> Hope you're alright, haven't heard from you since
> Saturday. Are you still hung over? LOL.

My eyes feel misty reading his message. I'm trying to get over him, yet here he is acting as if things between us aren't strained.

"You must be Charlotte." A woman in bright blue comes strolling over to me. "Ellie has told me so much about you."

"Hi. Yes. Maryann?" I slip the phone into my bag and put my full attention on her.

"Yes. Please. Come follow me, we'll do the interview in the stock room."

Lily gives a wink and a wave as I follow Maryann back behind the register to a solid white door. Inside is a bit messy, reminding me more of a warehouse than a chic clothing store in the mall.

In the far back behind a rack of clothing sits a round table, some shelves, and a counter with a microwave and a fridge. She pulls out one of the metal folding chairs at the table for me, then finds one for herself. She's got paperwork on the table ready to go, and as she sits, she shuffles through.

"So, Charlotte. Why don't you tell me a bit about yourself."

Placing my bag on the table, I take a deep breath. It's been a while since someone asked me to tell them about my life. Other than I'm a teacher I'm not sure what else to say. "I worked in education previously, but the market is tough right now. I've been a stay-at-home mom for a few years, but I'm looking to find a job part-time until the right opportunity comes along."

She smiles. "That's perfect, we have a worker who went on maternity leave and I'm needing someone to fill the void for a while. Your résumé is really great, and you have worked in retail before. It says in high school?"

"Yeah, in high school and my first few years of college I worked at the music and movie store."

"Great. So, you have some customer service experience under your belt along with money and register experience. We aren't much different, only the product. So, if you're interested, I'd love to hire you part-time, a few days a week to start off. If you could get me a list of hours you're available, since I know you have a little one at home."

"Oh, well my mom has open availability for babysitting so pretty much anything you throw at me, I think I can handle. What about sick time and such? With a kid it's hard to pinpoint those things."

"Yes, I remember those days. Mine are grown, fifteen and nineteen, but I get it."

She goes into all the dirty details of days off and coverage. Maryann seems like an easy woman to please, and I don't feel like I'll have an issue. When I discuss the vacation for Christmas, she doesn't mind, and tells me I can start right after I return home.

I stand to get ready to leave when Lily's voice echoes through the stacks of clothing. She finds us by peeking her head around a tall shelf of handbags.

"Maryann?"

"Yes, Lily?"

"Rebecca called out, she's vomiting, like the projectile kind, and even while we were on the phone…"

Maryann holds up a hand. "Lily, please spare me the details," she says.

"Right. So, um, I can't stay late today, and Ellie's not able to come until five."

"If you don't have anyone, I'm willing to step in," I say. "I'm a quick learner and I'm sure the registers aren't much different from the ones at the music store."

"I can train her," Lily interjects. "It's still quiet right now, and Heather is here too; she knows the ropes."

Maryann contemplates this, tapping her bright red painted lips with her pen. "I can get you in the system now and set you up with your associate number. Lily, can you and Heather handle the floor for another fifteen minutes while I do that?"

"Yeah. Like I said, it's quiet for now."

"Perfect. Okay, Charlotte, let me show you to a locker and get you all situated."

I wasn't expecting to work today, but it's getting me out of the house, and honestly, I don't mind. Plus, I get to talk to adults all day; it's a win–win. After Maryann sets me up on the computer, I find my way back up front where Lily is opening a box of shipment. She runs me through a training course in the register, and it doesn't take long for me to get the hang of it. Before the first two hours are over, I've already rung up four customers and have done three returns. Those are tricky, but I don't think I'll have an issue.

"So, how are you liking it so far?" Lily asks, as she slides one customer their bags with a smile. "Have a good day."

"This is great," I say, handing the customer on my line her product. "I may have talked a few ears off, but I don't get to have much adult interaction outside of Logan and Ellie."

She chuckles. "Adults aren't all they are cracked up to be."

"True, but when you ask someone 100 times a day if they did poopy, and to not put objects in their mouth, it can get a bit lonely."

I miss Hunter, but I'm feeling almost human again. More hours pass, the day going by pleasantly fast. By the time five o'clock hits and Ellie walks through the door I'm exhausted but happy.

"What are you doing here?" she asks, finding me folding some jeans.

The foot traffic in the mall has picked up, but I don't mind at all. "Well, surprise, I got the job. I'm filling in for someone who was projectile vomiting. Lily got an earful on the phone."

Ellie laughs. "Well, that's good. Not the vomit, but you working. Your glowing, Char," she says.

"Am I?" My cheeks burn.

"Yeah. I haven't seen you this cheerful since…" she trails off, and for once I almost don't feel the wince of pain, it's there, but much easier to handle than usual.

"I'm enjoying myself. I mean I know the irate customers will get on my nerves eventually but knowing that there will be money I made in my account makes everything better."

Ellie wraps her arms around me, and I drop the pair of jeans I'm folding. "Seeing you smile again makes me happy," she says, sniffling.

"Are you crying?" I ask.

She laughs as she wipes some tears from her eyes. "Work looks good on you, Char."

"Thanks."

Ellie and I work together for an hour until my shift ends.

Before I leave, Maryann has my shifts all planned out for when I return. I'm excited to start after the holidays and finally feel like my life means something again. It would make things better if Bryan and I reconnected, but it can't and shouldn't happen. We aren't the same people we were when we met or married. It happens to the best. We just have to get through the week. I've got this.

CHAPTER 10

My phone is filled with a few more messages from Bryan, a voicemail, and two missed calls. I should check them, but I'm on such a high from work I decide not to.

For dinner, I get Hunter his favorite fast food and we both spend the evening in a good mood, minus one meltdown from him over wanting an extra cookie for dessert.

Once he's down for the night, I slip into the bathtub, needing to unwind from the day. Across the tub is the caddy with my wine, some chocolates, and my phone, which starts going off the minute I look at it. Bryan's calling again, I get it, he said he's leaving Wednesday so that gives me until tomorrow to decide.

"Hey, Bryan." I leave the phone on the caddy and put it on speaker.

"Oh, Charlotte, y-you finally answered." There's a slight stutter in his croaky tone. He was worried about me?

"Yeah. Sorry. I got a job today," I say, like it's no big deal.

"You what?" The surprise in his voice almost makes me angry.

"Ellie told me about an opening at the store. I've been honestly searching for a while now, and with the divorce I can't always rely on you."

"Char, I told you I'd take care of you and Hunter until—"

"I know," I cut him off. "I know what you want to do, but Bryan, if we aren't together, you don't have to. I want to do this. It's the first time I've felt like myself in months. Please, don't fight me on it."

He sighs into the phone but stays silent. The quiet isn't uneasy, and I allow myself to lower my body into the tub and close my eyes. My free hand rests on my inner thigh.

"I'm sorry." He pauses for another few seconds. I listen to his breathing on the other end, remembering the way it felt to have the warmth of it lingering in my ear, and over my mouth. The thought sends shivers down my spine. "Have you... have you made your decision yet?"

It's not so much his question that catches me off guard, more the subdued tone in his voice mixed with a little roughness. I rub my hand along my inner thigh out of pure anxiety, the motion feeling good enough for me to moan under my breath.

The idea of spending the week with him makes my body feel things, ache for things. It wasn't all about the sexual parts of our relationships, but he satisfied me in a way no one else ever could. His love too. I never once questioned it. Never had to worry about him straying. He was fully invested in this... in us. That's the part I don't understand. Even now he seems so committed to us but still keeping himself at a distance.

I scrunch my face to stop the hollowness in my chest, making my throat dry and eyes itch. "I'll go with you, but we have to tell them."

"We will, I swear. Can we maybe get through Christmas?"

"Bryan!" My eyes fly open.

"I promise we will. Please, can we keep it on the down-low, for a little bit longer. It's Christmas, our first, you know, and..."

He's breathing in and out, and for a second I swear he's whispering to smell the flowers and blow out the candles, like I tell Hunter to when he gets upset. I laugh to myself.

"Charlotte." Bryan's quiet tone is more sensuous than it should be.

My fingers slip and I can't help the gasp that escapes my lips. "Mmm."

"Char..." I wait for him to say more. "Are you..." More quiet. "Are you..." He groans. "Never mind. It would mean a lot if we, uh... if we spent Christmas as a family normally," he whispers.

I respond with a low tone, "Okay."

Again, silence passes between us, but it's more calming than I expected it to be as I allow myself to feel things. It's oddly satisfying, and I find myself fighting back a moan as my fingers work around down there. What I'm doing is insane but it's the most we've talked in months and I can't help it.

"I'm gonna go, Bry. I want to finish my bath—"

A loud thump on his end makes my fingers slip. There's some static, a curse or two, and then his voice finally filtering back in. "S-sorry, I dropped the phone."

I hold in a snicker building in my chest. "Goodnight," I say, softly.

"Night, Char." His tone matches mine.

He doesn't hang up right away, there's a few extra minutes of dead air before the line cuts out. Releasing a trembling breath, my fingers continue to dance low around my center. I sink into the bubbly water, even lower, allowing the tension to build and my mind to slip to a happier time.

The first time we had sex started with me babbling about an old story of when Ellie, Logan and I went ice skating. I was nervous as hell, because we'd been on the verge of rounding all the bases but hadn't quite gotten there yet. That night I'd felt it in the air from the moment he picked me up, as we ate dinner and his foot tangled in mine under the table, then as he invited me back to his place.

We stood outside his apartment on the steps. Me using my full body to tell the story, and him smirking.

"Char," Bryan said quietly.

"Mmm."

He grabbed hold of my face, and kissed me, like he really meant it. His hand wrapped around my lower back, and he pulled me into him. He was so hard against me I whimpered as his hips thrust forward. He bit my lip and tugged.

"I want to hear you whimper like that again," he growled, low and deep.

"Okay, so take me inside, and I'll show you what other noises I make."

Bryan's brows shot up. He was taken aback by me being so forward. I'd played the shy card, because I was afraid to feel, but with Bryan everything felt right, and after a month of imagining how it would feel to have him inside me, I was ready. His hands shook as he attempted to open the door. While he did, he checked over his shoulder several times like he was making sure I wasn't going to vanish into thin air.

I closed the door behind me, and he made it two steps before he turned around and pushed me up against it. I moaned louder as he pressed his erection against my body.

My hand rested flat against his sturdy chest. The need to touch his skin jolted sparks of tingles into my fingertips. His eyes snapped to mine, and I sharply inhaled at the sight of his fervent irises dilated with hunger.

"Please tell me you have a condom?" I panted, in a desperate frenzy.

"I got them after our first date in hopes we'd get this far."

He reached for my jawline and wrapped his hand around it. God, I loved when he would grab me like that. My center twitched with a blissful tickle of wetness between my legs. I tilted my head back against the door and sighed as his lips smashed against mine.

I pulled away slightly. "It's been a really long time…"

"Don't worry, Char, I'll take care of you," he panted.

His hungry mouth devoured mine, as our tongues danced along with each other. I couldn't help myself as I reached between us and grabbed hold of his length where it pressed through his jeans.

"Shit, Char. That feels so fucking good." The rasp in his voice was everything. He always spoke with a deeper tone when we were intimate. Such a turn on.

"Bed… room." His words were said between each kiss.

He took my hand and tugged me towards the room. Inside, the lights were out, and it was dark, but it didn't stop him from reaching for me. We stumbled through the room.

"Where's the bed?" I could hardly see less than an inch in front of me.

"It's here." He started to sit, but then stopped himself.

He was off by an inch and faltered. We almost fell, but still somehow made it to the bed. Our laughter filled the dark space as we grabbed for each other. He reached for the waistline of my leggings. As he tugged them down, I attempted to unbutton his jeans, but couldn't. He shimmied my pants down my leg, and it got stuck on my boot.

"I didn't take my shoes off." I laughed as I kicked them to the floor.

"We're fumbling our way through this, aren't we?"

"It keeps things more interesting."

"It sure does," he said, as we continued.

Eventually after some more fumbling around in the dark, Bryan got up and turned on the lights. They were on a dimmer switch, so he kept them low, but bright enough to see each other.

I stood as he whirled around towards me. His eyes roamed over my entire body as the last piece of my clothing dropped to the floor. No man had ever looked over me the way he did. It was like every part of me was perfect in his eyes.

The second he crossed the room his mouth closed tight around my hard pebbled nipple and in an instant my body shook with pleasure. His tongue flicked around, and my body arched up and into him. His moan was deep and low. I let my hands run over his shaved head and pulled him into me as he sucked harder.

He carefully helped me lie back onto the charcoal comforter. His lips were on the move the second I was flat on my back. He was between my legs and caressing every inch of me with both his rough fingers and soft lips.

When he reached my center and glanced up through his lashes, I was done for. He watched me while I took in what he was doing. His tongue touched my insides, and moaning was not enough to relay how it felt when I released all the built-up tension. I yelled for him to let him know I was about to do something I've never done before. He didn't even lift his head as I let go.

I'd never been touched or licked like that before. It was the most erotic thing I'd ever experienced. I gripped his shoulders because I needed to give him something in return.

"Bryan, come here. I want a turn on you now."

He slowly made his way back up my body, making sure to plant tender kisses on every part on his way up. I was met with his picture-perfect grin as he reached my chin and pulled back.

I grabbed for him. He fitted nicely in my hand, and my mouth easily covered his length. I'd only done this one other time, but it felt right, and I went with it. He didn't complain, as his eyes rolled back, and the tip hit the back of my throat.

"If you keep that up, we won't get any further," he said.

I chuckled. "I'm ready when you are."

"God, you're amazing." He adjusted so he could kiss my lips again, then reached for the condom inside the bedside table.

When the tip of his arousal hit my entrance a heart-pounding zing pushed through me. I thrusted as he filled me, meeting every need.

"You're so tight around me. So wet, and tight, and—" Unable to finish his words he yelled out my name and the sound coming off his lips alone had me on the verge of letting go again.

I tightened around him, and his wide eyes met mine in anticipation of each impressive thrust. The thing I remember most was the way it felt when we connected. I wrapped my legs tight around his waist and he burrowed his face into my neck. He nibbled along the sensitive skin and kept moaning my name.

"I don't think I can last long, Char. Not with how fucking good it feels to be buried inside you."

In one panted breath I said, "Then don't. Come for me, Bryan."

I'm brought back into the present with an orgasm so intense it feels like he's here with me. I half-whimper and half-scream with a mixture of pleasure and sadness all rolled into one.

"Bryan." His name leaves my lips in a panted whisper, and I allow myself a second to bask in the pleasure of the memory, while shedding a few tears.

Life is about to get interesting, and while I know it's time to move on, there's still a piece of me that has faith things will work out and we can somehow slide back into each other's lives and be happy.

CHAPTER 11

"Hunter, can I have the big block?" I hold my hand out waiting for him to respond.

Bryan is picking us up in an hour and my living room looks like a tornado has struck. Hunter felt very over-stimulated this morning. We went through so many toys and he's been stuck in repetitive motions.

Over the last day I've attempted to prep him for our week away. I quickly whipped up a social story with pictures of the cabin and the family members we'd be seeing. If I take him somewhere and it's not routine it stresses him out and he will have meltdowns. Providing him with the stories helps ease his fears.

For the past twenty minutes he has been focused on blocks, and I'm afraid if I move it will ruin his calm mood. His lips are pulled into a straight line as he arranges the blocks, attempting to build.

"Hunter. Give Mommy the big block." I try again and he puts another smaller one on top.

He lifts his gaze and for a second focuses on something before returning his attention to the blocks. "It fits." He says to himself.

He doesn't look me in the eye but turns in my direction. "It's castle, Mama."

Smiling, I help him add more blocks. The doorbell rings and Hunter doesn't seem fazed at all. I get up and answer it.

"I'm sorry, I know I said I'd be here at nine, but I picked up some coffee along the way at the place you like." Bryan holds out a small cup from a shop in town. It's a local family who owns it, and their coffee is a hundred times better than what those chain stores offer.

I take the cup and allow him in. "Thanks, Bry. It's okay. I'm sort of ready. We had a rough morning, but if you hang out with Hunter, I can get everything ready."

"No rush," he says, taking a sip of his coffee. His lips hold steady on the cup as he watches me. Images of the other night in the tub flash before me. For a second I'm caught up in him and the way his muscles flex as he brings the cup lower.

"Great." My voice squeaks.

He makes himself at home. As he should. This house is still technically his, but as he told me when we finally calmed down enough to discuss our separation, he wants it to be mine, so Hunter doesn't have to reroute his entire life.

While he and Hunter play, I make myself scarce and finish cleaning up from breakfast, and then go around collecting all the toys we've played with. By the time I'm done, and have our bags by the door, I'm spent.

I find my way back into the living room and sit down on the floor with them. "Wow! You guys did a number on that block castle."

Bryan has an eye for building things. I think he secretly bought a ton of blocks for himself. There's even more in the basement. He ordered them when I was pregnant stating, "You can never have too many." His colorful building is nearly as tall as Hunter when he stands and has enough space for him to walk inside.

"Hunter, you want to put the last block on?"

Hunter stares off. Sometimes he gets these random bouts of zoning out. Another thing I've discussed with the pediatrician. She wants us to get some neurological testing in the new year, but she said for now keep an eye on it.

"Hunter?" Bryan asks again.

"Hunter, sweetheart, look Daddy has a block."

Instead of answering us, he jumps to his feet and scampers across the room to his soft Paw Patrol couch and buries his head into it.

"We should go," Bryan says, placing the block down beside what he built.

Bryan gathers the luggage for me to put in the van, while I prep Hunter for the trip. I layer him in a sweatshirt for the car ride, then lock up. Before I know it, we're out the door and on the road. Hunter falls asleep quicker than expected.

It's been so long since we've driven somewhere together as a family. The old familiar feeling creeps up, and it almost feels real. Bryan's quiet as we drive our way through the Queens border. I'm not even sure what we can talk about. We used to talk about so much. We'd fight over the radio playfully and chat about our favorite movies. Both of us are huge Ryan Reynolds fans, so we had that, but now there's nothing.

"When do you start your job?" he asks, breaking up the silence.

"I had a shift yesterday. They needed someone to fill in, but I start officially after the holiday when we come back."

His hands grip on the wheel like the thought of me going out and working bothers him. I love that he wants to help, but if I don't find myself without him, I'll never be free from the pain.

"So, what's the plan once we get there?" The question has been weighing on my mind, and I want to change the subject.

"We act married." He keeps his eyes on the road. His posture is stiff and not like the Bryan I fell in love with. "Hunter has his little room, so it will just be you and me."

When they found out we were expecting, Bryan's dad redid an entire room in their large cabin for Hunter. It had everything we needed for him, including a crib, a bed, a diaper changing station, and toys.

"Should we come up with rules and boundaries? Your mom knows us as a touchy-feely couple."

"We should probably continue to act in that way."

I swallow hard. Touching Bryan again won't be good for my heart. A familiar slow steady beat comes on the radio. Without thinking I reach for the knob. A hand knocks into mine, electric jolts shooting up my fingers. Bryan and I lock eyes. It's only brief since he has to watch the road. I expect him to turn the song off, but instead he spins the volume control louder.

A soft smile dances on his lips. "Sorry, we can shut—"

"No." I almost shout but hold back the volume of my voice. "I mean, I still love this song."

"I do too. Especially because the first line is so you. *You say you'll be down in five*, but we know it takes you twenty years to get ready."

"Hey." I give his shoulder a light, playful tap and take notice of the blush forming on his cheek. "I'll have you know the past few months I have learned to become quicker at getting ready. In fact, Hunter and I did a few library classes last month and guess who was on time?"

"No. You? On time? You were practically late for your own wedding."

"Hey!" I counter-argue keeping my tone light. "That was not my fault. Abigail had a wardrobe malfunction."

It's one hundred percent the truth. My friend from work, Abigail, who was also a bridesmaid, had a slight tear in her dress, so thankfully Ellie, being the amazing MOH she was, had a sewing kit ready for action. I sat there sewing Abigail's dress ten minutes before I had to be at the church.

"I vaguely remember us being late for the dinner we had made reservations for on our honeymoon, and it wasn't my fault. I had all my makeup on and was dressed and ready."

"I had to take a shit."

I roll my eyes. "Men. What do you guys do in there? I mean seriously. Do you take a crap and then just sit there scrolling through social media? How many texts have you sent, or phone calls have you taken while sitting on the john?"

Bryan chuckles and it's a sweet sound like honey, and it vibrates through me.

"Remember the time I called you on Christmas Eve saying I was going to be late because of traffic?"

I vaguely remember last Christmas. I had dinner all set out ready to go. Logan, Ellie, Mom, and I were all waiting for his arrival. Then he called and said the traffic was a nightmare.

"No! You were in the bathroom?" I pretend to gasp. "At work too?"

My shoulders shake with mirth. I've missed this more than I care to admit. His laughter grows louder, and I bask in it, taking it all in before I no longer have the privilege of hearing it.

"That's sick. I'm telling El."

"You know it's bad when I resort to taking a dump at work."

I gag and reach over, this time pushing at his leg. The hand closest to me retreats from the steering wheel and briefly brushes over mine and gives a little squeeze. I inhale deeply, shuddering at his touch.

He pulls away and his laughter fades a little, but a smile still holds. Maybe he and I can survive this week together. And as much as it would hurt me, I hope that after we sign those papers, the two of us can co-parent and still be friends. It won't be easy, seeing him with someone else, but Bryan is a catch, and any woman would be lucky to have him. If only my chance hadn't ended so quickly.

CHAPTER 12

We pull up to his family's beautifully renovated log cabin. It was originally a six-bedroom house with an attached three car garage, but within the past few years they have made a huge reno on it, turning it into two smaller rooms.

Some cars are already parked in the large gravel driveway leading up to what once was the garage. Bryan finds a spot along the grass closest to the front door.

Being here makes the reality of the situation come crashing down. A tightness forms over my chest making it hard to breathe. Keeping my eyes focused on the dashboard is kind of helping, but at the same time if I close my eyes and imagine being anywhere but here, I'll open them and know this isn't a dream. I can do this. I can get through the week with Bryan and his family and then go back and start my new life without him.

Before we shut off the car, his mom is already waving to us from the steps. She rushes towards our van and Bryan's hand slips over mine. My eyes flick over to him. I hope he doesn't catch the hitch in my breath at his touch.

"I'm sorry." His melancholy tone throws me off.

"Sorry?"

A bang on the passenger window startles me, it's his mom. Bryan removes his hand from mine. A coldness rushes over the spot he held. I check on Hunter, whose eyes fly open at the sound. Confused, but not upset he blinks at me, trying to get his bearings.

"Hey, Hunter. We're at Gammy and Pa's house."

"Gam-Gam?" he asks in a daze.

I nod. Gayle—Bryan's mom—tugs at the back door and Bryan flips the lock and opens the sliding door. She doesn't waste a minute and crawls into the captain's chair beside Hunter.

"Hunter!" she shouts.

He doesn't look at her right away, but when he does his eyes light up. He loves Bryan's mom. She doesn't get to see him often, but he knows exactly who she is.

"How do I get him out of this contraption?" she asks, glaring at the five-point harness on the car seat.

Bryan chuckles. "I got it, Ma." He slides out of the van and opens the other side. Once he's out, Bryan's mom takes Hunter in her arms and gives him big squeezes. He squirms and she lets him down. Bryan comes around and follows after him.

"My sweet daughter-in-law, come here." She wraps me in her arms.

My eyes sting at the thought of every lie I have to tell this week. I hold on a little tighter than intended and she immediately pulls away, holding me at arm's length to gauge what's happening. She's a retired psychologist and that's what worries me the most. She can read anyone faster than most people.

"Charlotte, sweetheart, is everything okay?"

"Yeah, of course, Gayle. What makes you think anything is wrong?"

"You have stress lines on your forehead."

I touch the smooth surface wondering where she sees any lines. Maybe it's an expression? Whatever it is I have to figure out how to make them go away. "We got Hunter's diagnosis the other day. They said he's on the spectrum."

She claps her hands. "That's wonderful news. You can move forward and get that sweet boy exactly what he needs."

She gets it. She always has. When I first told her the news on a video call, she was on board. Being a psychologist, she knew the signs and agreed with me, even though most of their interaction was through the internet.

"I'm just worried. I shouldn't be, because I'm well equipped to handle anything thrown at us, but it hits home a little harder when it's your own child."

She touches both my shoulders and squeezes. "You know we had Bryan evaluated. I would have done it myself, but I wanted a colleague to check him out."

This was all news to me, and I kind of wonder if he has any idea. Back when we were growing up it felt almost taboo to talk about neurodiversity.

"And what happened?"

"He had a speech delay. A stutter. He was afraid to talk in fear of being made fun of. He had services, but my boy, he was the smartest of the bunch. Straight As from the very beginning." She casually watches Bryan following Hunter and his curious little mind.

My brows knit together. I feel the pull. I'm sure my forehead is full of confused lines now.

"He never told you?"

I shake my head. "No."

Thinking about it, it makes sense as to why Bryan had a hard time coming to terms with the appointment.

Hunter giggles and Gayle and I get distracted for a second. He seems enthralled by the expansive space. He's not used to such a large area without buildings or roadways.

My heart swells with so many different emotions. I wish Bryan would have come and talked to me about all of this. Our fights started around the time I mentioned making the appointment. Maybe he was trying to avoid the subject and taking extra hours at work was a way to keep the conversations at a minimum. It breaks my heart to know he was afraid to tell me. Me, of all people. The woman he once loved.

"Don't tell him I told you."

"I won't. I'm trying to understand why he didn't confide in me."

Aside from this lie burdening me, I now have this whole new issue. It will bother me the entire time we're here. I don't want to go against Gayle's wish, but at the same time I want Bryan to be honest with me. Maybe it's a little too late since we are separated. He's not obligated to tell me anything.

Bryan's head tilts, like he's aware something is wrong. He always could read me well. His mom gives my shoulder a squeeze before returning her attention back to her grandson. Bryan happily gives him over to her. His eyes land back on me.

I shake my head. I can't show him there's something wrong. I give the best smile I can muster and make a motion like I'm tapping the key fob to open the trunk. He jogged over, clicking the button. We pull the luggage out together, a heavy silence falling between us. A silence filled with secrets that if we're not careful might destroy us all over again.

CHAPTER 13

> Ellie: Fuck me! Logan has a man cold.

> Me: Oh no! My condolences to you.

I spin around and settle down onto the red and green Christmas quilt neatly pressed onto the bed. Three dots appear on the conversation, and I wait.

It's been a while since I've been up here in this cabin, and I'd forgotten how beautiful it is. White Christmas lights are hung around the room, and although it's still daytime they are lit, making the room glow behind heavy dark forest green curtains.

> Ellie: Come save me, please. Why do you have to be so far away?

I chuckle, shaking my head. Leave it to my brother to get a "man cold" a few days before Christmas. Mom is going to be pissed. She's already a little upset with me for skipping town on

Christmas, but she also does understand that Bryan's mom needs time with Hunter too.

"What are you laughing at?" Bryan asks, bringing in the last suitcase.

"Logan has come down with the 'man cold.' Maybe I should send flowers, and a sympathy card."

Bryan narrows his eyes, but there's a hint of playfulness in his stare. "Hey, 'man colds' are legit. I had one a month ago and didn't get off the couch for four days."

I roll my eyes. "They are not legit. Remember when I was pregnant and caught the flu, and you got it too. I was up doing dishes, making us dinner, while you pretended you were dying in bed."

His laughter echoes through the room. I bask in it some more. It's odd how much you crave something when you've gone without it for so long. I'd compare it to being pregnant, not eating sushi, and then devouring a whole spicy tuna roll the minute your baby pops out. At least that was my experience.

Maybe I shouldn't compare Bryan to food, but his voice alone has me a little more relaxed than I was this morning and it's pleasurable to hear.

"Not funny, you guys are all the same."

He shrugs, a casual grin crossing his lips. I growl at him, then put my attention back on the text with Ellie.

> Me: I wish I could. Go to your mom's and let him fend for himself.

> Ellie: LOL! I should. He put this app on his phone that sounds like a bell and every time I walk away, he presses it a hundred times to annoy me.

I snort. Logan was always a baby when it came to being sick.

Mom was a sucker though. She was all, *Oh my poor baby*. Then she'd baby him.

> Me: Actually. Drop him off at my mom's house. She'll take care of him.

> Ellie: You're a genius!

I chuckle and rest the phone back on the bed beside me. Bryan has a far-off gleam in his eyes, but it's focused in my direction.

"Where's Hunter?" I ask.

He blinks several times before speaking. The base of his neck flushes and the pink creeps up onto his cheeks. Bryan fidgets with his fingernails before replying. "He's playing in the living room. Sydney is here. Morgan and her wife should be here shortly."

"Oh." I pop up. "I'll go say hi to Syd. I haven't seen her in ages." I start for the door, get halfway there, when Bryan's soft touch rattles me. His hand wraps around my arm in a gentle caress.

One simple touch can say so much, and his says millions of unspoken things.

"Thank you, Char." His voice climbs barely above a whisper. His hand slips lower and right into mine and over the spot where my rings should be. Shit. His own ring finger swirls over the spot, and a hard piece of metal presses into my skin lightly. Peering down, I notice the black tungsten circle still on his left ring finger.

I bite on my bottom lip and pull my hand away. "I should go say hi to everyone," I say softly.

He nods, a lethargic, heavy movement. "I'll be down in a few."

I open my mouth to say okay, but the word never leaves my lips. As I retreat from the room, he shuts the door behind me.

There's a pang of guilt in my heart. My ring had been on my hand a few days ago. I took it off to clean, put it in the jewelry box my late father carved by hand when I was twelve, and forgot to put it back on.

Reaching the top of the stairs, I hold on to the banister. It would be easy to surrender to the tears and anguish I feel over forgetting. The old Charlotte would have brushed it off, stormed into the room and given him an explanation, but as I peer at the shut door, I know it's not what he wants.

I'm about to take a step but stop myself as a round of giggles echoes through the cabin. Glancing over my shoulder at the closed door tugs painfully on my heart. I stare down at the empty spot on my left ring finger. The memory of the day he put it there surfaces, holding me in place.

I should have known I'd be the one to plan my own proposal. Bryan was sneaky like that. I asked him if he'd like to do a couple's photoshoot. He was on board, and jumped at the opportunity a little too eagerly, but I thought nothing of it at the time.

It was a brisk December afternoon. Light snowflakes were falling, but it didn't stop us from having the photoshoot.

We had already decided to take pictures at the school where we met. Luckily the playground was open, and we took several photos on the swings. The best part was the trees in the woods behind the school were covered with falling snow. It was like nature was decorating for us.

Our photographer was amazing. He captured all the bloopers, from me falling into the snow because we attempted to perform a dip, to the snowball fight and Bryan getting blasted in the face with a snowball.

It was at that moment I felt like there was something Bryan was hiding. His glassy eyes reflected a hint of fear as they darted everywhere.

Bryan took my hand; his was cold and sweaty, and there was a slight tremble in his touch. The sun had started fading and we were both cold, but when I rounded the corner of the school my entire body heated up. Along the sidewalk was a pathway lined with beautiful lit lanterns. A small round table with a white cloth was at the end of the path. It was covered in red rose petals and in the center was a beautiful ornate wooden box.

On the other side of the bus circle on the snow-covered lawn, two familiar faces stepped out from behind a tree. A familiar Jonas Brother tune came to life, as Ellie and Mom closed in on us.

Bryan had a few stray tears cascading down his pink cheeks.

"Bry?"

"Char." His voice was rough, edgy, and a little wobbly.

When we got to the small table, he opened the box, and pulled out a smaller blue one. I took a step towards him and underneath the freshly fallen snow was a patch of ice. My foot slipped, and he grabbed me, almost taking himself down in the process, but his quick reflexes saved us.

"Don't need you going down too, officer," I said.

He chuckled. "Trying to recreate the moment we met?"

I laughed, cried, and snorted all at the same time. I hugged a hand to my mouth, and with his free hand he tugged it away.

"Charlotte Rae Fields."

"You're not gonna call me ma'am?" I teased.

His eyes sparkled not only with tears, but with a love so strong I could feel it buzzing through me like an electric current.

He got down on one knee and popped open the box. The beautiful diamond sparkled in the soft light from the lanterns beside him.

"Being your officer in shining blue was the best moment of my life. I knew I'd met my soulmate. I had never once brought someone I helped flowers or something to eat. It hit me while I was in line ordering your hot cocoa."

At that point I couldn't tell whether I was laughing or crying.

"With your mom, Logan, and Ellie's permission…"

"Logan?" I asked, my voice broke.

I searched for him, but he was nowhere.

He nodded. "I got his number from your mom. We talked and he gave me his blessing."

I cried harder, but in a good way. The fact Logan had answered the phone and spoken with him made my heart soar. At that point in time, Logan was still in Pennsylvania, and rarely spoke to us.

"So, with their permission, Charlotte, will you be my wife for the rest of our lives and beyond?"

I had never been so speechless. I nodded. My mouth formed the word, yes, but nothing came out. The second the ring was on my finger he stood, and I jumped into his arms and cried into his shoulder.

"I love you, Char. Forever."

"Forever," I whispered.

There's no time to let the tears fall. Jack, Bryan's dad, catches me in my daze as he comes up from behind me. He's taller than Bryan by a few inches. His hair has receded since the last time I saw him.

"Charlotte, sweetheart. I'm so glad you and Bryan made the trip. He scared us, acted like you two weren't coming." He pulls me into a bear hug. His usual peppermint scent wafts through my nose. His favorite tea flavor. I bite down on my lip, the tears teetering on the edge of my eyes. I blink them away before he pulls back.

"We could never miss Christmas," I say.

A grin dances along his clean-shaven face. "I'm glad to hear it."

Jack pats me on the back. I follow him down the wooden staircase into the living room. A fire is roaring, heating up the room. By the stone fireplace are Sydney and Hunter. She is studying to become an elementary teacher and was so happy to have a little nephew to do learning activities with.

Between the two of them is a peg board, one I've used many times in my therapy sessions with kids. He's ignoring her, doing his own thing, but she keeps encouraging him and telling him what a great job he's doing. I watch the two of them from the bottom step. The empty spot on my hand suddenly feels heavier than before.

Sydney's green eyes light up when she sees me. I take the last step down as she stands and rushes to hug me. "Hey! I've missed you." She holds on for a second longer, then pulls away.

"It's so good to see you," I say. "How many toys did you bring?"

"This one was supposed to be his Christmas gift." She chuckles. "But I couldn't wait. Oh, don't worry, every toy for Christmas is educational."

I love the way she thinks, and how she's so determined to shape little ones' minds. She was meant to be a teacher. I've always seen her potential since the day she told me she got into the early childhood program she'd been working towards.

The stairs creak and the two of us turn our attention there. Bryan stops at the bottom.

"On top, on top!"

We all stare down at Hunter, who's casually in his own little world as he stacks a red on top of another red.

"On top. On top."

Forgetting that Bryan's gaze is glued to me, I kneel on the floor beside Hunter and hug him. He doesn't respond much and continues to concentrate on his blocks. It doesn't matter because my son saved me from breaking down and telling them all.

"You're a smarty pants like your dada," Sydney coos at him, as she takes a seat back on the floor.

There are footsteps behind me, but they walk in the opposite direction instead of towards us. I catch the back of Bryan's head as he goes into the kitchen, where the scent of mixed cheeses and burnt breadcrumbs slips through the threshold and into the living room.

His sister Morgan and her wife Sam arrive a few minutes later. She's all dressed up like she came straight from work in her gray pants suit. Sam is the complete opposite, preferring some sweats and an old sweater for the trip.

"Hey, Char." Sam hugs me. She towers over me, even more than Bryan.

"Hey, Morgan, how are things?"

"Well…" She grins. "We may need some hand-me-downs from you soon…" Morgan locks eyes with Sam, a beautiful sacred exchange passing between them.

Gayle is already touching the small protruding stomach Sam is sporting under her sweater. She's got the right idea for her outfit. Being pregnant and traveling for several hours is a lot.

"Oh my God. Congrats. When did you find out?"

"I told Bryan like three months ago. Did he really not tell you? How did he keep it a secret for so long?"

Three months ago, we were both still healing. We didn't joke around the way we have been lately. It was an even darker period than now. I'm still a little offended he didn't tell me though. "He uh, he never told me," I say, trying to keep a smile on my face. "I haven't donated any of my clothes yet, I wanted to hold on to them in case, but now with the sep—"

Her eyes narrow, and I stop myself from talking.

"Just in case we had more, but I'll gladly go through everything and send them your way."

She squints at me, like she's onto me, but if she is, she doesn't call me out. "That sounds great."

After they say their hellos, they head upstairs to settle in and for Sam to take a short nap.

I keep myself busy with Sydney and Hunter, until lunch is

ready. If there is one thing Hunter loves, it's mac and cheese. I help set up the dining room table, and we all sit down together to eat. To make things less awkward I set Hunter's chair between Bryan and myself, but even so there's still a heaviness hanging over our side of the large oval table. I hope no one notices.

CHAPTER 14

The day passes quickly, and within a blink of an eye I'm in the kitchen with Bryan's mom and sisters preparing the coffee and organizing some after-dinner snacks. Morgan and Sam brought donuts on their way over from the airport. They smell delicious and they're from the most raved about bakery in the area.

I help with wiping down the countertops. My mind is anywhere but in this cabin. It's going over my schedule for when we return, and the fear of the divorce papers that will probably be waiting for me in a pile on my own countertop. Also hoping a teaching job will pop up so I can make even more money for Hunter and me.

"You're quieter than usual." Morgan's voice startles me, pulling me from my erratic thoughts.

I smile, but it's weak. "My brain is flipping through all of the things waiting for me after the holidays."

She nods. "I hear that. Taking time off for me as a lawyer is not a good thing. I know when I return, I'll have a ton of paperwork to sort through. I brought my laptop and some files with me in case, but man, I'm going to be swamped. Are you sure there's nothing more going on?"

"No. I'm okay."

"You know postpartum depression can hit many years later too. Are you seeing someone? Mom can ask around for a counselor in your area, I'm sure she has friends…"

"Thank you, Morgan. I—It's nothing I can't work through on my own. I saw someone after my dad passed and have mostly been okay since."

She steps closer to me. "I know we aren't close, and it sucks I'm all the way in Colorado, but I love you like a sister, and I want you to know that I'm here for you." There's a half-knowing look in her eyes. "Are you and Bry okay? You tiptoe around each other like one of you might burst."

I grab hold of the counter, allowing my hand to rest there. *Smell the flowers, blow out the candles.* All I have to do is get through the week and then this will all be over. "We had a stupid fight on the way up here. Nothing some makeup sex can't solve."

She chuckles. Morgan has always been easy to talk to, so joking about sex wasn't taboo. "Well, you have a house full of babysitters. You can have all the alone time you need."

"That was the plan all along," I say, trying to make the conversation lighthearted, because any more serious small talk might spill everything we came here to hide.

After dessert, I take Hunter up to get a bath. There's a bathroom attached to our room, which is useful, and private. Although tonight might get a little awkward.

Sydney knocks at the open door. She peers in around the frame as I dump a small cup of water over Hunter's head. "Hey. Can I put him to bed tonight? I found an amazing book that I'm convinced he'll love."

Morgan was right, I do have a ton of babysitters here this week. Maybe it's what I need; and maybe Bryan and I can have some time to sit down and talk without the burden of rushing out to work and without an excuse to leave. We are both stuck here and although I could get up and leave at any time, it's a lot harder than when we're home.

"Of course. He's almost done. I have to get all this soap out of his hair first."

"Awesome! I'll wait in the room."

When Hunter is well cleaned, I take him out and dress him in our room. Sydney is waiting on the rocking chair for me to bring him in.

"What book are you reading?"

She pulls up one with the Pigeon on the front cover.

"Oh. Pigeon, we love him. We don't have that one."

"Please, stay and listen. This is a good one!"

"Don't mind if I do," I say, placing him on her lap, and taking a seat on the floor beside them.

"Hunter, look it's the Pigeon."

He's busy playing with a string on Sydney's university sweatshirt, but Hunter kind of pays attention to the book. "Pigeon silly. I like pigeons." He holds out his feet and wiggles his tiny toes inside his red socks.

Sydney chuckles.

When the book ends, he's still a little wired, so she offers to read him another story. I'm exhausted. I give Hunter a quick kiss on the head before heading out. It's quiet in the house now, the downstairs lights have been shut off.

As I close the door to our room, the bathroom door opens and a half-naked Bryan walks out. A navy-blue towel is wrapped low around his waist. I don't know where to turn my attention. My eyes dart everywhere around the room. It's hard not to peek, because my hus—ex-husband is a beautiful human being and still is.

"I forgot my soap," he says with a rasp.

I lift my eyes to the ceiling and attempt to walk, but he heads in the same direction. Our bodies bump, then our gazes meet. I suck in a harsh breath, as we do a little dance. He goes one way, and I somehow go the same. It takes us a few seconds of scooting back and forth, along with a soft chuckle to figure out how to go in opposite directions. He gets what he needs then goes back.

If things were normal, he would have taken me in his arms and dragged me into the shower with him. I want to cave and forgive but there's so much more to it than that. Isn't there? With a sigh I settle onto the bed and reach for my phone on the bedside table. I text Ellie to help keep my mind off the fact that the man I'm still insanely attracted to will be naked on the other side of the door.

Me: How's Logan? Should we prepare for his funeral?

Ellie: I don't think the cold is what will kill him.

She ends her response with an emoji sticking out its tongue. I snort.

Me: LOL! Make sure you hide the body well.

Ellie: He says, real funny. We are watching some action movie and now I want to die.

Me: Ugh, make him watch a rom com that will get him out of bed.

Ellie: How is it going up at the cabin? You and Bry okay?

Are we okay? I can't tell. He told me we had to pretend we were still lovey-dovey, but since our arrival and his discovery of my missing rings, he hasn't said much to me. If we don't step up our game his family will find out sooner rather than later.

> Me: It's going. I forgot my ring, and he noticed. His mom and sister are onto me. I'll keep you updated.

Unable to sit still I stride across the room to where my suitcases sit beside the wooden dresser. We are going to be here for a while, so I put my things in the top two drawers.

Bryan steps out a few minutes later. He's fully clothed now, must have brought all his stuff in with him so we didn't have another naked encounter.

"So, your sister and mom have both said something to me," I say.

"Which one?"

"Morgan. She asked me if I had postpartum depression."

"And what did you tell her?"

I stop folding my clothes and stare over at him. The muscles in his back are tense; even through his black T-shirt it's hard to miss it.

"It doesn't matter." I pause. "Look, I can explain about—" I briefly stare at my empty finger.

"No, don't. It's not like we're together, I should have expected it."

When I check out his hand, my heart drops into my stomach. He took his off too. There's a building sob crawling up my throat, but I push it down best I can, turning it into a painful hiccup instead.

"Are you coming to bed? I'm tired, I want to shut off the light." His heated tone doesn't help the queasiness in my stomach. He pulls back the quilt and the covers on the bed.

"Bryan, if you want them to believe we are still together you might as well play along like we are. This was your idea to begin with, not mine. If you don't want to pretend, I'd be happy to tell them."

"We can't tell them. We can do better tomorrow. I'm done talking now, shut the lights when you're done."

There's no hiding it now. A few gentle tears fall down my cheek, landing on my lips. I wipe them away, but more fall. I turn away from him, grab some pajamas from the drawer, then head into the bathroom. I don't slam the door, I'm more sad than angry.

To drown out the pending sob, I turn on the shower. I grab a towel from the closet, wrapping it over the bar outside the tub. When I hop in, I unleash the tears. Holding my face in my hands, I lower myself and bring my knees to my chest, allowing the water to fall over me Harsh echoing sobs surround me, and I hope the water is loud enough to drown them out.

Why did I agree to this? I knew this would happen; that I'd spend every night crying my eyes out after a day of pretending. It's all too much, but I know Hunter needs time with Bryan's family. I won't ruin it for them. After a good cry, I stand and finish my shower.

Feeling wide awake, I make the decision to go downstairs. Bryan is under the covers. He isn't snoring, but his body moves in a fluid motion as he breathes.

I'm not sure what I'm going to do downstairs, but all I know is I'm not ready to slide into bed next to Bryan. It's been six months since we slept in the same bed, and there's no telling how my body might react.

There's a scratching noise coming from the kitchen. I lean against the door frame. Jack is hunched over the table with some tools. He's staring down at what appears to be a wooden toolbox. I'm quiet as can be, but it doesn't stop him from lifting his gaze to find me watching.

"Hey, Charlotte. Everything okay?"

"I couldn't sleep. Mind if I come in and grab a bite."

Jack smiles, lowering the goggles off his face. "Don't tell Gayle I'm using her kitchen for woodworking."

I chuckle. "Your secret is safe with me. What are you making?"

I browse through the cabinets for something simple to munch on, find one of those mini bags of pretzels and open it.

"It was supposed to be a surprise, but do you think Hunter will like it?" He turns the wooden box around and carved into the top corner are the words, *Hunter's Tools*. Laid out on the table are handcrafted realistic tools.

Sometimes when I'm having a rough time my brain likes to throw memories of my dad at me. The toolbox brings back one of him and Logan working in the garage when we were young. He had this "real toolkit" and would imitate Dad. When I asked to play too, Logan told me woodworking was for boys only.

One night while Logan was sleeping, Dad brought me downstairs to teach me how to use a few of the tools. Seeing Bryan's dad create something out of wood hits me hard.

"Charlotte, are you alright?" Jack stands from his seat, his brows narrowing on me.

I'm dizzy but hold my own against the spin of the room. "Yeah. Sorry. It's beautiful. You did it all yourself?" I ask, trying to keep my voice from cracking.

He puts all the handcrafted tools into the wooden box. "I sure did. I love woodworking, something Bryan never got into much. Morgan though, she's got an eye for it, but you know she wanted to be a big-shot lawyer, so she doesn't have the time anymore."

I take the seat across from him. "May I?"

He slides the tools over, then gets a sponge from the sink to clean up the sawdust he's left on the table. Every few seconds he's checking over my shoulder, probably waiting for Gayle to catch him.

I forget all about the bag of pretzels I've laid on the table while admiring his work. "This— Wow. I'm in awe. My dad and I…" I start to say, but my voice wavers. "He loved woodworking.

He made me a jewelry box, and even showed me how to make a few things. I'm not good at it, but it was fun. He built me this beautiful shelf. In fact, it's still in my childhood bedroom. Some days I miss him more than others." I spin the box and lift out each tool. There's a hammer, a saw, a bolt, a wrench, all perfectly crafted and sanded down.

"I wish we could have met him. What else did you like doing with him?"

"Vacations. My dad was the kind of guy who wanted to see the world. Before Logan and me, my parents did some traveling. He even loved staycations. We went to so many places all over Long Island. Greenport was his favorite. Have you ever been?" I ask.

He nods. "Oh, yes. Gayle and I spent a lot of our summers there as well. She loves eating crabs and walking through town."

I run my fingers over the carving of Hunter's name. Jack and Dad would have gotten along well. They are similar in many ways. A tear pools at the corner of my eye.

"I lost my dad too. I was young. Fifteen."

Bryan rarely talks about his grandparents, mostly because he really didn't know them.

"Some days are better than others," I admit.

"It's been a long time for me, and I still have days like that."

"It's so hard. There have been so many times, I'll think about him, and the memories bring smiles and not a single tear." My voice breaks, as I wipe away some of the wetness starting to drip. "Then sometimes, it hits me, and when things are bad, I just wish he were here."

Dropping my elbows to the table, I rest my head in my hands. "I'm sorry," I say. "Life's been a little rocky lately, so I'm a bit emotional."

His laughter is kind and gentle. "I understand," he says, pulling a chair up beside me. "My favorite memory of my dad was probably our fishing trips. He had this boat and every

Sunday we'd go out in the bay and fish. I do wish Bryan had gotten to meet him too. So, I get it."

A sob escapes, making my cheeks burn.

"I know my wife is prying, but I can't help but notice a little rift between the two of you. Everything okay? I know marriage isn't all sunshine and rainbows sometimes, but I've never seen you two so..." He rubs the silver scruff on his chin. "So distant."

I shake my head. "I promised not to tell, but if I don't tell someone here, I might burst."

"Tell us what?"

In one trembling breath I spill it all. From the fighting to the big blow-up and the divorce papers. He tugs a napkin from the silver holder in the center of the table and hands it to me. I dab at the corners of my eyes and wipe my cheeks. "I'm sorry, Jack. It's been a long few months."

"I won't tell anyone. You can count on that. My son isn't very good at talking about his feelings. Getting anything out of him is like pulling teeth. There's still something there though, isn't there?"

I shrug. "I don't know. Sometimes I feel it, other times, I don't."

"You still love my son." It's not a question. It's a statement.

"So much," I say, through trembling lips.

His hand touches my shoulders, and then he pulls me close. I feel closer to Jack than I do my stepdad. He and I have never really talked. Talking to Jack feels different: there are so many things he understands better than even my mom.

"Do you want my opinion?"

"Can't hurt," I say, through a sniffle.

"If he didn't still love you, why would he invite you this week? I know my son, and I think he hasn't told us because he doesn't want it to be real. Once it's out in the open, it's no longer a thought in his head. It's his reality. He looks at you the same way he did when he told us he was marrying you. Nothing's changed."

Rubbing my temples, I blow out a harsh breath.

Jack squeezes my shoulder. "You should get some rest, it's late."

The time on the stove reads 2:04AM. He's right, Hunter will be up in a few hours, and I don't think anyone wants to see the "mombie" I turn into if I don't get enough sleep.

"Thank you, Jack. For listening to me babble, and for this beautiful gift for Hunter."

Smiling, he pulls me in for a hug. "Anytime, Charlotte. You're like a third daughter to me. Don't be afraid to come talk to me. I know I'm not your father, nor am I his replacement, but if you need some fatherly wisdom, I'm your guy."

A small smile tugs at my lips. I pull away, and stand, sniffling to erase the tears before I crawl into bed.

"Goodnight," I say.

He wishes me goodnight, then returns to his cleaning. Back upstairs, I make my way through the darkened room, the nightlight plugged into the wall illuminates a pathway for me.

I slip under the covers, and although Bryan's on the other side of the queen-sized bed, I can still feel the warmth of his body. I lie the opposite way, so I can't see him. He adjusts and I know he's moved to face me. I want to so badly to reach out and touch him, but don't, because he's not mine to touch anymore. The thought makes my heart constrict. No matter how much of what Jack said might be true, I'm not so sure Bryan loves me, but I can hang on to some more hope now. I close my eyes and push myself to fall asleep.

CHAPTER 15

I wake to an empty bed. I haven't slept with Bryan in months, and out of instinct I reach for his pillow and tug it towards me. His soapy scent lingers, mixed with the cedarwood of the over-priced shampoo he buys.

Beside me on the bedside table is the monitor. Hunter is gone, but the high-pitched voices on the other side of the door let me know he's running around.

Groaning, I get out of bed. I have to start this day eventually. Yesterday was somewhat of a nightmare, and I fear what today will bring and wonder if I can handle it. I dress warmly. Even with the heating on in the house and the number of bodies, there's a chill. Pulling the heavy curtains aside I sneak a peek at the light snow flurries floating around the gray morning sky.

After taking some time to enjoy the scenery and remembering how damn lucky I am to be spending the holidays with people I consider family, I head downstairs.

"Good morning, sweetheart." Gayle is the first to notice me, her gaze immediately flickers to my eyes. When I checked the mirror heavy purple bags drooped underneath.

"Morning," I say in the most chipper voice I can muster.

Gayle is sitting to the left of my chair at the end of the table, while Jack occupies the spot opposite me. It feels like a normal morning, and it gives me some relief. Jack waves as he shovels food into his mouth, and continues his conversation with Sydney, who gives me a sweet hello.

Bryan stands and walks behind Hunter's seat. He pulls out the chair for me. My feet feel as if they've grown bricks on them. I can't move, but when I look over at Hunter and his arms outstretched for me, it gives my body the kickstart I need.

As if things were normal, Bryan tugs me into him. His warm hands wrap around my waist. I hold back a gasp as he presses a kiss on my cheek, but it lands at the edge of my lips. His body is flush against me, and I attempt to regain my composure as his family's eyes land on us.

With trembling hands, I take a bowl of scrambled eggs from Gayle and scoop some onto my plate. From the other side of the table Morgan is watching me with cautious eyes.

"So, what's the plan for today?" I ask, finally feeling somewhat calm.

"Oh, Bryan and Jack are going out to get our tree. When they return, we'll decorate it. I need all the ladies' hands on deck: we're going to decorate the whole place."

"I get the outside," Morgan says. "I want to Clark Griswold this place."

"Please don't." Bryan chuckles.

"Remember when Dad got the tree that was too big? Mom nearly had a heart attack."

Jack joins in the laughter. "Hey, I measured correctly, it was the guy who cut down our tree who measured wrong."

"No, Dad, you were off by several inches. They even had it written down," Morgan cuts in.

"Great, now my kids are going to gang up on me." Jack smirks.

"No, dear, they are making sure you don't make the same

mistake. Bryan, please make sure your father doesn't bring home a gigantic tree again."

"I can't make any promises. I mean, my boy needs a real beefy tree. Right, buddy?"

"Tree, Daddy?"

"Yes, buddy. We are going to get the biggest tree in the lot."

"So big," Hunter says, arms wide.

"Oh, Charlotte, I think you'd be perfect to set up my village over the fireplace."

"I love Christmas villages. Bryan and I—" I suck in a harsh unintended breath, freezing up at the words. The room gets too quiet, and the piercing silence brings me back. "Bryan and I have one we set up too in my favorite hutch. We have an ice-skating rink and a train."

For a second no one speaks, but then Gayle breaks the silence. "A train! Why didn't I think of that? You know I might have one put away from years ago that we used under the tree. Wonder if it still works. Little Hunter would probably love it like his daddy did."

"We had a train under the tree?" Bryan asks.

"Yeah. You had this Thomas the Train obsession. In fact, I think I might have stored it away with the old metal trains."

"Those are collectibles, probably worth a decent chunk. I took care of them."

"Maybe you can display them on Hunter's shelf in his room," I suggest.

Bryan contemplates this. "That's not a bad idea."

"Oh, Charlotte, we'd love to see your house. You gave us a small tour before the wedding when there was no furniture, but we didn't see it all put together. Maybe next year we could come to your house, during the holiday break. Or maybe we can stop by on our way down to Florida this year."

I hold my breath and peek over at Bryan.

"Yeah, Ma, I'm sure we could work something out, right,

Char?"

My cheeks flush warm, burning like the yule log on Christmas. "Yeah. Yeah. Of course, we can."

She clasps her hands, a bright smile on her wrinkled face. "Well, it's settled then. We will work something out. I'm so excited now!"

Bryan clears his throat. "Dad, should we get moving."

Jack checks the sports watch on his wrist. He pats his face with his napkin. "You're right, son, with it being so close to Christmas I doubt there will be much left."

Jack makes his way around the table to give his wife a kiss. She glances up at him lovingly, and follows him out of the room, with some dirty plates. They make some kind of gesture at each other, like they are both still in the honeymoon phase, and I have to turn away to protect my heart.

Morgan and Sam start up a separate conversation, and Sydney asks if she can take Hunter into the living room to play. I wish she lived closer, because I'd hire her in a heartbeat to watch him so I could work again.

Bryan's hand touches my shoulder. I'd been so wrapped up in my own thoughts I hadn't realized he was still in the room. My attention flickers to the hand where the ring has magically appeared again. I hold my breath before finishing the journey to his eyes.

His brows knit, and he presses his lips, like he wants to say something. The floor creaks and we both snap out of it. He leans down and kisses my forehead, our eyes meeting again, and our gaze lingers longer than I expected it to. He's the first to veer off in another direction.

"Bryan, you ready?" Jack asks, before leaving the room.

"Yeah, Dad. I'm coming." Before he releases my shoulder, he gives me one last kiss. I wait for him to move away. I dread it. It's not until Jack clears his throat that Bryan finally retreats, leaving the space beside me feeling emptier than it ever has before.

CHAPTER 16

The village on the mantle was a lot of fun to create. I've been working on it while Hunter is napping. He and I played a little outside in the light coating of snow and by the time we came back inside he was exhausted.

I put the finishing touches on the skating rink made of tinfoil, and then step away to make sure everything is perfect. The white fabric snow sticks up in some places, so I shift around a few of the small buildings to help make it look better.

The front door opens and Bryan and Jack slowly carry the tree inside. It's pretty large, but the living room has high vaulted ceilings, so it should be okay. His mom helps by bringing in the stand and the water, and together they manipulate it.

Hunter stirs on the monitor, just in time to decorate the tree. Gayle gathers everyone back inside. Morgan and Sam have done the outside lights and decorations and I can't wait to see them tonight when the sun goes down.

"Hey, baby boy." Inside the room, Hunter lies staring up at the stars plastered on the white ceiling.

"Daddy's here with the tree," I whisper.

Hunter blinks up at me. He stares off as if his mind is

somewhere other than here. I pick him up and set him on the ground to change his pull-up. Toilet training him has been a nightmare. He's fine during the day but for naps and overnight I use the pull-ups for any accidents.

"Are you ready to decorate the tree?" I ask.

He bends and reaches for the pack of wipes on the ground beside him and plays with it, his mind once again enthralled by an object. I let him keep it, as I finish changing the pull-up.

"You have to go pee-pee on the potty?"

He shakes his head. His pull-up had some in it from his nap, so I'll have him try later.

"Decorating is going to be so much fun. You get to go first and pick a special ornament to hang up there for Gammy and Pa."

"It green?" he asks.

"The tree?"

"It's green."

"Yes, baby. Green."

I grab the wipes, placing them on the small dresser next to the crib. A loud piercing scream comes from his mouth. He cries and lashes out by hitting the dresser.

"Come on, Hunter. Let's go decorate the tree."

He screams again. Tears stream down his bright red cheeks as he lifts his arms attempting to grab the wipes.

I reach for him, touching his arms. Sometimes running a hand up and down his arm helps him relax, but he's not having it. I try to keep my cool. He's in a new environment and his schedule is thrown off by our trip.

He's screaming loud enough for everyone downstairs to hear. The door to the room squeals open. Bryan crosses the room and sits cross-legged on the floor beside him. In his hand is a bright azure ornament with his favorite dog Blue on it.

"Hey, Hunter," he says calmly.

Hunter ignores him. Bryan dangles the Christmas ornament in front of Hunter. His scream fades as his eyes land on the ball.

"There we go, buddy. Do you want to hang this on the tree?"

Hunter doesn't answer but keeps trying to grab the ball. Bryan gives him the ornament, then takes his hand. Bryan's eyes lift and meet mine. I close mine and nod to thank him.

Back downstairs everyone is waiting for Hunter.

"I want a family photo. The three of you go and hang it."

"Gayle, sweetheart," Jack whispers, placing a hand on her shoulder. He leans down whispering something in her ear that makes her chuckle. His eyes find mine, and I realize he's trying to distract her. It doesn't last long because she's adamant about getting the shot.

I try not to show my lack of enthusiasm for the idea and expect Bryan to try to get out of it, but instead his hand slips into mine. He pulls me over to the tree and lifts Hunter. Gayle takes pictures while we hang the ornament together.

"Guys, look this way."

"Daddy's new house has tree," Hunter whispers to himself out of nowhere.

"Hunter," Bryan says, his cheeks flushed red. "Look at the camera."

My eyes meet Bryan's, and his wobble with worry. If anyone is going to spill our secret, I never imagined it being Hunter. He doesn't understand what's happening. He knows he goes to a different house to hang out with his dad, but I don't know what he's interpreting it as.

"Hey, Bryan and Charlotte, this way," Gayle encourages.

I'm afraid to see what kind of smile Bryan has on his face. My attention is solely on Gayle, who is snapping a ton of photos. I'd ask her to send them, but if this is our last Christmas together as a couple—a fake couple—I don't want pictures.

"Oh, what's above you two love birds?" Sam remarks, her eyes glancing up at something above us.

I'm positive it was Gayle's doing. A small piece of mistletoe hangs on a string from the lower point of the ceiling.

"Here, give me Hunter," Sydney says, reaching for him.

Bryan's gaze flickers to me, then back at his sister, and to me again. I nod. If he wants to keep up appearances, we have to do this. Sydney happily takes Hunter and brings him over with the rest of them. They all stand there like we are famous, and they are the fans waiting for a show. Gayle is the paparazzi waiting for the money shot.

Being here in front of them reminds me of the day we took our vows. We said we'd make it through anything life threw at us, but clearly, we lied in front of everyone we love.

"I chose you the day we met. When I reached you and almost got taken out by the same ice patch, I just knew. I called you ma'am and in your dazed state your response made me laugh. Something clicked for me then, but how can someone know from one simple conversation?"

In front of our friends and family Bryan's voice broke, a few tears slid down his cheek. I let go briefly to wipe them away. He leaned into my touch and lifted his hand to his cheek, covering mine. "I love you," he mouthed. We stayed in that position while he finished his vows.

"I'll never understand it. Maybe it was your smile, or the beautiful sound of your laughter, but while I stood in line at the coffee shop waiting for the hot chocolate, a bouquet of flowers tucked under my arm, it was like I pictured myself doing this every day for you. I think that's how I knew. Charlotte Rae Fields, my heart was yours from the moment I stepped out of that police car. And my heart will forever remain yours. Through whatever curveballs life throws at us, I'll always be your knight in shining blue."

When it came time, we both leaned forward, without

hesitation, without reserve, and when our lips met, I melted in his arms, hoping never to leave them.

I open my eyes as the memory fades. Bryan's stare jolts my body, causing my shoulders to twitch. My lips part, eager to say something, but I'm unsure of what. The kiss on the head this morning was one thing, but to feel his lips pressed against mine. I have to inhale and hold it before release. I close the gap between us.

He lowers his mouth to my ear. "If this is too much, Char…"

With the side of his face nearly flush against mine I tilt so our cheeks rub together. The scruff on his face is so familiar and nice. Bryan's breath catches in his throat. I swear he doesn't let go of the air for a few seconds.

My knees wobble, but I'm saved by him slipping his whole arm behind me to hold me up. My eyes focus on his lips again. I've kissed them millions of times and allowed them to do things to me that I shouldn't even be thinking about in front of his family. It's hard not to remember, even if it's been months. I haven't stopped fantasizing about them.

"I'm okay. Kiss me, Bry." The words are out of my mouth before I can stop them. They're low, raspy, and not like me.

We crash into each other with urgency. Neither of us opens our mouths, not at first anyway. It's a family photo and there's no need for it. I expect him to pull away, but as their attention wanes from us to Hunter doing something cute, his mouth opens first.

"Charlotte," he murmurs into my lips.

I can feel the ache in every part of me pining for this. For us. Even the butterflies I felt when he first smiled at me return with a vengeance. I want to fight for this man, I want him to fight for me. God damn, I have missed him.

For a short-lived moment our tongues meet, and electricity zaps us both into reality as we jump away from each other.

"Who's hanging the next ornament?" Jack asks.

Bryan's cheeks glow pink.

"Oh, that's me!" Sydney yells out.

Speechless. We're both speechless. Ironic, as that was our wedding song. As Sydney comes to the tree, she bumps into me and hands me Hunter. It's over before it even begins, and when I search for Bryan amidst the chaos of the entire family bombarding the tree, he's no longer in the room. I don't have a chance to find him, because I'm given two more ornaments to hang on the tree.

Jack hands me one of them, but keeps it in his grasp, as if he's waiting for me to tell him I'm okay. I shrug because I know I will be, but right now, I'm not really doing well. He squeezes my hand in understanding and gives me the ornament. I spin to throw the ornament on the tree when Bryan's eyes find mine from across the room. He knows.

Instead of confronting me he heads for the box with ornaments, and casually steps back into the mix. I let Hunter down to continue decorating the tree.

As Bryan and I help, we exchange a few words, he holds my hand, and bravely goes in for another kiss on the cheek. The worst part is that it really is fake. There's no passion behind any of it, not like the one before. At least, that's what it feels like, until I lift on my toes to put one last ornament on the tree but fail to get it on the branch, I'd like it to go on. He easily slips his fingers over mine. His other hand rests on my waist where my shirt is rising. His hands on my skin are like fire, and I'm burning up from the simple touch. When I land flat foot, he freezes in place, and I swear he stops breathing. My body tingles. His eyes are focused on my body, like the touch has ignited something in him.

❄

I'm glad for the chaos of the afternoon. The decorating, and the extra cooking for tomorrow's big dinner to distract me from how badly I need him. But as night falls and everyone slowly trickles to bed, I'm in the bedroom, alone with my own thoughts. I don't know where Bryan is, but I'm thirsty and can't sleep.

I reach the top step and two distinct male voices are whisper-yelling below me. Bryan paces in front of the stairs, so I throw myself back against the wall so he can't see me.

Footsteps pound heavily on the floor below. "Wait, how did, how did you—? She told you, didn't she? Did Mom squeeze it out of her?"

"No, son, no one squeezed it out of anyone. It's obvious you two are in some kind of disagreement. Doesn't mean I don't see the love in your eyes."

I have to remember to thank Jack for not ratting me out. It sounds like Bryan stops at the foot of the stairs. Peeking around the corner, I'm right. He runs a frustrated hand through his hair.

"No, Dad, you don't get it. We aren't compatible, there's nothing holding us together, except for Hunter. Why are you drilling me anyway? I'm a grown man and I don't need to hash out my feelings."

Jack sighs. "First, you're never too old to hash out your feelings with your dad. Secondly, I know you don't believe that. You look at her as if your whole world revolves around her. Even now. You still love her."

"I-I… uh—I uh… of course I love her, that's not the point. I'll always love her." His words are a bit broken, like a few times when we've argued, and he couldn't clearly get his thoughts off his lips.

He's quiet, and there's no movement from either of them.

"What happened, Bryan? You two were the happiest couple I know. There's nothing you can't work through."

The silence is deafening. I don't know if Bryan will answer his dad. Again, I check on him. He's sitting on the bottom step now, head in his hands. Jack leans against the wall his hand braced on Bryan's shoulder.

"I failed her."

His words are piercing. Failed me? Is that what he thinks?

Jack says nothing, like he's waiting for Bryan to go on. I've never heard him express himself in this way. We have had serious conversations, but I've never heard him talk like that about himself.

It takes everything in me to not trudge down those steps and tell him that he never failed me.

"Son, you didn't fail anyone. That woman loves you as fiercely as you love her."

I shouldn't be listening to this. If Bryan wanted to tell me all of this, he would have. I attempt to tiptoe across the hallway, but the floorboards creak and both men shoot their gazes up to where I am. My eyes catch theirs, but instead of sticking around I run back to the room.

Slamming the door, I race to the bed and crawl inside. I expect nothing to happen, but the door to the room flies back open, and bangs against the frame as it shuts again.

"You told him, Charlotte. I know you did. My dad doesn't assume things, he's not Mom. What did you say?"

Here we go, another fight. I've been through enough that the tears don't even come, all I feel is anger. I throw the comforter off me. I'm tired of this, tired of Bryan getting the upper hand in our arguments, blaming me for things.

"YES! Are you happy? I told him. I came downstairs and he was making..." I pause, because talking about my dad is a trigger for the tears that I've fought back so far. "He was making Hunter's Christmas gift, and I told him about my dad, and it all came out of me. I needed a father figure to tell me it was all okay."

"I told you I d-didn't want any of them to-to know yet. We were supposed to do that together. Now my mother—my..." He growls like he can't get his words out, and that's when what Gayle told me comes to light. "Now she's going to try to throw her therapy strategies at us."

"Your dad said he wouldn't tell her. What's wrong with her throwing them at us? Maybe it would help. Like instead of holding things in about your childhood and your feelings, you'd tell me what's going on. Our communication sucks, Bryan. There's nothing wrong with getting help."

Again, his hands are in his hair. He tugs at the ends and growls in frustration. "Why can't you listen to me."

"I have been, Bryan. I always listen to you, but I can't read your mind or your thoughts. I confided in him because, when he spoke to me it felt like I was talking to my dad again. He sat with me and listened, as mine always had for me."

"Well, you didn't need to hash out our secret."

My mind shifts focus from us to something different. Living without my father has been the hardest obstacle I've ever had to navigate. I wish he'd understand. I never told Jack out of spite to hurt Bryan.

"I felt it was a safe space. He was there, our conversation was comforting, and I spilled. You don't know what it's like to wake up every day and wish you could pick up the phone and call one of your parents only to realize…" Now my lips are quivering, and I can't stop the tears. "Only to realize they are no longer there to give you the advice that helps you grow. You don't get it."

I'm finding it hard to focus on him. The anger and sadness mixing are a lethal combination. It's why we ended. Why we couldn't see past what the other was saying.

"The reason why this—" I point between us "—why this didn't work, was because you kept everything to yourself. Seems it's not only me you like to keep secrets from. I know you didn't work just because you wanted extra money for diapers and shit. We were fine, there was something else that you were working hard for, but you chose to keep it a secret, and then let it destroy us."

Bryan is quiet. His hands are at his side, I expect them to be balled into fists, but they aren't.

"I'm tired of secrets, Bry," I whisper.

His shoulders slump forward. I still can't meet his gaze, because as Jack had said, there's still love there. I know there is. Looking at it will only make walking away harder.

I point to the bed. "I don't want to fight anymore. Please don't make me fight anymore. I'm tired." I mean physically and mentally.

Not allowing him to say another word to me, I slip under the covers and pull them all the way up to my chin. Rolling myself into a ball I shut my eyes tight.

There are several beats of silence before his footsteps head for the bed and the mattress shifts under his weight.

Even with my eyes closed I know he's facing me. He's closer than last night. In the stillness I swear I feel his hand movements. If I wasn't so sleepy, I'd think he was drawing the shape of a heart with his fingers on the mattress.

It's hard to hide the trembling rush of air leaving my lips. If he notices he doesn't react. I listen to him breathing and eventually my body no longer fights the heaviness and succumbs to a restless, yet dreamless sleep.

CHAPTER 17

Today is Christmas Eve. There's so much to be done tonight, especially after Hunter goes to bed. I'm not sure what Bryan got for him, but I brought a few gifts here myself, and left the rest under our own tree, so he can see Santa visited there too.

I stand behind Hunter while he's perched on a chair leaning over the counter helping me roll dough. It's Christmas cookie time, and the first batch has already been thrown into the oven. Hunter is making cookies specifically for Santa.

Santa is coming later—well Jack is. He volunteered to do it for Hunter. Last year's picture with the mall Santa was horrendous and I told myself I would never put my child through that again. I'm willing to bet it was the setting and environment which caused him to have a meltdown and left us $70 poorer. He's also older this year so hopefully luck will be on our side.

"Good job, buddy," I say, as we take the roller and gently push it back and forth together.

A warm body presses up against me from behind. I know the feeling of Bryan from anywhere. He sweeps some of my hair behind me, sending shivers coursing through me. My shirt is one size too big, so the hair he brushes away exposes the skin of my shoulder. I'm not expecting the chill as his fingers slowly trace a heart over the exposed skin. Maybe I wasn't imagining things in bed.

It's been over six months since I felt him do that. Any time we'd fight, even minor ones, after we'd cooled off, he'd come over and trace a heart on my body wherever he could touch. Sometimes my hand, my back, other times right over the real one pumping inside me. It was his way of saying sorry.

Bryan's woodsy scented shampoo radiates off him, surrounding me and mixing with the sweetness of the cookies baking. After tracing a heart one last time, he reaches around and places his hand over mine and Hunter's on the sides of the rolling pin.

His scruffy cheek rubs against mine. I love how it scratches along my skin. It's like he's rubbing away an itch I didn't realize was there. My eyes shift to the side, and he does the same. Our gazes hold steady for a few lingering heartbeats before we both turn our attention to Hunter.

He pulls back allowing cold air to surround me as he steps beside the chair. "I think your dough is flat, here's some cookie cutters."

Bryan slides over the Santa shape, the star, and the Christmas tree. Hunter doesn't take it, he just stares. I step back an inch. Bryan takes Hunter's hand, holding it gently in his own, and places the star in his tiny palm.

"Hey, buddy, press it down on the dough. Like this."

"Ten cookies, Da-dy," he says.

Bryan silently counts them. "There sure are, Hunter."

Bryan takes the Christmas tree and presses it into the top part of the flattened dough. Hunter stares, flaps his hands with excitement then plops the cutter down onto the dough.

He presses his lips together and blows, making a motor-like

sound, as he happily stabs the dough several times with the cookie cutter.

Bryan chuckles beside me and takes Hunter's hand, showing him again. "Nice job, buddy," he says.

Hunter ignores him and continues to press the cutter down. Bryan leans over and kisses the top of Hunter's blonde locks, then stares up at me. I almost feel as if he's leaning closer, like he wants to kiss me too. I can feel it and my eyelids lower as he grows closer.

A high-pitched squeal comes from Hunter, and he bashes down on the counter with the cookie cutter.

"I think someone is ready for a nap. Santa is coming later, and he needs to be well rested."

"May I?" Bryan asks.

"He's going to need a good bath. He's covered in flour and cookie dough."

"I'll do both," he offers.

"You just want to get out of baking cookies," I say, teasing him.

Bryan's lips pull up into a smile, one I haven't seen in ages, but even so, it doesn't reach his eyes. There's a heavy sadness lingering. "That is the plan." His hip bumps into mine, stalling there for what feels like a lifetime. "Come on, you." He pulls away and holds Hunter's hand to help him off the step.

Hunter's arms wrap around Bryan's middle in a bear hug. I watch him happily hugging his son. As they walk out, I can't tear my eyes away as he makes Hunter giggle.

There's a pang in my chest over how things should be. How we planned on having a baby, and how happy we both were. How did it go from that to this?

Bryan loved the idea of being a dad. He had a good role model, so it made sense. I devised this silly plan to tell him. Ellie and I got Bryan's friend, another officer at the precinct, to help. Keith graciously agreed.

He picked Ellie and me up in his police car and we waited for Bryan to drive by. I love Ellie, and as much as I was embarrassed to be dressed in a sexy cop costume, her idea got the best reaction out of him. I opted for the pantsuit with the short-sleeved top, and the V opening at the top instead.

"Under arrest for knocking you up, now that's classic," Ellie joked.

"What should the criminal charges be?" I asked.

"You don't want me to answer that with Officer Keith in the car." Ellie snickered.

Keith chuckled and shook his head. He opened his mouth to say something when Bryan's car came around the corner. "He's here. Are you ready?" Keith asked.

"As ready as I'll ever be."

I was grateful my nausea was under control but sitting in the back of the cop car on that cold afternoon it returned with a vengeance. As Keith stepped on the pedal, I almost vomited all over the back seat. Thankfully it passed as Bryan moved his car to the side.

"You ready, best friend?"

"No." I laughed.

"Go get him," she said.

Keith glanced over his shoulder. "If it makes you feel any better, Charlotte. I think he's going to love it. I've known Bryan since he started on the force, and for one thing I've never quite seen him smile as much as he does now with you in his life."

"Thanks, Keith. And thank you for doing this. I hope you won't get in trouble."

"Nah, these things happen. In fact, an officer recently did a proposal and pulled over his wife."

It made me feel slightly better, but my blood pressure was probably the highest it had ever been. Despite the cold my body was on fire.

"Here we go," I said as I stepped out.

Ellie followed and stayed behind me with the camera. Keith got out of the car too and leaned up against the driver's side door. They urged me on.

Bryan's eyes met mine through the rear-view mirror on his car. He grinned, but his brows furrowed in confusion. "What are you doing?"

"Sir, please let me do the talking."

He leaned out the window staring at where Keith and Ellie were, then turned to me. "I'm sorry, officer, did I do something wrong?"

"You're damn right you did!"

I could hear Ellie from her spot beside Keith's car laughing.

"Charlotte, we don't talk like that."

"Shush, I'm nervous." I chuckled. My hand rested on the door, and he covered it with his. It made me remember how cold it was outside. "I'm going to need you to step out of the vehicle."

Standing against the cop car, Keith turned the chalkboard sign he was holding. It read:

Daddy's backup is on the way. Duty starts September 10.

"Okay…"

I stepped aside and Bryan got out, hesitantly surveyed the situation, then grabbed my hands. His eyes were trained on me. "What's going on, Char?"

"Sir, I'm going to have to handcuff you for being handsy with an officer," I said, in the best sultry voice I could manage.

My eyes sting. I knew what was coming, and I was kind of afraid of his reaction, but at the same time excited for him to finally know. This was going to change our whole life.

"What about if I do this?" He leaned forward and planted a kiss on my lips, then backed up. "What will you do to me then, officer?" His low tone made my insides shiver with pleasure. I didn't know if it was the hormones talking, but I made it a point to tell him how much I was turned on by our little roleplay. It was kind of sexy.

"Well then, you're just going to have to come sit in my police car."

I gave Keith a simple nod. He held the sign higher. Bryan's attention zeroed in on Keith and the sign. He read it to himself, his lips moved along with each word. Then when realization struck, he turned.

"You're having a—we're having a—I'm gonna be..." he stuttered. His attention landed on my stomach. His hands were grabbing hold even though there was only a small bump.

I nodded and could no longer keep the tears at bay when I saw the tears in his own eyes.

"Baby, that's... I'm so happy." He moved his hands to my face, and then gave me an exceptionally sexy kiss in the middle of the street.

"Hey, you zoned out there."

Morgan steps in front of my view.

"Didn't get much sleep."

"Does he still snore? Oh God, it's awful, isn't it?"

I chuckle. "Yes. Sometimes I want to smother him with a pillow."

Morgan laughs. "So, we used to have these big sleepovers in the living room. Mom and Dad would help us make forts and we'd sleep under them. I remember being mean and making Syd sleep in the fort beside him because the whole night it sounded like a chainsaw in the room."

"He sometimes does," I say, remembering those nights. "But some nights it's not so bad."

"Good memories." She pauses and observes my face. "Are you sure everything is okay?"

"Yeah. I'm good."

I fix up Hunter's cookies and put them in with the next batch into the oven. When they're done, I take them out and bring them to the small table in the center of the kitchen. While they cool, I help Morgan and Gayle with the cleanup. It's a mindless task and I don't find myself zoning out as much.

Once they have cooled, I pick up the pipettes of frosting, and start on his cookies, so they are ready to leave out for Santa tonight.

As I squeeze out some green for the tree a finger reaches around from behind and gets the frosting I'm squeezing. Turning around I come face to face with Bryan. I whirl and he rests his hands on either side of me on the table. I'm trapped in his grasp.

"And what do you think you're doing? You say you don't want to make cookies and then you steal the frosting? Nah-uh. You don't get to steal anything because you didn't help."

As if there was nothing bad between us, I squeeze some out onto my finger then boop his nose.

"You didn't just boop my snoot, did you?"

"Oh, I did."

Bryan leans to the side, but his body stays pressed against mine. He grabs the white and squeezes it in my direction, drizzling it on my face. His eyes light up like dirty thoughts rage in his mind... and okay maybe through mine too. There's a hint of the old us shining through the darkness. Half of me wonders if this is really a show for his family or if this is real. Flutters form low in my belly itching downwards causing my insides to ache in want.

"Hey!" I squeal. "You're making a mess."

His attention lingers on the white frosting now slowly oozing down my cheek. He wiggles his brows and squirts some more, and I fight back squeezing out the green. My heart feels like it's been magically sewn back together from the smile lifting his lips. He removes his other hand from the table, then lifts a finger to my face, wiping some of the frosting and licking it.

"I might be making a mess, but I got you to smile." Our eyes meet and I swear I've stopped breathing.

He squirts some more out and some lands in my eye. It stings.

"Ow," I moan.

"Shit, I'm sorry, Char."

"It's fine, it just stings."

"Here hold still."

I'm about to protest when his fingertips find the corner of my eye. "Keep them closed, okay."

I don't know how close he is because I can't see him, but I can feel him. We're flush against each other. I try to squirm in his hold, but he doesn't allow me to wiggle away. As a few fingers attempt to remove the frosting his thumb casually strokes my jawline. My breathing becomes staggered, and my body relaxes into his touch. I'm watching him through one eye, while he's concentrating on the task at hand.

"How is that?" His words come out in a tight whisper.

I blink a few times, it stings a little, but after a few seconds it eases up. His hands haven't left my face, and his thumb continues to make small circles in the same spot. I'm overwhelmed with an urge to pull him closer and to hold on and never let go, but I fight the feeling, because this isn't real; we're pretending.

I'd love for this to last forever. I move out of his touch and grab the paper towels. Behind me he quietly observes my rigid movements. I turn for a second, offering a few paper towels for his own face.

"Thanks," he says, softly.

"Mmmm."

"Hey, Char."

"Hmm…" I can't bring myself to face him, so I crumple up the used paper towels and get back to work on Hunter's cookies. He stands there silently watching. I listen to the conversations between Sydney, Sam, Morgan, and Gayle, like it's muffled background noise.

"I'm sorry about last night. I sometimes forget and take what I have for granted."

My voice catches in my throat. "Okay."

A few more beats of silence pass between us, while the room is lit with conversation, the voices becoming louder again. He still hasn't left, so I muster the strength to look at him.

"I really am sorry," he repeats.

"All I ask is that you put yourself in my shoes before you judge my reasoning for things." Biting my lip, I feel the sting of tears pressing against my eyes. I sniffle, but nothing falls. My attention lands on the cookies. And for a few more minutes he lingers there behind me. When the coldness infiltrates the space around me, I know he's walked away. I put the frosting down and momentarily become lost in my thoughts.

"Charlotte, sweetheart?" Gayle comes over and rests her hand over my shoulder. "Is everything okay?"

I'm honestly tired of everyone asking me. But I can't be mad. They can see the strain clear as day. We aren't fooling anyone.

I give a lackluster smile and nod. "Everything is good. Do you think Hunter will like these?" I ask.

She squeezes my shoulder. "Darling, I think that boy will love anything his mama makes him. And I'm here if you need to talk. Okay?"

My lip is going to be sore after this week as I bite down again to suppress the knot in my throat. "Thank you," I whisper before she walks away.

CHAPTER 18

Gayle gasps. "Hunter, do you hear that?"

I've got him in my arms just in case. We're all gathered in the living room. From storage, they pulled out this ugly red velvet chair. It used to be a part of the decor here. When they renovated Jack couldn't part with it, so it ended up in storage. For one night only it will be used as Santa's seat.

Bells jingle and a thud on the roof catches our attention. Hunter responds to the sound and his eyes flick up towards the ceiling. Bells sound off again. The front door bursts open as a hearty chuckle floats through the room. Hunter is intrigued now. Boots clomp along the wooden floors and a few seconds later a jolly old man appears.

Jack went all out. His beard looks so real I have to do a double take. Hunter has his full attention on the man in red.

"Ho, ho, ho. Merry Christmas," Santa huffs.

From behind I feel a hand on my shoulder. Bryan is standing over us, watching his son's reaction.

"I got word that there is a young boy named Hunter who was put on the nice list this year. Ho, ho, ho."

I can't tell if Hunter is scared. Bryan's hand slides down to my hip as he stands behind me. His body is a mere inches away.

"Ho-we-sheet!"

The entire room comes to a halt. No one speaks, not even the fire crackles. We all look at the four-year-old staring off as if nothing happened. I'm sure it only sounded like it, there's no way. He has trouble forming some words, and understanding directions, yet here he is cursing like his mom. I have used that choice word a lot, especially over the last few months.

Sydney is the first to crack. Her high-pitched cackle starts a wave of laughs.

Hunter squirms in my arm, unaware of what he said. I allow him to get down. He cautiously makes his way to Santa.

Leaning down, Jack kneels on one knee getting to Hunter's level. Bryan nods and encourages Hunter to go for it. Tears prick at my eyes. He's never once tried to seek anyone's approval.

"Go ahead, baby. It's Santa," I whisper, the words catching in my throat.

Hunter flaps his hands and waddles over to him. Jack's arms are stretched out waiting. He releases a high-pitched squeal, flaps a few more times, before running into his arms.

"Oh. Ho, ho, ho. Hello, young Hunter. Come, come sit on my chair."

Even Jack's voice is the perfect octave for Santa. He's got the deep low rumble that gives you a warm feeling of Christmas. Funnily enough, Dad did the same for us growing up, until Logan ruined Santa for me, but that's a whole other story.

Jack lifts Hunter onto his lap. "So, young man, what do you want for Christmas?"

I pull out my phone, taking several pictures. It's amazing to see him take so well to Santa this year. Around us the soft melody of my favorite Jonas Christmas song plays. In my ear Bryan matches Nick Jonas's tone. I'm not surprised he knows the song. Ellie and I literally wore their Christmas songs out last year.

My attention lands back on Hunter, who still hasn't cracked a smile, but he also hasn't shed a tear yet. We try to get him to look our way to take a nice photo, but his attention is always off somewhere else.

Santa is a familiar figure in his life, so Hunter curls up on his lap and snuggles into his arms like he's ready to take a nap. My eyes sting as I take in my surroundings. These people are as much family as my own. Knowing I won't be part of it for much longer once Bryan and I separate tugs on my heart.

A sniffle catches me off guard and I wipe my eye.

"Char?" Bryan's lips tickle my ear.

My body reacts by leaning into him instead of jumping away. How did we stray so far from one another? It went from us talking every day to our conversations being only to say, *I love you, goodnight,* and *goodbye.* That and *Oh Hunter needs this,* or *I'm going to the store, what do you need?*

Even the sex died down. Bryan would be exhausted from work, and for me the idea of being touched after a whole day with a baby was just… ugh. He'd work for hours doing one of the hardest jobs out there, while I struggled at home to take care of a baby and keep myself sane. Push came to shove. We bickered about stupid stuff, like me not taking in the mail, or not having dinner ready.

If I could go back in time, I'd tell past Charlotte not to lose herself in the black hole of motherhood. I'd yell at her to tell her husband how much she appreciated him, even when he wasn't home.

And then I'd remind her to text him more often, even if he didn't answer. Not to nag him but to simply say things like, *I'm thinking of you.* Not texts like, *Where the hell are you? And why aren't you answering.*

That woman fell down a rabbit hole and couldn't find her way out. She got buried so deep she lost more than herself.

"I'm—yeah, I'm fine. I just need to pee."

I don't run, because if I do, he'll follow.

CHAPTER 19

After a good cry in the bathroom, I step out into our room and jump. Bryan is sitting on the end of the bed. His attention is buried in his phone, but with the click of the en suite door his eyes flicker up to me.

"What are you doing in here?"

"I got something for you. I thought you might want to play."

My forehead scrunches as he stands and rummages through his things. Out of his black duffle bag he pulls a rectangular box covered in Christmas wrapping paper.

"I didn't—You... you got me something?" Dread settles in my stomach. I got a gift for him, but it's buried at the bottom of my sock drawer at home. I didn't expect him to have anything for me, so I didn't bother bringing it. Now I feel like the bad guy.

"It's okay if you have nothing for me," he says.

"I can't accept this." Stepping back, I crash into the closed door, and wince from the impact.

Bryan isn't letting up. He trudges forward, gift in hand, until he's only inches away from me. The present sits between us as he holds it out.

"Bry—"

"Char—" His tone is demanding yet playful. He places it in my hand, and as much as I protest my hand wraps around the smooth silky paper. He urges me with a silent nod. Stepping around him I settle onto the bed with the present. I know when Bryan has his mind set on something he won't give up.

I tear through the paper slowly. It's wrapped without wrinkles. I almost don't want to open it. Laughter fills up my lungs and I probably sound crazy. "You're still a better wrapper than me," I say.

His warm chuckle heats me up, and suddenly the heavy sweater I'm wearing feels like it's strangling me. "Always better. I saw the presents you wrapped for Hunter. Was Santa drunk when he wrapped those?"

I give him a friendly nudge with my hand. "Hey, they've got my signature touch."

His laugh grows deeper, and my body a little hotter.

His laughter fades, but his smile remains. There's sadness in his shining eyes, and once again I'm left wondering what he's thinking. There's something there, but as usual it's hidden in his own head, and I'll never know.

I open the parcel at the sides not tearing an inch of the paper, and it pulls off exactly how it was fitted to the box.

"So, you can open gifts neatly, but not wrap them."

"Stop teasing me," I say, my voice light, airy and playful, which sucks some of the tension lingering in the room. The inside box has a plastic feel. It slides out easily and my eyes widen as the words appear under the wrapping. My mouth makes a sound between a gasp and a sob, but I'm not crying.

"The original Game of Life?"

"It really is the original. I got it on eBay. Don't worry I checked all of it and had it wrapped nicely. I uh… I know it's not the one your dad—"

It doesn't even matter. I drop the game beside me on the bed and wrap my arms around him. Bryan grunts as I barrel into him. His shoulders shake with mirth.

My dad and I played the game for hours on end. It was our thing. Logan used to get mad because he'd always lose, and he could never handle games if they lasted longer than ten minutes. So, it was me and my dad's thing. And when he passed, Mom, not realizing it donated the game in a purge and I lost it. I thought I had it safely in my room, but it was on the game shelf downstairs, and she didn't think anything of it. It haunted me for years. The one in my hands might not be my dad's copy of the game, but it's the thought that counts.

Bryan's hands are smoothing out my hair as the tears fall. They aren't sad, they are happy. Guilt piles down on me, here Bryan got me this amazing sentimental gift, while the one sitting back at home is a bottle of his favorite cologne.

"Thank you," I say, pulling back and wiping my eyes.

He reaches for the tears but stops halfway. I run my hands over the plastic.

"Do you want to play?" he asks.

"But we have to get back downstairs."

"Syd and Mom said they'd handle Hunter. He was happily enjoying playing with one of his early Christmas gifts from Morgan."

"Okay then, let's play."

First, before we start, we head downstairs to help Hunter set his cookies for Santa, then grab some snacks and drinks. I indulged in a fruity wine cooler, and Bryan has his usual beer. We binge on holiday popcorn straight from the tin, and extra cookies from the baking session earlier. Half an hour turns into an hour, and for the first time in months we haven't yelled at each other once. It's like it was in the beginning, nothing but laughter and teasing.

"Hmm Sunnyside Acres or Millionaire Estates," I say, tapping my chin.

A twinkle sparkles in Bryan's eyes.

"What?" I ask.

"Nothing. You're so serious, it's kind of cute."

My neck warms, and the feeling creeps up to my cheeks. I can't help touching my face and rubbing along the heated spot.

"Oh, shush! This will determine how I spend the rest of my life; just give me a minute."

His chuckle vibrates through me.

"Okay, stop, you're distracting me. I'm going to go with... Mill —no Sunnyside," I say.

I move the tiny red car to the spot on the game board, our hands graze as he reaches for the spinner. We pause, glancing up. His lips twitch and I find myself biting down hard on mine.

Bryan spins the spinner. It slows to a stop, and he yells out in excitement as he joins me, sliding his green car right beside mine with a satisfied smirk. We count all the money, repay our debts, and all that comes with the game.

"Winner!" I hold up the fake money and shake it.

"You really are the master, aren't you?" he asks.

"Of course. Dad taught me well."

"He sure did."

Memories jog me of the time Logan stomped away after losing one of the only games he'd ever fully completed with us. Dad and I shared a laugh. There were so many laughs, smiles, and hugs. If only I could, I'd go back in time to have an extra moment or two with him.

"Hey, you okay over there?" Bryan asks.

I shake my head. "Duh—I won, of course I'm okay."

He leans forward over the gameboard slightly, his head tilts to the side, and he grins. "I lost you for a second. Where did you go?" he asks.

I shake my head. "I'm good. Really."

Music and laughter come from downstairs. It bleeds through the partially open door. A familiar holiday tune echoes through the speakers. Bryan stands and dusts off his jeans. For a minute he seems a little lost, but then he holds his hand out. "Dance with me?"

I feel hesitancy in the tug of my brow.

"Come on," he says.

I reach for him, and he pulls me to the side, so I don't step on the game board. It's a slow tune, one that gives you shivers and brings back memories of Christmas past. This song always brings back memories of when Dad was around, when Logan and I were kids. It also makes me think about all the firsts I've had with Bryan.

With ease we fall into each other's steps, and I rest my head right in the spot between his shoulder and neck. I'm surrounded by his scent. It hangs in the air enveloping me in its grasp. Listening to the thump of each beat of his heart I close my eyes. I let the sound take me to another place, a place where Bryan and I are still together.

He's singing along to the song again. It's like he's trying to bring back the spark between us. I don't want to get my hopes up because I'm already hanging by a thread. I grip him tighter.

"Charlotte." The rasp in his tone makes my lower half tense in response.

When our gazes meet, I'm lost, lost in a sea of solid blue and gray. My words never surface. They don't have to. He lowers his head, dipping further, coming for me. I lick my lips to prepare for when his connect with mine. Our eyes hold steady. I'm overwhelmed by the light brush of his lips. I sigh into his mouth, needing more. When I'm about to open my mouth, a giggling Hunter rushes through, and he grabs a hold of our legs. It's then I realize he's naked with the pull-up in his hands.

We stare down at the person we created. This beautiful human who will keep us part of each other's lives—forever.

"Hey there, buddy."

A winded Sydney comes into the room. Her eyes landing on

how Bryan and I are still connected, and then down at Hunter at our feet. Bryan pulls away from me, and the air chills around us. He bends down, adjusts the diaper, then picks Hunter up.

"He's fast," Sydney breathes.

Bryan and I chuckle. "He sure is," I say.

"We'll take it from here. Thanks, Sydney," Bryan says.

"Oh." Her eyes widen and brows wiggle. "Got it."

"I guess we shouldn't break family tradition on Christmas Eve. Help me get him to bed. Did you bring the book?" he asks.

I nod. We made it a tradition, even before Hunter was born, to read Bryan's copy of *The Night Before Christmas* every Christmas Eve. It's from when he was a little boy and he wanted to pass it down to Hunter so maybe one day he could do the same.

We get Hunter into a clean pull-up and his holiday jammies, then slide into the rocker in the far corner of the room. It's a tight, but comfortable fit.

Bryan's grasp tightens on me, and for the first time in months his eyes light up. I don't want to get my hopes up that things are changing, because he did file for those papers. So, I'm not holding my breath, but something feels different tonight. It's as though as a couple we've made progress, but then there's the fear of heading back to the real world, and once work starts up again things will go right back to how they were.

I wish I could forget it and deal with his long hours and me being alone all day. Maybe I'm being childish, and I need to grow up and accept that we can't live a fairy-tale life. But I don't want a fairy tale or happily-ever-after, I want to be together, through it all.

"Lost you again," he says.

I shake my head, not even realizing he's finished reading, and Hunter has passed out between us.

"I'm here. Just tired." I lie to him. "We're stuck, aren't we?"

His laugh is short and sweet, but it still helps me feel better.

"While that wouldn't be terrible, my back won't be very happy in the morning."

"No. Definitely not. Okay, I'll get up slowly."

As I move to get up, Hunter stirs, rolling deep into Bryan's arms, allowing me some space to get out. I slide off the chair, stand and reach out for Hunter, then take him and put him in the bed.

"Easy-peasy," Bryan whispers behind me. He leans down and places his cheek beside mine. Watching Hunter sleep I'm taken back to how things used to be.

"If you want to get ready for bed, I'll put the gifts under the tree," he offers.

"That would be perfect."

"Okay, I'll be up in a few," he says, but doesn't move.

"Okay," I say, not moving either.

I don't know how long we stand there staring at each other, maybe both waiting for the other to make a move. I can't help imagining what it would be like to kiss him for real again, uninterrupted. The sinking feeling of knowing the divorce papers will most likely be at home when I get there hits me hard.

"I'm going now," he says, awkwardly pointing over his shoulder.

"Okay."

"Okay," he repeats. He's not blocked by me. I'm being blocked by him. I could step around, but I don't, I'm not literally stuck, but I feel it. Finally, he turns and walks for the door. My heart drops into my stomach as disappointment fills me. Once he's out I turn back to Hunter, run a hand through his beautiful hair, then head back to the room to clean up and head to bed.

CHAPTER 20

It's Christmas morning, and there's a lot of commotion all around us. Hunter is in a cheerful mood but stimming a lot. He's making a chaotic mess on the living room floor around him. Jack brings over the toolbox he has made.

"What's this, Dad?" Bryan asks.

We are sitting on the floor with Hunter. Bryan is doing the dad thing and tugging out all the toys as if they were for him, while I'm collecting the wrapping paper and making neat piles of all the unopened gifts and clothes.

"It's something special I made for Hunter." Jack winks at me.

"Hey, buddy, look what Papa got you," I say.

"Daddy's tools!" he says, as he notices the wooden pieces sticking out.

"Yes, baby. Tools. Look," I say, spinning the box around. "Your name is on it too." I point to the carving.

Hunter takes each wooden tool out and lays it down on the carpet lining them up. He grabs the saw, and saws the carpet, watching the back and forth movement. It's relaxing for him, and his eyelids fall heavy with each motion.

While my attention is on Hunter, Bryan stands and embraces Jack in a side hug, thanking him for the work on the box.

"I made this for the two of you. Before." He says the word quietly so only we can hear. "I hope it's okay."

In his hand he holds out a holiday bag with green tissue paper sticking out of the top. I get to my feet and stand beside Bryan as he searches through it. He tugs out a circular object that looks as if it were made straight from a tree trunk. In the center is a large tree carved into the wood. Above it sits a quote, *"Where life begins, and love never ends."* On the branches are not only Bryan's family, but mine, including my dad, and even Ellie with Logan, and all the branches are connected.

Misty eyed I stare at the present. "It's perfect." I step into his open arms and hug him tight. It's hard not to cry. Even if Bryan and I aren't together, it will be the perfect family heirloom to pass down to Hunter. The room is quiet, and I'm probably giving myself away, but I can't help it.

Pulling away, I wipe my eyes. Bryan goes in for a full hug too, thanking his dad, then putting the gift safely back into the bag. He sits back down with Hunter and me and shows him the different tools, and together the three of us bond as a family again, lost in our own world.

It's not Christmas without seeing my family, and since I can't be with them, I escape to the kitchen to call Ellie.

"Please tell me he's not wearing the Santa suit?" I say into the phone camera.

They are at Mom's house. I'm happy to see Logan's man-flu did not put him six feet under, and he's back to his old self again.

As the commotion over there combats with the one here, there's a pang in my heart and I wish I was with them today. I know Mom is surrounded by her new husband, her best friend Ellie's mom, Ellie, and Logan, but I can't help wanting to be there with her.

"He's even wearing the Christmas boxers," she says, cringing.

I chuckle, as strong warm hands connect with my shoulder. Ellie's eyes widen and she makes a squinty face, her eyebrows wiggling with delight. I shake my head to try and tell her there's nothing happening, but her brain has other ideas.

"Hi, Bryan! Merry Christmas!" she says, cheerfully.

He leans down and rests his chin on my shoulder. I inhale deeply to capture the moment with all five senses. His soft breath in my ear. The woodsy smell and slight hint of aftershave; his light scruff since he shaved this morning; the way I can see him in the corner of my eye and how he's half looking at me while his attention is on the screen. The only part missing is the taste, but I remember that too. His warm inviting lips on mine. *Shit.*

"Merry Christmas, Ellie."

In the background I catch sight of a blob of red again. Ellie grabs the suit and pulls Logan down. "Wish your sister a Merry Christmas," she says.

"Charlotte!! Ho, ho, ho. Where's my nephew?"

"That's all I get is a ho, ho, ho?"

Bryan chuckles beside me. "Hi, Logan, Merry Christmas."

"Hey, man, how's it going?"

"It's actually going pretty great up here." He snakes his arms around me and pulls me into him.

"Oh, really?" Now it's Logan's turn to make the face, and I almost get to throw him the finger when Hunter's tiny voice starts talking. Bryan steps away, grabs Hunter, and hands him to me.

"Unca Logo. Aun Ellie."

"Hey, buddy! Did Santa come?" Logan asks.

I think he says yes, followed by some more gibberish. Logan is fully invested in the conversation, and I love that about my brother. Even as Hunter's attention is everywhere but the screen, Logan continues to ask him questions.

"Here, let me take him, you can finish your conversation. Brunch is almost ready," Bryan says.

"Okay. Be there in a minute."

Our eyes lock. If I were a snowman I'd have melted from the heat of Bryan's gaze. He pulls away first, and I'm glad he does. I'm hoping it was quick enough, so Ellie and Logan don't catch on.

Bryan takes Hunter, then gives a wave to Ellie and Logan. I take a deep breath, and when I turn, I expect them to have a bucket of popcorn while my life unfolds in front of them like a movie. I'm about to get roasted.

"So, what's with the snuggles? Did you two? Oh my God, you had sex." Ellie is so loud I cover the phone speakers. I peek over my shoulder, thankfully no one is sneaking up on me.

"El! Sh. We did not!"

"Who had sex?"

"Mom!" I shout as she comes over to the phone, her head trying to peek over Ellie's shoulder.

She's in her red holiday dress that she's been wearing for years, and she's paired the outfit with her favorite Santa hat, the one with the oversized white ball on the top.

"Oh, hey, Char. How's your trip going?"

"Hi, Mom. Merry Christmas. It's fine. Hunter is busy opening gifts. I can have him call you later."

"Oh. No worries, darling. I'll see you guys when you come back. I'm going to burn the lasagna, let me get back over. Have a good Christmas."

"Love you, Mom."

It's the first Christmas in a long time I've seen Mom glowing and smiling. She would put on a front for the holidays after Dad passed. Logan was never there to see it, but I was. It was awful.

But since Tommy came into her life, she's been smiling and happy again.

Mom rushes away leaving Ellie's and Logan's questioning faces.

"I didn't have sex with him. At all. I swear."

"You'd tell me though?" she asks.

"Okay, maybe I'll bow out of this convo. I don't need to know about my sister's sex life. Anyways, have a good holiday, and don't have too much sex."

"You guys!" If I was a cartoon I'd burst into flames.

"I should go help your mom since your brother is running around like a child and is no help," she says.

"Heard that!" Logan yells from a distance.

"Sounds about right. Merry Christmas, El. I promise I'll update you if anything happens."

I hang up the phone and head to the dining room. Hunter is already in his chair, and this time instead of him being between me and Bryan, he's off to Bryan's right, while my chair is beside his. My heart skips several fluttering beats. Bryan catches me waiting, his head twists to the side, and brows narrow.

I cross the room and take the seat beside him. Everyone is excited and the conversations are loud and crossing each other at the table.

"Oh, Bryan, you'll never guess who I saw in Colorado," Morgan says, over the rumble of voices.

Bryan seems lost in thought.

"Michael Jennings."

"Mikey J?" He perks up a bit. I sneak a peek under the table at how his hand is flat on his lap but every once in a while, twitches in my direction. If I were certain he'd want it, I'd rest my hand over his and hold on, but I'm not going to push my luck. Not when we've had a good streak going for the last day.

"Yes. And the best part... he's married and expecting number five and six."

Bryan's eyes widen and I almost think he's going to choke on his food.

"Mikey J has kids?" Jack asks, nestling his way into the conversation.

"Who's Mikey J?" I ask.

Morgan grins. "Mikey was Bryan's first friend. He was a bit out there, a troublemaker. One year for the talent show—"

"Morgan, no. We don't need to relive junior year talent show," Bryan groans.

"Oh, this has to be good then," I say, rubbing my hands together waiting for the juicy details.

"So, do you remember the 'Jingle Bell Rock' dance from *Mean Girls*?" she asks.

"I think every millennial does." I pause to stare at Bryan, and note his rosy red cheeks. "Wait a minute. You didn't…"

"Oh, they did," Gayle says, joining in.

"Not you too, Mom. I thought you were on my side."

"In fact, I think your father has the DVD here. Don't you, Jack?" Gayle asks from across the table.

"As a matter of fact."

"No, you guys. No, no, no," Bryan says in a defensive yet playful tone.

"Well, I have to see this now."

There's an eager tone in my voice. Bryan shoots me a teasing look. "You're just as bad as them." He chuckles.

After everyone shovels their food in their faces, Morgan and Jack make it a point to head out into the storage room to go through the old family DVDs. I'm not expecting them to find it, but they come traipsing in a few minutes after Gayle and I finish cleaning up and doing dishes.

"No, you didn't find it," Bryan groans.

Hunter, Sydney, and Sam's giggles filter in from the living room as we all make our way in. Bryan and I met when we were twenty-two, so while we've told each other things about our childhood, neither of us have had a chance to peek a glimpse into it.

"Oh, we did. And your son and your wife get to see your dance moves." Morgan grins, rolling her hips.

I still love the way *wife* sounds when it comes to Bryan and me. I can't help it.

"Oh, I'm excited too," Sam says.

Bryan scowls at everyone, but still manages a small smile.

Morgan cackles like a witch. "You are all in for a treat."

I walk up behind Bryan and grab his arm. "Was this part of your Lindsey Lohan phase, or the blonde?"

As if things between us were perfect Bryan pulls me into his grasp and tickles my sides. It feels good, no matter how much I hate to be tickled. I know I said moving on is best, but for right now I want to be here present with him. When his fingers stop moving, he continues to hold me. And for a second a passing swarm of butterflies flutter in my belly. Hunter's giggles pull us from our embrace.

We all get settled into the living room, and Bryan swoops Hunter up and sets him between us. He's investigating the bumpy wheels of another new truck. Sam, Sydney, and Morgan are all perched on the floor waiting for the show, and Gayle is beside us on the far end of the couch with Jack.

There's fuzz on the screen and then finally a high-school auditorium stage pops up. The deep forest green curtains move aside, people clap and cheer. It's a bit of a grainy picture, but when the stage comes into full view, I can tell which one is Bryan right away. There are four of them, Bryan is the tallest in the dead center. They're all wearing bright red Santa pants that glisten in the light, with white cotton along the bottom of the shorts, a black belt, and tight white T-shirts.

A few seconds into the dance, they slap their knees, and the entire audience erupts in laughter, including all of us watching.

As the dance continues, they point out Mikey, who's on the far left, dark hair and muscles bulging through his tee. The song is over in less than a few minutes, but it leaves us all in tears from laughing.

"That was the best thing I've seen all day," I say, between breaths.

Bryan is laughing along with us. "Hey, don't judge. Logan showed me the video he took of you and Ellie pretending to be the Jonas Brothers while standing on a picnic table and lip-syncing their songs."

Now it's my turn for the embarrassment to creep up my cheeks. Bryan fully accepted my first love, the Jonas Brothers, from the day I told him. I swore Logan got rid of the tapes. It was the summer he claimed he wanted to be a film director, and we literally had to pry the camera from his hands because he always had it with him.

"He didn't," I say, as we inch closer.

Hunter squeezes out from between us to play amongst the mess of wrapping paper still littered on the floor.

"He's getting an earful when I get home."

"Aw, but it was cute. Which one were you? The curly haired one, right?"

I growl and reach for him. He grabs hold of my hand and tugs me towards him. Instead of tickling me he holds me close, allowing me to rest my head on his chest. I adjust and bury myself in his warmth, like I used to. Somehow the butterflies migrate back and settle low in my belly. We sit there in the quiet while his family rattles on about the video.

"He should have done that at the wedding," Sam cackles.

"Oh, she would have left him at the altar," Morgan cries out.

And while that comment was meant to be a joke, my whole body goes stiff. Bryan must feel it because his grip around me tightens, and he holds on. His hand wraps around and settles over mine. At the slightest touch his breath hitches. I close my eyes allowing the sounds of the house to drown out while I try to focus on the beating of his heart and listen to every staggering breath he takes.

CHAPTER 21

Hunter was exhausted, worn out by the day. He fell asleep quickly and didn't put up much of a fight. Downstairs is empty, but voices trail in through the sliding glass doors in the kitchen. Large flames flicker in the backyard. It's cold and there's a thin layer of snow on the frosted ground, but Bryan's whole family is out there right now.

Stepping outside onto the deck I take in everyone gathered around the fire laughing. The only empty seat is beside Bryan. They probably left it for me. His mom is the first to hear me walking across the deck—she's the closest. She turns, her eyes meet mine and she waves me down.

I take the three steps down onto the lawn, already feeling the heat of the flames as I approach. Bryan's head lifts as I slide into the chair and tuck my legs under me to warm them. Smoke billows up from the metal pit in the center. Morgan and Sam are laughing, while Sydney and her parents are deep in conversation about something that happened at school.

My chair is flush against Bryan's.

"No jacket?" he asks.

"It was upstairs."

Bryan, as usual, is layered. He peels off the first layer—his coat —and helps me push my arms through. Underneath he's got double sweaters, and although his cheeks are rosy and he looks cold, he's packing some intense heat under there. I always called him "my space heater."

"Thanks." I grin.

A hesitant smile tugs on Bryan's lips. "This is for you. Candy-cane hot chocolate."

My hands wrap around the warm smooth surface of a black thermos. I lift it to my nose to smell. The sweet minty taste tickles my senses. I shiver, still freezing even with his jacket, the hot chocolate, and the fire.

"How's Hunter?" Sydney asks from across the fire pit.

"Out cold. You guys made this Christmas so special for him." My voice hitches and to avoid crying I take a sip of hot chocolate. My eyes close as the delightfully smooth mixture coats my throat. I hum at the delicious taste. The hair on the back of my neck stands and it's not from the cold.

Bryan's gaze is frozen on me. "Good?" He chuckles.

"Amazing." I shiver again.

"Come here, Char. You're freezing."

"No. I'm okay. Really."

"Oh, Charlotte, don't be embarrassed, we know you two love your PDA," Morgan teases.

Now I'm warm as my cheeks burn. She's smiling at me, encouraging me. Bryan moves his legs resting his feet flat on the ground. He pats the spot on his lap. I contemplate the move. His family has witnessed us doing this weird divorce dance around each other, when we are the most affectionate of couples.

My body is stiff as I pull myself off the chair, but as I place myself onto Bryan's lap, everything loosens. I should be offended by the way his hand grasps my hip dangerously close to cupping my ass cheeks, but I'm not. His touch sends my heart into a frenzy. He tugs me closer, and I settle into him. He's taller and my head fits perfectly in the crook of his neck, like it always has.

I allow myself to feel again. To unleash some of the chains strangling my heart. When his lips graze my head, I release a single tear into the darkness. Not even he notices or if he does, he doesn't say anything. His grip tightens around me, and I settle in basking in the warmth.

"I wish we could do this every year," Gayle says, sipping on her own thermos. "Charlotte, we could invite your family and it would be one big event."

Bryan and I stay silent, but I nod in agreement, because if things were normal my mom would love to be a part of this big happy family. I hate not being with her this Christmas. I remember the first one after dad passed and it was so hard for her. The realization makes my heart ache in another way. Their love was truly a fairy tale.

Mom and I both held a similar story. Just as Bryan had come to my rescue after slipping on ice, Dad saved Mom from a spill in the cafeteria of their high school. I used to love it when they'd share the story. Growing up, I'd ask repeatedly to hear it. When they did, they would cut each other off to tell their side, and never once did they look away from each other. God, I miss Dad. Their love is what made me fall in love with the concept of love. I knew it was out there and thought I'd found it for myself. Truly I did. My throat aches with the desire to cry but I hold back.

Relaxing into Bryan I drift, listening to the conversations around me. The atmosphere is relaxing and for the first time since we got here, I'm calm.

"Char," a soft whisper pulls me from my thoughts.

I search around, no one else is there, it's only us against the roaring fire. I rub my eyes. They are heavy with sleep.

"Oh my God, was I snoring?" I ask.

Bryan's entire body shakes with laughter, and the deep sound reminds me of the first time we met. "You don't snore."

"Oh, right that's you."

He grips me tighter, reaching for the most ticklish spot on my stomach again. My giggles echo into the night. Our laughter swirling together is like music to my ears.

"How long was I out for?" I ask, as we settle down.

I adjust to get a better glimpse of Bryan. I'm no longer trapped in his warmth, but I shouldn't do that anymore. The reality is too much to handle.

"A good thirty minutes."

"I didn't realize. Everyone went to bed?"

"Yeah. I told them I'd take care of the fire, but I got caught up in it."

"It's colder than a witch's tit out here," I say. "But I don't mind hanging out for longer."

His smile almost reaches his eyes. Tonight, under the light of the fire they're a bit duller than usual, but they light up at the prospect of me staying with him.

"Are there any marshmallows in the house?"

"I dunno, want to go check?"

He's all bright-eyed and bushy-tailed as he nearly knocks me off his lap to go and check. We rush inside, hit the jackpot, try to contain our giggles with everyone sleeping, then make our way back out to the fire.

It's a little before midnight, but it doesn't stop us. Bryan is used to being awake at all hours. We put the ingredients for s'mores on a random Christmas platter, and he hands me a stick he picks up off the ground.

He moves the chair a bit closer, and I move too.

"Hey, why don't you come back over here, it's cold, body heat will help keep us warm."

There's a devilish gleam in his eye and it gets me all hot and bothered. It's like everything is okay again. I want to bask in the moment. Everything feels right and comforting, and I almost don't want this night to end.

I reach for the platter we placed on one of the chairs and hand him the marshmallows. He preps them onto the sticks. My hands are ice cold, but I don't care, sitting here on his lap the rest of me is warm.

The fire crackles and the marshmallows begin to melt. I keep my concentration on the flickering flames and the white gooey mess on a stick. I want him to tell me the past six months have been a nightmare and right here, right now we've finally woken from it.

"We should set up a fire pit in the spring for Hunter. He'd love it," Bryan says, stealing me from my intrusive thoughts.

"Yes, I know he'd love that."

"We said we'd get one. Remember when we took that camping vacation the first summer we were dating?"

"And you tried to bet me that I couldn't put a whole gigantic marshmallow in my mouth." The memory sparks joy in me.

Bryan shifts and for a flicker of a second, I feel something hard against my ass. I fix myself so I'm not remotely close to having it push into me again. My insides throb with an ache so bad.

He clears his throat. "And you did it."

"I did," I say, sticking out my tongue.

He lifts his marshmallow; it's a little browned, and I reach beside me and grab the other ingredients for him with one hand, while keeping my marshmallow over the fire.

"You're not burning it again, are you?" he asks.

"But the crispness of the marshmallow is the best part."

"Gag," he says, making puking noises.

"No, it's not." I chuckle, leaning into him enough to feel his hardness pulsating into me again. A gasp escapes my mouth. His face shifts, and his eyes focus on me, and then on my lips. I release short, staggered breaths, then distract myself with my burnt mallow.

"Ah, perfect," I say, trying to ignore the urge to drop the marshmallow and stick, turn around and straddle him.

"You are so gross," he says, his voice is light, but there's a tightness in there too.

I make my own s'more and we eat them in silence. As I scarf down the last of it, I yawn, the craziness of the day getting to me.

"We should get to bed," he says.

"Yeah."

"Um. Can you take this stuff in? I, uh—" He swallows so hard I can hear him gulp. "I-I'll be up in a minute."

I nod, afraid to use my voice. It'll sound weak and desperate if I do.

I put everything away and wash the platter. Before heading up to bed I peek out the door. The fire is still roaring, and Bryan is sitting in the chair with his head in his hands. He runs a hand through his hair and glances up in my direction. I don't think he's able to see me at that distance. I pin myself against the wall beside the doors. My breathing becomes labored and heavy and my knees are weak.

After a minute or two I leave the kitchen, but before I do, I turn back around. Bryan's now pouring water over the fire and standing there watching the flames flicker out. I don't hang around. I can't. So, I run upstairs, check on Hunter, then get myself ready for bed quicker than I ever have before.

It takes some time before the door opens. The bed shifts with Bryan's weight, and he grunts a little as he lies down. Tonight, he's closer, and I swear I feel him tracing a heart on my back. He lets out a long shuddering breath, and minutes later he is snoring lightly. It doesn't feel like there's much room between us. Resting my head back on the pillow I allow my own body to pull me into a deep sleep with the comfort of his hand on my back.

CHAPTER 22

O ur first real fight was hard. Hunter was three months old and suffered reflux and was constantly crying at night. That, and the poor kid still had another two weeks in his harness for his hip dysplasia. Thankfully it resolved within a few months.

"All I'm asking is for you to call out for the night. Please."

I hated the night shifts; they were the worst. The tension was only starting to build. I'd never asked Bryan to call out, ever, not until that night. Hunter screamed in my arms.

Bryan rubbed at his temples. "I can't just call out. This isn't a teaching job, Charlotte. Hunter isn't sick, I'm not sick, you're not sick, there's no good excuse to call out."

"What's that supposed to mean?" I bounced Hunter in my arms and patted his back in hopes the gas pains would soon subside for him.

"Forget it. If I don't get moving, I'm going to be late," Bryan said, tying his shoes.

"You do have an excuse. How about the fact that your wife needs you? I have not slept well in almost a week, and your son's reflux isn't getting any better. He has his appointment tomorrow, and I thought maybe we could go together."

"I'm sorry, but I can't. I've got a job to do, and a responsibility to not only you and Hunter, but our community." He threw on his jacket, and checked himself, making sure he had everything he needed. His hand touched the door handle.

"Do I make you unhappy or something? Do we make you unhappy? Is this not the life you wanted?"

My words caught him off guard. His shoulders tensed under his uniform. It was the cranky lost version of myself seeking my husband's attention. I should have dealt with it.

He didn't look at me when he spoke his next words either. "I'm not unhappy, Charlotte. He's been to specialist after specialist for reflux, and the hip dysplasia. We have bills to pay. I'm sorry, okay? I'm saving my days off for sickness. I have faith you can handle this. I have time off from work this weekend. The three of us can go out east or do something fun. Okay? Let's just get through the work week."

He slammed the door and left, leaving me with a very upset Hunter. I still regret not saying *I love you* that day, but would he have even said it back?

Hours later I was pacing the living room. It was almost six in the morning, and I had yet to fall asleep. Bryan's shift was supposed to have ended at three. Him not being home threw me into a frenzy.

Over Hunter's loud cries, the news channel was reporting about some gunfire a few towns over. I felt dizzy and sat on the couch. My phone went off and I reached for it. It was tangled between the blankets on the couch. When I finally answered, Keith sounded out of breath.

"Hey, Charlotte. It's Keith. Bryan is okay, but there was a small incident; he's at the hospital."

I gasp for air as real tears stream down my face. I wipe and wipe, and sit up straight, making the world spin.

Beside me the spot is empty, as it had been for the last six months. Realization strikes. I'm not home, this isn't my bed. We're at Bryan's family's cabin upstate. The sound of running water catches my attention. A speck of light peeks out from under the bathroom door.

It wasn't a dream, but a memory from the morning when Bryan had an injury from a knife wound and needed stitches on his arm. When I got that call, I expected it to be much worse. The memory of those words makes my chest tighten and my heart ache all over again.

I release a trembling breath, as Hunter's cries catch me off guard. I throw the comforter off and sprint down the hallway to him. When I open the door, tears slide down his pink cheeks. Picking him up, I walk back and forth trying to calm him down. Both of us are crying. I know why I am but have no idea why he is. I wish he could tell me.

"Oh, baby boy, it's okay. I'm here. Did you have a bad dream, huh?" I sniffle. "Mommy did," I say in his ear. "Mommy had the worst nightmare, but it was real."

Hunter keeps crying and sniffling. He coughs when it becomes too much, and I fall into the rocking chair beside the bed.

"Holding you helps Mommy feel better. You seem to be the only one who does."

Hunter relaxes a little at my voice, so I continue to talk. "I could have done better for you. You deserve to have your mommy and daddy under one roof. I messed up. I messed up so badly. He gave up because I did. I let my tired state dictate my emotions and I shouldn't have. I am so sorry I did this to you, that you're going to grow up with a broken family."

I hold him tighter, and he remains quiet. His eyes close. The dream or memory has surfaced so many emotions and I can't stop.

"I'll make sure even though things aren't good between your daddy and I, that he and I will give you the best life. I promise, Hunter." I sob into his shoulder as he rests his tiny head on mine. Life has slipped by so quickly and I should be doing what young Charlotte would have done. She wouldn't be crying over it. She'd have taken a breath to figure it out. Where did she go?

Hunter is snoring lightly by the time I've pulled myself from my head. I press a kiss to the top of his head and place him back into the bed. For a few seconds I watch his back rise and fall with each breath. I need to do better, not for myself, but for the little life Bryan and I created.

I exit the room quietly and start down the hallway. As I reach for the knob, the door opens and I'm face to face with Bryan. Worried lines crease his forehead. His hand reaches out and he brushes it against mine, but the briefness makes it feel ghostly, like it never happened.

I peek down at his fingers, the ring is still there, and for some reason all the pain of the nightmare vanishes. He might only be doing it for appearances, but seeing it there makes the divorce less real.

"Good morning," he says.

"Morning," I whisper.

"I'll meet you downstairs, okay?" The sincerity in his voice catches me off guard.

I nod. "I'm taking a shower first."

He steps aside, allowing me to go in. When I shut the door, I rest my back up against it for a few minutes to relax and collect my thoughts. I survey the room, my eyes landing on the baby monitor that's on with the volume up. I gasp and cover my mouth. He heard everything I said. Glancing back at the shut door over my shoulder I imagine him on the other side waiting for me to open it. But when I do, there's no one there, only muffled voices downstairs.

Disappointment creeps up in me, and I know I shouldn't let it. Expecting him to be there was a ridiculous thought, and only happens in movies and books. This is neither.

Gently, I shut the door. I don't find the urge to cry. From here on out, I need to push forward and move past Bryan and me. Nothing is going to change his mind, and I have to accept that. No matter how hard it is.

CHAPTER 23

"Hey," Bryan whispers, nudging my shoulder.

My eyes flutter open to the most beautiful sight, one I thought I'd never see again. Bryan sits on the bed beside me with Hunter on his lap. Not only seeing them together but getting to witness the biggest smile on Hunter's face, makes this whole trip worth it.

After my shower I felt run down from the nightmare and instead of going downstairs I hid under the covers to read a book. Eventually, sleep overwhelmed me, and I passed back out.

"Mama, wake up!" His words are clear as day. And my eyes tingle with tears.

"Hey, buddy. What are you both doing here?" I ask.

"Hunter and I wanted to show you something." The genuine gleam in Bryan's eyes piques my curiosity.

Pushing back the nightmare, last night's memories come rolling back in. The fire, the way his body reacted to me, and how his hand touched my back as he fell asleep. Then halfway through the night his arm wrapped around me, grabbing my hands, and pressing them against my stomach.

When we were together, it was my favorite gesture. Being

woken in the middle of the night even when I was so tired, I couldn't move, having him hold me made me feel alive. I hate that it was ruined when I woke up in a panic, but now staring at the two most handsome guys in my life, makes it all better.

"Oh yeah. What's that?"

"Hurry and get dressed. We'll wait downstairs."

Bryan lifts Hunter from the bed.

"Mama there's…"

"Don't ruin the surprise," Bryan says, tickling him. "Just hurry."

Bryan takes him out of the room, and without hesitation I get ready. Lately, it has been taking me several tries before I can convince myself to leave my bed, but this morning being woken by Hunter and Bryan gave me a little extra motivation to get up and move again.

It's quiet downstairs, but I catch a sweet chocolate aroma, mixed with the greasy sound of bacon popping. I head to the kitchen and the sight before me almost brings me to my knees. I brace myself on the wall. It feels like forever ago we were doing this in our own kitchen. Part of me wishes I could take back the last six months and change it by never letting Bryan go. I should have held on tighter.

Bryan stands in front of the stove wearing his mom's red Christmas apron, while Hunter paces at the door staring out at the white wonderland that was created overnight. His hands flap, stimming with excitement.

"What's all of this?" I ask.

"Well, it's been a bit of a crazy morning. Dad and Morgan went down the street to help the old neighbor shovel the snow, Sam is under the weather from the pregnancy, and Mom and Syd are out in the shed searching for the old sleds. Everyone ate a quick breakfast, and I figured while we had time it would be nice to have a family breakfast. Just the three of us."

Bryan has a soft smile on his face. It's uneasy and hesitant, half turned up. And his eyes. They flicker across the room, unable to meet my gaze. I close the gap between us and let my lips settle on his cheek. He closes his eyes and inhales.

"I think it's a great idea. For Hunter, right?"

Under my touch he tenses. "Yeah. Yeah. For Hunter. And afterwards we can go sledding on the hill."

His smile fades and he turns back to cooking. We could totally spend days like this, even if we aren't together, we can do this. Co-parenting isn't always easy, but I know Bryan and I can get past all the drama and focus on our son. No matter how amazing the little moments are, it doesn't negate the fact that we fight—A LOT. The thing that kills me is the small glimmer of hope in his eyes, because I want it too, but realistically, I fear it won't work.

The kitchen table is much smaller than the large table we've all been eating at, but it's perfect for the three of us.

While I get Hunter settled, Bryan brings over the food and Hunter attacks the pancakes right away. His face is covered in the melted chocolate from inside the fluffy cakes.

"He eats like you, messy," I tease, attempting to ease the tension in the room.

There's a smidge of chocolate on the top of Bryan's lip.

"And like I always say, like father, like son."

"What?"

I tap the left side of my lip and Bryan mimics my fingers, but on the wrong side.

"No, up. No down." I attempt to point him in the right direction, but he's not getting it. "You're gonna make me do it, aren't you?"

"You're not pointing in the right spot." He chuckles, making another valiant effort, but it only makes the smudge of chocolate worse.

Giggling, I shake my head and bury my face into my hands. Peeking through my fingers, I find him grinning at me.

"What?" he asks again.

"Do I really have to do everything? You're as bad as Hunter." I let out a playful sigh. "Come here." I lick my thumb, lean over the table, and run my thumb over his upper lip. A shaky exhale escapes from his lips, and for a split second, that feels more like a lifetime, I hold myself there. My thumb against his warm face, and my eyes steady on his.

Hunter's gibberish brings me back into focus and I settle back down in my chair. I catch a devious smile on Bryan's face. His demeanor has changed from a few minutes earlier.

"Better?" he asks.

"Much," I say.

"When did it even start to snow? We were out there pretty late."

I watch the snowflakes descending to the ground through the frost-lined sliding doors.

"It was right after you went upstairs. It was a light snow too, the type that makes the grass sparkle, and when I woke up this morning it was everywhere."

"Guess I should watch the weather. I had no idea it was going to snow."

"Me neither. Guess it's a good thing we are still here for a few more days; looks like it's going to continue through tomorrow," he says.

"You and I were always terrible at watching the news. Remember the time we got stuck on the train coming home from the city? The snow was so bad they cancelled all the trains and we had to take a taxi."

"The scariest taxi ride I've ever been on." His laughter fills the room as we reminisce over the terrifying ride over the black ice and freezing snow.

We spend the next thirty minutes having random conversations and never once does it turn into either of us fighting or getting upset. And now the hope he felt has ignited inside me too.

"The snow is white. Daddy, the snow," Hunter says.

"I think someone is ready for some snow. You think they found the sleds?"

"Guess we should find out. I'll head out and you get Hunter ready?"

I'm glad I brought a snowsuit. Being up here you never know what the weather might hold. I finish getting him ready and he stands there, his arms out and legs spread apart.

"Great. My son looks like Ralphie from *A Christmas Story*."

My attention floats back in the direction of Bryan's voice.

"Funny. He's got to be warm."

He points at Hunter. "The boy can barely move. What do you have under that snowsuit, ten jackets?"

Bryan comes over and scoops Hunter up. "We shouldn't trust Mommy with snow gear ever," he says.

I pucker my lips and throw him a shady scowl. "Har, har."

"Har, har to you too! Sleds are ready. Are you?" he asks.

"Yup!"

Hunter nods. "Mama, it's white."

"You are all ready to go. We could literally just push him down the hill and he'd fly down and be protected with all the layers."

"Oh my God! You're an A-S-S," I say, shoving him lightly on the arm.

He laughs again, making everything feel as it once was.

In the yard, Gayle and Sydney have four sleds, red, green, blue, and yellow. Behind the property is a small hill, not too big, and the perfect size for Hunter to enjoy it too. He and Bryan step into the green sled when we get to the top.

"Come on, you too," Bryan says, patting the spot between him and Hunter.

"There's no way, that's so dangerous. You two go. I'll race. Blue is my good luck color anyway." As I say it, my gaze lands on his eyes. I'd always said blue was my good luck charm because any time I'd find a blue item something good would happen.

The night before I got engaged, I found my dad's old golden wedding band with a blue sapphire ring around it. He had lost it a few months before he passed, and somehow it ended up in the garage inside one of his toolboxes. I had gone down to grab a hammer, because Mom wanted to hang a new photo on the wall, and as I combed through the old metal box, on the very bottom was his ring.

Bryan and I line up the sleds. Hunter isn't paying much attention to our antics; he's got his own thing going on in his head. Gayle and Sydney stand at the bottom of the hill and count down, telling us when to go. Bryan and Hunter start off strong, only because Bryan got his sled going first.

"You're a cheater!" I yell as I slide up beside him.

Neck and neck, I pull ahead, but at the bottom my sled tilts. I tumble out rolling through the snow, laughing.

"Good luck, huh? You might have won, but we didn't tumble," he jokes.

"Ha, ha, you going to help me up?" I ask.

"Nah!" He walks away and sways his hips as he does.

"Bryan! I don't take my statement back. You really are an ass!"

He turns and heads back to me, a Cheshire cat grin on his face. The corners of his eyes wrinkle. Leaning down he holds out his hand. Being spiteful, I grab a hold of him, and tug hard enough to make him lose balance. He crashes beside me and when he falls, I scoop up some snow into my hands and drop it onto his head. The snow breaks apart and some pieces go down his jacket. He shivers, then turns to me.

Behind us Hunter's excited shouts distract me. Bryan takes this opportunity to strike, and I'm hit with a snowball down the front of my jacket. I scream and giggle from the frigid ice raining down my chest.

I lie down against the cold ground. Holding my arms and legs out I create a snow angel. While I'm doing my own thing, Bryan retaliates a second time smacking me in the head with a snowball. His laughter echoes over the hills.

Sitting up, I grab his jacket to shove him when his gloved hand captures mine. With his other hand he wraps it around my back and pulls me into him. I'm suddenly captivated by his eyes. Instead of icy cold, they are more of a warm blue ocean on a hot summer's day. His lips part and the more they do, the closer I get to him. My giggles taper off into nothing. The noises around me still. I know Hunter is laughing and screaming, but my ears have chosen to only hear my name on Bryan's lips.

"Char..."

I cut him off by pressing my mouth to his.

We gasp together in sync. I can't help the way my mouth forms to his. He releases a shallow breath and when his tongue meets mine again, I'm done for. I'm lost in him all over again. His body melds with mine in a way no one's has ever had before.

It takes me several long-drawn-out kisses to realize this can't be happening. My muscles in my lower half tighten, pleasure rippling through as if we were doing more than kissing.

I'm torn away from him by Hunter's giggles. We stare at each other for a few lingering seconds, trying to catch our breaths. Shaking my head, I stand all too quickly and the world spins, but I manage to hold my balance. Bryan gets to his feet, dusts off, then rushes back to Hunter laughing at how he and Syd wiped out on the sleds.

I need a few moments to collect myself. My body is buzzing like never before. His kisses set me off, every damn time. He's the only guy who has ever made me hot and bothered with a simple kiss. I've always felt fireworks, but there was also that rollercoaster drop feeling that makes you want to scream, cry, and be excited all at the same time.

"Char, snowman?" Bryan asks.

Blinking myself back to the present, I stare at him. How long had I been in my own head?

Bryan and Hunter have already started a snowman. I can't say no to a snowman. Hunter is throwing the snow but then patting it on the large round bottom Bryan made.

"Hey, I lost you again," he says, as I jog over.

"Yeah, sorry. I got distracted."

My eyes wander up meeting his own, and he grins like he knows. I shake the thoughts and the memory and spend the rest of the afternoon building a snowman, sledding, drinking hot chocolate, and being with my family. There's no other place I'd rather be this holiday than right here with them.

I go to bed first making an excuse about feeling worn down. Gayle is happy to take over with Hunter, and so is the rest of his family. I left them creating animals with playdough.

There's tingling below, one in desperate need to be taken care of. The way Bryan's lips fell on mine tonight was electric. It's the first time we've been close in months. The fire between my legs needs to be extinguished and needs to happen fast. I don't know how much time I have alone.

I get comfortable under the blankets and grab one of my smaller toys from my suitcase. It feels weird to have brought it here with me, but I knew at one point I'd need a release. Bryan was my husband and there's not a day that goes by I don't fantasize about the way he'd always come up from behind and press himself into me when he thought no one was paying attention.

The toy roars to life, it's small and the buzz is light, but enough to help me release the pressure. I lift one hand above the covers to swipe along my lips where he kissed me tonight. I try to remember the feeling of them and the way he'd kiss my thighs and then linger over me, and how his tongue would enter me ever so slightly. The buzzing doesn't intensify but I squirm under the tightness raging through my lower half.

Is it weird to be fantasizing about my soon-to-be ex-husband? I have no clue. All I know is the way he touched me tonight set me off. I go back to the memories and try to flip through one that will send me over the edge. One. I keep telling myself. One orgasm is all I need, and I can forget him and his touch.

I reach under my shirt and roll my nipples the way he would, between his pointer and thumb. His large coarse fingers had the perfect roughness to them that always sent me over the edge.

Thinking about it brings me close, although my hands don't quite feel the same. I close my eyes and imagine it's him. I picture him as he kisses my body, wraps his lips around my nipple and—holy shit I think I'm—the door swings open and my fingers fumble with the switch. It's off, but I'm left unsatisfied.

I keep my eyes closed and hold the small vibrator in my hand. The footsteps stop, but I don't move. I wait and wait, and a few seconds later I finally hear them retreating into the bathroom. The door shuts and I let out the trembling breath I've been holding back. I thought it would fix this desire I had, but now it's only made it worse.

CHAPTER 24

Beside me Bryan shivers in his sleep, and moans like he's in pain. I roll over to face him. The only time he ever moans in his sleep is if he's not well. I press my lips to his forehead, he moans again. He's on fire.

I start to get out of bed to search for some medicine when his voice stops me in my tracks.

"Char. Char, I'm so sorry, baby," he calls out.

In the dim light of the night light across the room, I see his eyes are still closed, but he restlessly moves around. His voice is painful to listen to. I settle back into bed and run a hand through his hair. He hums at the contact.

"Hey, Bry, it's Charlotte. I'm right here. I'm going to go find you some medicine: you're burning up."

In his dazed state he sings a few lines of "Burnin' Up" by The Jonas Brothers.

I chuckle. "Leave it to you to actually remember lyrics to my favorite song while you're in a fevered state."

He grins in his sleep then groans. "Everything hurts."

"The man cold has begun," I say.

"Not funny." He puckers his lips and opens his eyes.

"Where does your mom keep the meds?"

"Kitchen, upper cabinet, in the corner." His eyes shut again, and he rests an arm over his head.

I kiss his forehead. "I'll be right back, okay?"

He mutters something incoherent. As I try to get off the bed his hot, clammy hand reaches out to grab my wrist. "You'll come back, right?" he asks, voice breaking. "Please."

I'm not sure if I should get all worked up about his question. He's in a weird state from his fever, but there's something about the way he's holding on to me. Maybe the truth is coming out. My heart is frenzied and refuses to stop its erratic beat.

"Yes. I'm not going anywhere, only leaving the room to get you some meds to bring down your fever. Okay? Promise."

I use my phone to light my way through the dark house. I don't want to wake anyone. The medication is exactly where he said. I fill a glass with water and head back upstairs. He's now sound asleep. For a few minutes I lay beside him watching his breathing.

"Rub my head?" He opens his eyes, and I don't miss the half-assed cock of his brow along with a wiggle. At least things are somewhat back to normal between us.

"Take this first."

He lifts his head slightly, enough to take the pill and swallow with a few sips of water. I put the glass back on the table.

The heat from his fever is hot against my skin as I run my hand over his forehead and through his hair. He moans once more, but it's a sound of relief. I rest my head against the headboard and massage his scalp.

"Char…"

"Bryan, get some rest. Okay? You're not well and if you start talking now, you'll regret your fever talk later."

I was so wrapped up in him I hadn't realized he was touching me. In an easy fluid motion, he draws a heart on my arm. Not only one. He draws several. I shiver from the gesture alone not the touch.

"I could never regret telling you how much I love you." His voice is barely above a whisper.

Holding in a breath I count to five, then release. Now I'm sweating, feeling feverish, but I'm almost certain it's the anxiety that comes with those words. I sniffle to make the itch between my eyes and nose leave. He drops his hand lazily, like he can't hold it up anymore. There's a strong need to forget this whole fighting thing and never fight with him again, but then there's a twist in my gut. Maybe I'm being stubborn.

"Hey, look," he says, pointing towards the window. The curtains are pulled aside slightly. Outside the first hint of light shines through, a pink, blue, and orange sky brightens the darkness. I don't respond to him, only continue to rub his head. My mind drifts to all the dark places it shouldn't. His eyes flicker open. He's so sick it seems to hurt him, and they are only half mast.

"Sleep. You need sleep."

"I can't help it, you're just so beautiful."

I touch a finger to his lips. "Shh… not another word."

"What are you going to do? Arrest me?" He's so delirious, even the grin on his face is loopy.

"You'd like that wouldn't you?"

"Mmm…"

I chuckle, but there's a hint of a sniffle. His eyes fly open again. I catch a pool of water at the corner of my eye. His brows narrow, and his mouth opens ready to talk, but I shush him again.

"You're worse than Hunter, go to sleep."

He scowls then closes his eyes. Within minutes he's sleeping again. It's not a very peaceful sleep. Every few minutes he rolls over back and forth, still groaning a little.

Once the day fully breaks and Hunter starts moving on the

monitor, I go to check on him. We head downstairs and everyone is already bustling around.

"Morning, where's Bryan? He's usually the first one awake," Gayle asks, concern in her voice.

"Man cold," I say.

"Oh God, you poor woman." The room erupts in laughter.

I allow myself to join in, but my mind is reeling over what was said between Bryan and I this morning. There's no way he meant them. My heart is even more confused than it was when we drove up here together or when we shared the kiss in the snow or beside the tree. In those moments it feels as if he still wants me, but then I rewind back to our conversation about the divorce papers.

"I'm so glad I married a woman, at least I'll never have to deal with a man cold. Those sound terrible," Morgan says.

Sam chuckles. "Totally."

I turn to Gayle. "I want to make him soup. He loves my grandmother's homemade one, but I'm not sure if we have all the ingredients."

She grabs some coffee from the machine and turns around, blowing on the steaming liquid in her *Favorite Grandma* mug. "Oh. I'll take you to the store. Roads seem to be clear. We'll wait for some sun to melt the ice."

Sydney offers to watch Hunter, and by late morning Gayle and I find our way to a store about twenty minutes away from the cabin. It's a small shop, and the produce section is a little empty, but I make do.

"So, darling. How are things going?"

"Okay I think," I say, as I lift some small red potatoes to check them.

"That's great. You two look happier than when you first arrived."

I fight the urge to tell her although on the surface everything is okay, inside I'm breaking. Sure, we could go back to living together upon returning home, but the heaviness of Bryan's decision to leave will always be there. It's contradictory to want to never regret my moments with him but push him away at the same time. Maybe it's me, the messed up one, not him.

"I think we'll be okay."

I'm not sure if she bought it. Her smile is light, but she doesn't push the subject, only makes her voice known.

"I'm relieved. You two had me worried. You are good for him. You cracked through his shell."

My thoughts drift back to what she mentioned when we first arrived. I still haven't had the guts to ask him about it. He was sensitive about Hunter starting therapy and knowing why helps me to understand his reaction. I'm not sure how I feel about carrying the secret around, but I hope one day maybe he'll trust me enough again to talk about it with me.

I change the subject to cooking and our favorite soups. While my cooking skills are subpar, this soup recipe my grandma passed down to me is made with love, because I feel if I don't make it as perfect as she did, I'd be disappointing her in the afterlife.

Back at the cabin, Gayle gives me full access to the kitchen. She and Jack have gone out to get some more firewood for the fireplace.

"Smells heavenly." Hearing Bryan's voice sounding almost normal startles me.

I slap a hand to my chest. "Jesus, you scared me. And heavenly?"

"It's Bryan actually, not Jesus. I smelled your grandma's soup. So of course, I'm here now."

By the way he jokes with me, it's easy to tell he's feeling better. He comes over and stands behind me at the stove while I stir. With his hands on my hips and his body pressed into me, I inhale.

When he doesn't say anything, I face him and press my lips to his forehead.

"Ah, you're cool as a cucumber again."

His hands haven't left my hips since I spun in his arms. He pulls me a little closer. "That's such a mom thing to say." He chuckles.

I grin. "I am a mom."

I go back to checking my soup. His fingers tickle my sides. My ass bumps into him and he hardens under my touch. My breath catches in my throat, allowing a small gasp to leave my lips.

"Control that thing. You're still sick."

The words come out before I can stop them. It doesn't seem to faze him though. He chuckles and thrusts into me, and my insides flutter. "Doesn't mean I don't want to mess around with my wife."

For a whole five seconds I stopped breathing. The world stills from him calling me his wife again. I know we never officially got a divorce, but I honestly thought it was over, and now here we are, and my emotions are running rampant.

"My wife," he repeats quietly.

I stir the soup and place the ladle down in the holder on the counter. For a few seconds I lose myself, staring off at the wall. The colors blur together to the point where I have no clue what color it is. Bryan startles me by adjusting my body to look at him and reaches up and touches his hand to my cheek.

"Thank you," he whispers. "For the soup, and for taking care of me this morning."

"Of course," I say, my voice wavering at the end.

He holds on to me so tight; I fear what will happen when he lets go.

"You should sit. The soup will be ready soon. You're looking a little pale."

It's not a lie. I lean in to check his head again to make sure the fever hasn't returned. He's slightly warmer but not by much. I'll have to make sure he takes some meds soon. He's forgetful when it comes to that.

"I'm dizzy as fuck." He chuckles.

"See, no sexy thoughts. Keep it in your pants until you're better."

"Okay, Doctor Holmes."

I swear this guy will make my eyes permanently roll. "Come on you." I carefully help him navigate over to the kitchen table, then finish the soup. We sit together and have a long conversation about nothing in particular, but even so, my heart soars with an intense desire, so much that I have to force it back, because of my own irrational fears. But sitting here with him without a care in the world is a step in the right direction.

CHAPTER 25

The week has flown by, Bryan is much better, and things between us are weird yet good. We spend our nights cuddling. Neither of us have gone in for another kiss. Thank God, because I don't know how many more of those I can take before I break.

For now, we have put aside our differences and have turned our attention to Hunter. He loves the countryside and I do hope maybe even if things don't work out for us that we can take time out and have these vacations.

There's a knock on the door. I came up to recharge and talk to Ellie. She and Logan are ordering in and enjoying the ball drop from the warmth of their home. It sounds lovely.

"Come in."

Four heads peek around the door frame. Gayle, Morgan, Sydney, and Sam. Wide smiles grace their faces. Glancing around the room, my cheeks heat under the uncomfortable feeling of their stares.

"Did I miss something?"

Gayle walks in first, she's got a dress bag. In Sydney's hands is a very intricate box of what I'm thinking might be makeup. Sam and Morgan seem like maybe they are just there for support, but Morgan is holding a large rectangular shoe box.

"What are you guys doing?"

"Giving you the kid-free New Year's you two deserve. Don't fight me, I can see the stress rolling off your body," Morgan says.

"Now, don't you worry about Hunter, he's in good hands."

I can't deny that I could use some time to relax, but the fact that I'll be relaxing with Bryan is more nerve racking than ever. Our nights are spent together but it's mostly sleeping. We haven't had real alone time in I don't even know how long. I might miss it too much.

"Which one of you devised this evil plan?" I ask, smirking.

"First, there's not an ounce of evil involved... well, maybe a little. It was Bryan's idea, but we might have gone a little overboard when he asked us to watch Hunter, and well... we pushed to help make it special," Morgan cuts in.

I bite my tongue because words of doubt are simmering at the brink of spilling out. *He wants to spend time with me. But why?* Tears build in the back of my eyes. Concentrating on something else helps keep them at bay, but they might rupture anyway.

"I don't know if I should be excited or terrified."

"Both are okay," Gayle says, plopping down beside me. She rests her arms around my shoulders. Our eyes meet for a split second before I look away. I almost feel as if she knows, but the moment passes, and she smiles.

"Okay. I guess doll me up. It's the second time in a month I've been pampered, but bring it on."

Sydney stands in front of me with her hand out. "Come on. Let's make you even more fabulous."

Reaching out I take hold of her hand and she leads me into the bathroom. I expect this to bring a pang of sadness rushing over me, but instead I'm greeted with a warmth that covers me in a blanket of love, and I couldn't be happier.

Over an hour later I'm all ready to go. It's nothing fancy, but my black curls are tightened a bit, the waves falling naturally against the fabric of the maroon sweater dress. Standing in front of the mirror, I'm several inches taller with the help of some tan suede knee-high boots.

"If my son doesn't fall in love with you all over again, he better watch out, because you are stunning," Gayle says, eyeing me. She pulls out her phone. "Say cheese."

I strike a pose. The old me shines through, making it feel as if anything is possible tonight. I never cared for the whole new year, new me, but this year I want to be myself again. I miss the confident Charlotte, the one who flirted with a police officer after hitting her head on ice, and still managed to win his heart.

"Guys, if you keep ogling over her the food's gonna get cold," Sam warns.

Gayle checks the time. "Oh, you're right. He's probably waiting."

At the top of the stairs, it almost feels like I'm in one of those movies where I'll walk down the steps, and everyone will be waiting for me.

I see Jack first, followed by Bryan's arms holding a bouquet of white daffodils. He's wearing a sweater vest I've never seen on him before. My heart does a triple—no, a quadruple beat as I close in on him. He could break hearts in the sweater, in fact he already has. My pulse is drumming a different tune than a few weeks ago. The words I need to say stick in my throat as my eyes land on Hunter in a nearly matching vest and khaki pants.

Bryan's calm blue eyes find mine, and it's like I've slipped on ice and hit my head all over again, because I'm delirious at the sight. He blinks a few times clearing the haze that's frosting over his eyes.

Stepping forward he holds the bouquet out and I take it, breathing in the aroma. With my nose buried in the flowers, I glance up at him. His grin makes my insides tingle with a pleasure I've missed.

"Hi," he whispers.

"Hi."

"Mama?" Hunter's little voice pulls me from my head.

"Yes, little man?" Kneeling, I get to his level. He's got a beautiful smile on his handsome little face. In so many ways he resembles Bryan, and I can't help the tear that slides down my cheek. He tilts his head, his attention on something behind me.

"Daddy wuvs you. Wuvs you." His eyes are darting up and around. The teacher in me wants to correct his Ls but the mom in me wants to bask in the adorable way he says love.

"Thank you for letting me know." I kiss his cheek and stand.

"Come on, Hunter, let's go play a game," Gayle says.

Hunter's eyes light up. Playing games, although sometimes it's hard for him to concentrate for long, is one of his favorite things to do.

"Oh, wait!" Sydney shouts. "Picture. Get together you two."

This feels different than the picture we took at Christmas. Bryan's fingers grip at my waist as he tugs me into him. The pressure of his fingers gives me a case of giggles. The camera shutter flickers as I toss my head back and his attention is solely on me.

Gayle presses a hand to her mouth as Sydney shows her the shot. Grabbing the phone she brings it over, and to be honest I don't hate the picture. My smile is loud enough to be heard off screen. My head is tilted back, curls splayed all over. Bryan's stare is solely on me, light dimples caressing his scruffy cheek.

"Send that one to me, Syd?" Bryan asks.

I snap my attention to him. He wants our picture. I need to shake all the bad thoughts from my mind. When he realizes I'm staring he holds my gaze. Tonight isn't about the fighting or the past; it's about the now. Where our future is headed, I don't know; but what I do know is, I want to live in this moment with him.

"Okay, have fun, you two," Gayle says, waving. She gives Syd her phone back, then takes Hunter's hand and shoos everyone out of the room.

"So, I hear this was your idea," I say.

"Maybe a little." His cheeks flush red. "You look absolutely beautiful, Charlotte."

"And you." I fan myself. "Never thought I'd ever see you in one of these," I say, tugging on the top button. "I like it though."

He chuckles. "Are you ready?"

"Oh, I forgot my bag."

"You won't need that tonight; we're not going far."

Narrowing my eyes, I stare for a few long seconds. "What do you mean?"

His hand slips into mine as if it never left and pulls me into him again. I wrap my other hand around his arm, holding myself against him.

"A coat?"

"Nah. It's warm where we are going."

We step out back onto the porch.

"Warm huh?" I ask, glancing at the leftover snow on the deck.

The night sky has already taken hold over the day. The darkness above gives way to shining stars twinkling. My eyes scan the sky as we take it in together. A medium sized pop-up clear dome tent sits in the center of the yard, beyond the fire pit.

"Is that like one of those igloo things?" I ask.

"Kind of. My parents found it on Amazon. You know my mom is always searching for absolutely ridiculous finds."

I laugh, like it's the first real laugh I've had in months. "Yeah. That's your mom alright."

Inside sits comfortable outdoor furniture with large blue cushions on the wicker seats, and on a matching table food is already out and prepped on it. Hanging around the perimeter of the tent are white twinkling lights.

As we walk, I shiver, and Bryan holds me a little tighter. He steps away to unzip the entrance, and when I walk inside, I'm no longer cold. Bryan zips the tent closed, and there's no sounds other than the soft music playing off a laptop in the corner.

I twirl around, my eyes trained on the expansive sky above. It's just as clear in here and with us being in the middle of nowhere you can see everything up there. It's romantic and beautiful and I might cry several times tonight. The gesture alone has me choked up.

"Why?" I ask, turning my attention to him.

He closes the gap between us and once again holds my hands.

"Because, you and I haven't had any time alone to just do something... as friends... as partners... husband and wife." He blows a slow steady stream of air from his lips as his hands tremble in mine. "Our interactions the last six almost seven months have been either spent talking about Hunter, schedules, fighting, or a simple hello and goodbye. I thought maybe if we spent time as Charlotte and Bryan, the two people who met and fell in love. Maybe we could have fun and let go. Even if it's only for one night, I think we both deserve some goodness in our lives."

Leaning forward I press a simple kiss to his scruffy cheek. I linger for longer than I should, but he holds me with an intensity that makes me not want to let go. When I do, he's watching me, like he's gauging my feelings.

"We should eat. I made lasagna."

"You?"

"Hey, at least I don't burn the edges," he teases, as he leads me over to the couch.

We sink down into the cushion and I bump into him. "Hey, that was one time. I'm a good cook ninety-seven percent of the time. Better than Ellie, that's for sure."

He pushes me back with his shoulder. We fall into a comfortable silence as he cuts the cheesy goodness from the dish and sets each portion on white ceramic plates. With ease he pops open the bottle of red and pours some into each glass.

"I still can't believe your mom bought this thing. It must have cost her a fortune."

"She got it on sale for only like 500."

I nearly spit out the wine I'm sipping. Bryan chuckles.

"You know who would absolutely have loved this?" One person comes to mind. "My dad. He and my mom used to do all these romantic things together, and I could see him doing this for her. He'd probably travel with it too. He always loved a perfect nighttime sky."

My voice grows hoarse, but there's no sign of tears. The memories are good ones.

"Have you heard of the heart nebula?"

"Heard of it? Dad and I were obsessed with stars and space. Aside from our plan to explore the Pacific Northwest and all its glory, we had planned on one day going to Alaska too. We had a whole itinerary planned around seeing the aurora borealis." A tug on my lips lets me know I'm smiling, and it's been a while since I've spoken about Dad and not cried. Like with Bryan's surprise Christmas gift.

Bryan's stare pulls me in, and I find myself once again lost in his gaze.

"What?" I ask.

"Nothing. You just looked so happy a moment ago, talking about your trips and your dad. You always get this soft smile on your face when you speak of the adventures you had together with him. It's also been a while since I've seen your face light up."

"Oh." I stare at the food on my plate.

"Did you try the lasagna yet?"

I hold up a finger, grab the fork, and dive in. The aroma of sauce and cheese blend together tickling my senses. I moan when the sensations all hit my mouth.

"You like it," he teases.

Laughter fills me, and I nearly choke on it. The low grumble in his voice shocks my body into a reaction that makes me wish this night could lead to more.

His hand grazes the skin of my cheek. "Char."

"This is really good," I say, my words trembling upon their exit.

"I'm glad."

The next couple of hours take me back to our first few months as a couple, when things were easy, and our responsibilities didn't stress us to the point of exploding. It's close to midnight, and the two of us are casually sipping on our candy-cane hot cocoa and stuffing our faces with Gayle's leftover Christmas cookies.

"Char?" There's a timidness about the way he approaches me.

Setting down my white mug onto the glass coaster I lean back and turn to him.

"Yeah?"

"Charlotte, I'm—"

The sliding glass doors behind us whip open and Morgan's voice carries through the yard.

"Hunter! It's too cold."

"Mama, Dada, big ball, the big ball it's gonna fall."

Glancing back over at Bryan, he runs a hand over his head and scrubs his face. When he catches me staring, he searches my eyes. For what I don't know, but whatever he finds he smiles.

"Well since he's awake, I want to ring in the new year as a family. What do you think?"

My words fall short again, so I nod. Never in the last six months did I imagine Bryan, Hunter, and I would have this moment again. I expected us to celebrate separately.

The door behind us closes. I try to wipe away the moisture pooling in my eyes so when I go in there, I'm not a blubbering mess. Without hesitation Bryan pulls me into his grasp and holds on. The gesture pushes the tears out and onto his vest. He runs his fingers through my hair.

Taking a few extra minutes to gain my composure I lie there in his arms and stare up at the sky above. We might not be at our best right now, but I'm thankful we are here together.

"Let's go celebrate with our son," I say, wiping my face.

Bryan takes it upon himself to get rid of some more of my tears, before standing and reaching out for me to take his hand.

CHAPTER 26

I n the living room blankets are strewn all over the place. The TV is set on the Rock'n New Year's show, and the countdown is in the final ten seconds.

I scoop Hunter up into my arms, and he immediately snuggles into my embrace and holds on to Bryan as well. Bryan leans down, placing a kiss to his forehead. As he lifts his gaze his eyes find mine. Around us the family is shouting the final countdown, along with Hunter who is following along really well, but even amongst all of it, Bryan and I are glued to each other.

When the ball drops, we both kiss Hunter's cheeks. He squirms out of our arms, and we let him down. Neither of us pull our attention away from the other.

"I'd really like to kiss my wife tonight, if she would allow me the honor?" Bryan cups my cheek, and I lean into the touch.

My lip trembles, but the tears have dried up completely. "I'd like that a lot," I say, quietly

Without hesitation his lips are on mine. They are warm and inviting. I want so much more from them. We ignore the sounds around us and I surrender to the kiss. His mouth opens for me and our tongues tangle. When I touch his face, I notice his cheeks are wet. Are they sad or happy tears? A mixture of both? I'd open my eyes, but I'm too wrapped up in him.

Seconds later Hunter collides into us. Reluctantly we pull away and stare down at our perfect child.

"Mama, Da-dy, the ball look—it's colors... sparkles."

Scooping him back up, Bryan and I both kiss him on the cheeks again, and he happily nestles into our arms. I can't help the yawn that escapes me. The weight of the emotional mess going on in my head grows heavier.

"Hey, let me put him to bed, you look exhausted."

"Are you sure?" I ask.

"Mhmm... I'll be up in a bit."

I give everyone a hug and wish them a happy new year before heading upstairs. I was going to wash my face and hop into bed, but I need a shower. The hot water will help me relax and think over everything that has happened the past week, and mostly tonight.

The water running over my skin feels amazing. Bryan always hated how hot I liked it, but I never cared. Sometimes the heat releases the tension in my body. I have had plenty of it lately, especially now.

The pressure in the cabin is better than at home. I bask in the way the water hits into my back and cascades down. As I wash my body with soap, I take notice of the detachable shower head. This is a much safer spot than the bed, to relieve the tension growing between my thighs. My thoughts rewind back to the way Bryan acted tonight, like he was inviting me back into his life, no questions asked.

The pure thoughts turn impure. I remember the night by the fire and how his erection pressed into me, and tonight the way his lips felt over mine, how it seemed as if he wanted more.

With soapy hands I scrub low, running my fingers over myself. I suck in a breath: the build-up to an orgasm is quicker than I expected. I'm craving the release again. I allow my fingers to casually dance over myself; it feels good, but it's nowhere near good enough. I rinse my hands off, so they aren't so slippery and reach up for the shower head. Sometimes it does the work better than a vibrator or my fingers.

I adjust it so that it's on the power pulse massage. I maneuver it, making the water hit at the right angle. When the spray smacks into me a whimper escapes my lips. Bryan's face comes into my head, and I imagine it's his fingers dancing over me, or his lips sucking hard giving me the intense pleasure I've missed so much. I want him to hold me and capture me in his touch.

The pressure builds and within seconds I feel the release. I slide down the cold white tile wall inside the tub. Tears of relief slip from my eyes. After giving myself some time to breathe, I go for it again. One wasn't enough, especially after my half-assed attempt the other night.

This time I stand and lift my leg on the ledge. Turning the shower head I find the spot again, it builds and builds, my moans getting more intense. I try to hold back, but I can't. As I'm about to growl from the pleasure the shower curtain opens and my foot slips. I drop the shower head and it bangs against the tub with a heavy thud.

Hot strong arms hold me upright. My heart pounds from the surprise. His light, intoxicatingly fierce eyes find mine. His shoulders rise and fall in long fluid movements. My breathing matches his. Heat creeps up my neck rising onto my cheeks, as he lifts one of his hands and presses it against my flushed skin.

His thumb dances along the spot beneath my eye. He draws a heart right there on my cheek. My senses ignite from his simple touch. More than anything I want him to take me right here in this bathroom. There's so much I want from him, but just having him like that even if it's a lie, even for one night, I'll take it.

His hand shifts to the spot I like, under my chin. It's a steady gentle grab, but there's a roughness behind it, sending a shiver down my spine.

"Can I have you tonight?" he asks, breathlessly.

I nod. His grip on my neck holds steady, and there's no stopping the light moan from tumbling out of my lips. "Just tonight, right?" I'm doing it to protect my heart. If it went on any longer, I'd be a wreck. His lips graze my jawline then work their way up to my ear. I can do this, I can do what Ellie did, I can handle no strings for one night. Right?

"Yeah. One time," he whispers.

"Okay."

He slides his lips down and when they touch mine, I'm done for. He pulls me from the tub and reaches over to shut off the water, which is spraying everywhere. We stumble through the bathroom. I slip several times on the white tile floor.

Inside the bedroom, he tugs off his clothes, pulling off the tight black shirt and exposing his taut, lean body. His muscles have gotten bigger, but as my eyes wander down, I notice his dad bod around his midsection, and I lose myself in how attracted I am to him right now.

My hands roam all over his smooth chest. His fingers find my nipple, and he slowly rolls it between his thumb and pointer. He knows where to touch me to drive me crazy, especially when he sucks on one while playing with the other. It's his next move; he's predictable but it's comforting.

I expect it to be like how we've always done things, but he shocks me by lifting me under my ass. My legs wrap around him. We've never done this before. I'd be lying if I said I wasn't turned on by it.

He nibbles on my neck, and I roll my head back so he can get a better angle. He spins us and tosses me onto the bed, a rugged look on his face. His eyes narrow as he lowers himself. "You're still taking your birth control, right?"

"Yes, of course," I say, as his head dips low and he kisses my thighs.

His pointer finger circles my center, as two fingers slide up

176

and inside me, and I feel him add a third. I throw my arm over my mouth to suppress the moan. It's easy for me to come for him, and he knows it.

As I'm on the verge he lowers himself so his lips can intervene. Clenching my teeth, I let out a groan and my hips thrust upward into him, making his lips move faster along with me. I absorb the feel of him as his tongue glides over my most sensitive spot. His name tumbles out of me. I repeat it over and over making him work harder and faster.

It's been a while since we've slowed down and worked on each other before committing to sex. I love the way he regards me in the most sensual way. I've missed this part of sex. Once we had Hunter it became our mission to be in and out of the bedroom as quickly as we could, just in case. Tonight, Bryan's taking his time. I don't blame him. What if it's our last?

"Bryan, keep going. Please, I'm so close, Bry. So fucking close."

"That's my girl," he says between breaths.

He gives me two orgasms before pulling away. When he lingers back over me, he holds down my arms, so they are spread out behind me on the bed.

"Your pants are still on," I growl.

"Oh, and what are you going to do about it, Char?" he barks back at me, his tone fiery, his brows rising.

I free myself from his grasp and reach for his jeans. Undoing the button is a simple task. He stands and I sit up to finish the job. With his pants off, he slides his hands up my side, gliding them up towards my arms. Our hands clasp together, and I pull them behind me again.

Climbing on top he hovers over me. Escaping from his grip, I reach for him and hold his length in my hands.

He throws his head back. "Charlotte," he cries out.

"Does it feel good, Bry? Did you miss me touching you?"

"Keep talking to me like that, baby, and I'll come before I'm even inside of you."

I can't help the smile. Dirty talk had been almost non-existent in the last few months we were together. It's like the people we were when we met are shining through. I'm not the only one who lost herself in the mix, Bryan did too. We both had new responsibilities and our time wasn't only for us anymore, especially after we had Hunter. It feels good to stop and explore each other again as we did in the beginning.

"Are you ready, Charlotte?" he asks as I sit up and allow my tongue to dance over him while my hand pumps up and down.

My greedy mouth wants more of him, but my middle aches for him to be inside me. I linger for a few more seconds before lying back down. He doesn't hold back. When he slides inside, I find myself needing something to cover my mouth, anything. It's only been a second, but I'm already dripping all over him. I feel it.

He lowers his body and buries his face into my neck.

"My girl, always so ready and wet for me. You still want me?" He mutters the words into my flesh, his voice gravelly.

"Yes." I nod the best I can. "Yes, please, Bryan. Take me."

I lift my legs up and around him and cup his ass, scratching with my nails. His moans are turning me on. I shut my eyes and lift my hips to meet his thrusts. When my eyes open, he's watching me, and I can't veer away. I want him to see how good he's making me feel.

I suppress a scream and instead groan low and deep. I don't think he's locked the door. The suspense of getting caught rages through me. I've needed this so bad it doesn't even matter.

He slides out almost all the way, watches for my reaction, and when I bite my lip, he thrusts back inside, and I let out a yelp. He sets one of my arms free, giving me something to bite on while he hammers into me.

Almost six months of pleasuring myself doesn't come close to this moment. Not even a little bit. He's close, I can feel him tense. It's fine, the quicker the better.

When he does, he collapses on top of me. We're breathing heavily in sync.

"Once, right?"

It stings more than I thought it would when he asks again. But there are no tears, only relief from the pleasure. I don't answer with words, my throat is hoarse, and it will be easier if I keep my voice unheard. It would sound weak if I said anything, and I can't let him know this was more than sex.

He finally pulls out of me. I wait a few minutes as he makes his way into the bathroom. The shower turns on, but I can't move yet. I try to push my emotions into the far back corner of my mind. I enter the bathroom and we take turns washing each other, and kissing. I'd forgotten how good it felt, and I'm grateful he wants more of me, just for tonight. At least faking it might be a little easier now.

CHAPTER 27

P*ick up, please.* It's our last day here, New Year's Day, and I've finally gotten a chance to sneak away into the room. I've been dying to call Ellie since last night. When her round face and dark eyes appear on screen I want to jump through and hug her.

"Bryan took me on a date last night. Well, his whole family kind of was in on it."

Her brows wiggle. "Shut the front door! And what happened on this date?" she asks.

"We talked."

She pretends to yawn. "Only talked?"

The thought of what we did makes my entire body quiver with want and need so strong I can hardly contain myself. I tried so hard to let my mind only think it was sex, but connecting with him again, it felt much stronger. There was something in the way we moved together last night signifying how much the moment meant to us. It frightens and thrills me at the same time.

"Oh my God, Charlotte Rae Holmes! You did the nasty with your husband!"

In the camera I catch my expression. I'm no longer pale. My

cheeks are flushed and underneath the confusion is a hint of a smile on my lips.

"Was it good?" she asks, her eyebrows wiggling. "Sorry. Let me backtrack. Are you okay?" Her playful tone turns serious as she eyes me.

"I don't know. I'm still deciding." I can't help but think that my decisions last night were out of pure lust. In my sex-deprived mind, it was okay to go ahead and do it. Today, however, my heart and mind are at war. Am I turned on by it? Yes. Did it feel great? It was more than great. It was like falling in love with him all over again. Do I regret it? Kind of.

"Char, I want to be there to hug you right now." She can instantly tell whenever my mind is racing. I can do the same for her. I felt it when she and Logan were secretly together. I didn't know it at the time but could tell something was up by the distant look in her eyes. I'm sure she sees the same in mine right now.

"I would ask you how you handled the one-time thing with Logan, but you didn't do a very good job of it being just one time."

"Hey!" She laughs. "Not funny. Okay, maybe a little. At least you didn't wake up in a hotel room unaware of what you had done."

I chuckle. "True. I was sober and fully knew what I was getting myself into. Oh my God, El, it was…" I sigh. "I miss him," I squeak.

She adjusts herself in the driver's seat of her car. She must be in the parking lot waiting for her shift to start. On New Year's Day she has off from her regular job, but it's usually her day to work at the store.

"I'm sorry, do you need to get to work?" I ask.

"Oh, no, I have like fifteen minutes. Got here early. What did he say?"

"We both agreed it would be just one time." My lip trembles at the words. One time. I don't know how it could ever be one.

"That sounds all too familiar. Do you think he actually meant it?"

I shrug, and slump down burying myself into the blanket. "It would be for the best if it was. I love him. I love him so much it kills me to not have him in my life, but I can't go back to that. Losing him was awful. The fear is never going to go away now. Every fight will have me on edge waiting to see the back of his head."

I need help. It's easy to find it for others but when it comes to myself, I'd drown before realizing it.

"You need to come home so I can hug you. Don't cry, Charlotte."

I reach up and wipe underneath my bottom lid. "I'm sorry to burden you," I say.

"You're never a burden. I'm glad you came to me. When are you coming home?"

"Tomorrow."

"I'm off Monday night. Let me know and I'll make some time for you."

I wipe some more tears as the door to the room squeaks open. Bryan peeks into the room. His eyes land on me and I hold my breath. "I gotta go, El."

"Okay. Please don't hesitate to call. Okay?"

"Thanks. Love you."

"Love you more."

Her face disappears and I'm alone with Bryan. He steps inside the room, shutting the door, then crosses over. My pulse jumps all over the place and I wish it would go back to normal.

"Hunter is napping. I uh… you've been up here for a while, and I-I wanted to check on you." He sits beside me, the bed dipping under his weight.

"I'm good." I smile but he's already caught me. My cheeks are wet and I'm still finding it hard to focus. The tears still blind me but are no longer falling.

"You're not. I know because I'm not okay either. So, I know you must have a ton of things running around your mind." He stops, collecting his thoughts. "Charlotte, about last night I—"

"You don't have to say it. I know, it was once. That was it. We can't do this again. I don't want to fall into the same pattern." I lied or my eyes have betrayed me. They fill to the brink, and I can no longer keep the tears from falling. Is it normal to cry all the damn time?

"I don't either. I don't want to fight with you anymore. I hated fighting with you, Char. It tore me up inside to yell at you, and when you yelled back…" He pauses, shaking his head, shuddering from the memories. "I didn't mean to make you unhappy."

"Unhappy? Bryan you were… are… the best thing to ever happen to me. I blame myself for the unhappiness."

"It wasn't just you. Work made me miserable. No matter how much I love being able to help people, seeing it tear us apart made me hate it. I only took the extra hours because I was afraid if I didn't, we'd lose it all. The house, our life. But we lost it all anyway, didn't we? I wanted to give you and Hunter the world and I thought by working more, I could. I imagined us taking vacations and going on adventures together."

I nod. "We had the resources to make it work. Plus, if things got bad, we wouldn't be alone. Our family is our support system and would have helped. They are always willing to jump through hoops for each other. I mean look at what Ellie and Logan did for us. They took time out of their lives to help us redo our dream room. It takes a village, and we have one."

He glances down at the small space between us and blinks.

"And I wasn't telling you to stop working, I was asking for more time with you. When my dad—" I bite down hard on my lip. My teeth chatter like I'm cold, but I'm not. "When he passed, I saw my mom grieve over a man she loved. She would say things like, *I wish I had spent more time with him; I wish I had taken that vacation day; I wish I'd bought those tickets.* I didn't want to live with all those regrets one day."

His warm hand gently glides over mine. His touch is lighter than a feather, but I would be lying if I said it didn't make me feel things again. Like make me want to hold on to him for as long as I can.

"When you took those extra hours, I saw them as moments we lost that we'll never get back."

Talking about my dad is stirring up more emotions than I expected. It's been several years, but I still can't get my mom's words out of my head. The hand he has over mine lifts and brushes against my face. With a light tender touch, he wipes the tears.

Leaning forward, he whispers, "Then I guess we have a lot of lost time to make up for." His head presses against mine and he nudges me with his nose.

I suck in a sharp breath. I love when he's close like this.

"Bryan, I can't—"

"I'm not saying I'm moving my stuff back tomorrow. I'm saying, let's get back all the time we missed. I don't want to miss any of it with you either." He leans further into me, keeping his hand against my cheek. I love the way his face aligns perfectly with my own.

"Bry—"

"Sh," he whispers. "Please. If I don't have you again the way I did last night I might lose it. I want to show you what our life should have been like."

"Yeah, and then when we go back home, POOF! It will all magically disappear and then it's back to the real world and we're fighting again and barely speaking. Like two ships passing in the night."

His free hand finds the other side of my face and his lips fit mine. My mind is racing with all these *what if* thoughts. What if we did this? Could we be better? Could we do better? Or would this ruin us forever?

His mouth opens and my body follows along like it's on autopilot. I know every part of him, as my hands start their wandering. First at the scruff on his face. I'm heated from the friction between us.

"I understand if you don't want to give me one, but I'd like a second chance. I won't move back. We can try dating again. I'll take you out, we'll have sex, lots and lots of wonderful sex." He chuckles, and when I don't his eyes glaze over. "If in a few weeks or months or however long it takes, if it's still good we can talk about being together again. For real."

It's not a good idea. This can only end one way. In excruciating pain. But then my head drifts to Mom and all the regrets she had when Dad passed. I don't want to regret my life with Bryan. I love him way too much. I hope I'm not burying myself deeper into a hole.

"Okay."

"Okay? Really?" his lips turn up into a smile under mine. "Oh, thank God." He releases a quaking breath and holds my face again.

He pushes me back down onto the bed, kissing me like I'm his everything, the way he always has. If this is going to work, I have to look ahead. I want to press forward and not be stuck. One more chance. Out of anyone I know, Bryan deserves one.

"I need to have you again, please," he says, and the words almost come out as a moaning plea.

I close my eyes and allow his kisses to take over my heart and soul. My everything. My Bryan. I push away the relentless tears and a smile forms. If we're going to do this, I have got to be stronger. "Oh, I got a new toy." I grin, trying to lighten the mood.

Above me his entire body shakes. His warm sexy laugh makes the comment worth it. "You and your toys. What is it this time? It's not monster tentacles, is it?"

I smack him playfully on the arm. "Okay, no. That was a joke. Ugh. Gross. Let me show you." I sit up, and he moves out of my way as I stumble over to the suitcase. I pull out a small pink box and bring it over. Sitting down next to him I open it.

"Did you lock the door?" I ask.

"Yeah. Not because I expected anything, but because I wanted privacy."

"Sure." My grin refuses to let up. I almost feel light again. Like myself.

"Hey, I'm not the one with the toys."

"Anyway..." I push into him with my shoulder.

Fooling around with him is a breath of fresh air. The best part is sitting beside him and seeing his eyes light up. I've always loved how when he's truly happy the rings around his eyes almost sparkle. It sounds crazy, but I swear it happens.

I pull down my pants slightly, and take the device out of the box.

"So, this goes here." I push it down into my underwear and with the click of a magnet it's in place. Grabbing my phone off the bedside table I hand it to him. "Press that one."

He touches the pink app button and then I point out all the different features. It goes off on the highest setting. I grasp the sides of the bed as it does. "Starting a little rough there, aren't you?" I ask.

"I've got a hell of a lot of time to make up for here. Why dip our toes in the water when we can dive right in?" He leans over allowing his warm breath to dance over my ear, and whispers, "That's right, baby, come for me." And I do. I come undone right there in my underwear soaking the fabric and my leg as it drips down.

"Again?" He growls in a low deep rumble that vibrates my ear drum.

His hand finds the hem of my shirt. Tugging it off he throws it somewhere into the far corner of the room. His eyes roam over my body sending waves of butterflies dancing through me. As the vibrator picks up speed again, he clamps his mouth over my hard and ready nipple, and I bite down and yell out for him as I come again.

"What do you want to do now, Charlotte?" he asks, roughly.

"I want you to make me come the same way you did last night."

"I really have missed that dirty mouth of yours."

He kisses me with passion, lust, and all the love in his heart. I'm scared of this new development. More than anything I want this to work out for us. If we could be a family again and work through our differences, we'd be stronger for it. As a couple and as parents. This isn't going to be easy, but if he's willing, I am too.

Life sure has a funny way of working things out. I hope I'm doing the right thing. Not only for my heart, but for his, and for our son too. Nothing matters more than him. All I can do is hope and try to move forward and maybe it will land us in a good place.

CHAPTER 28

"We'll call you in a few weeks," Gayle says, hugging me tight. "That's when we should be making our trek down south."

"Sounds good," I say, but my voice wavers.

Not knowing where Bryan and I will be at that point startles me more than I care to admit. I love how we are trying to overcome this mountain, but it doesn't mean we'll make the climb over it and come out on the other side.

Gayle takes my face in her hands. The gesture is calming, but the tears are already there. "Please take care of yourself, Charlotte. Hunter needs his mama to be whole again. It's okay to reach out, and it's okay to get help. We may soon be a plane ride away, but I know when someone is hurting, and my darling, your heart is on fire. Please, don't ever hesitate to call me."

I nod, unable to speak. She really does have a knack for reading people.

"Hey, Char, you ready?"

I sniffle and wipe my tears as I pull away from Gayle. Bryan steps beside me, glancing between his mom and me. His hand rests on the small of my back and I lean into him. His reaction keeps me grounded as he curves his hand around my waist and pulls me into him.

"Everything okay?" The suspicion in his voice is clear.

His mom replies, "Perfect, son, just some girl-talk."

I step out of his grasp as he goes to hug Gayle. My eyes find Hunter and Sydney playing in the snow. She told me last night she was so sad we were leaving. She loved her time with Hunter, and let me know if we were available, she'd love to come visit during her next break. I of course had no objections.

"Take care of yourself." I hear Gayle say to Bryan. "But also, your wife too, she needs you more than you know. You're strong, but sometimes stubborn, and I know there's only so much someone can fight until they break, so don't be afraid to be vulnerable; you're human."

I know Gayle's words were meant for him, but I also know she meant for me to hear them as well.

After a tearful goodbye, we get in the car and drive away from the place that brought us back together. Now we're headed to a new reality and it's terrifying. I don't know what's waiting for us when we return. My heart flutters, making my chest ache, but the feeling is numbed as Bryan's hand slides over mine. I turn mine over and our fingers intertwine.

"I have work tomorrow, so I'll have to run when we get back. But maybe I can come over in a few days..."

"Yeah. That's okay. I get it." I bite down on my lip.

"Do you and Hunter maybe want to drive out east one day soon? I know it's cold, but there's nothing like a good drive and east end food."

His words make me smile.

"I'd like that, a lot. Hunter would too."

I check on Hunter, whose eyes are barely staying open. It's been so long since we've had a vacation and it was probably a lot for him. Although, I think more than anything he enjoyed it.

"Perfect. I'll make sure I have the day free." Bryan is quiet for a few seconds. His fingers moving and rubbing against mine as he thinks. His breaths are short like he's trying not to panic. I squeeze his hand, letting him know I'm feeling the same way.

"Charlotte, I want things to be different. I know you're afraid the magic will vanish once we get home, but let's not let our flame flicker out. I'm not ready for it to die, not yet."

I want to scream out, *Me too!* My throat is parched and it's like the words are stuck. In my wildest dreams I never imagined we'd be driving back holding hands and contemplating our future together. "Mmmm," is the only thing coherent I can say.

When we arrive home a few hours later, Hunter and I wave to Bryan from the porch, and when the door closes, calm rolls over me. I'm hoping it means things will be better, but I won't get my hopes up. I have to take one day at a time. I can steer myself in a good direction, but I can't control where I will end up.

"Hunter? Hunter?" I attempt to get his attention but he's staring beyond me into the porch at the door. When Bryan left the first time, Hunter didn't seem to take notice, but now after a week, I know he wants his dad here. Maybe I'm being selfish not allowing Bryan to move back in. As I glance down at my son, the worry doesn't vanish.

He sits on the floor, moves his body back and forth and stares.

I clear my throat. "Hey. Daddy has to work. You want cookies? Mommy has to go food shopping, but I think we can splurge on something fun for one night."

At the word cookie he perks up. After Hunter is satisfied with his cookie he walks away and plays with some toys in the living room. While he does, I go through the large pile of mail Ellie brought in for me while I was gone.

Junk, bills, junk, Christmas cards, and a large envelope addressed to me from a lawyer. It takes me by surprise so much my heart lurches. With trembling hands, I bury it under the pile of junk to save it for another day.

My phone buzzes and in a hazy fog I reach for it.

Bryan: Thinking about you already!

Me: XOXO

It goes off again and I expect it to be Bryan, but it's Ellie.

Ellie: Friday, date night. You and Bry should come out with me, Logan, Lily, and Jett. Maybe a night out with friends will help move things along. I can't wait to squeeze you tomorrow!

I chuckle. The papers are sort of forgotten. They aren't pushed to the far corners of my mind, but for now they're tucked away to be revisited later.

I text Bryan with Ellie's offer, thinking it will probably be a while before he responds, but within seconds he does.

Bryan: Yes! I'm in for Friday. Will you wear the tight red ¾ sleeve dress?

He adds a winking emoji, and my face heats up. Last year for my birthday, he bought this beautiful dress I've only had the chance to wear once, and when I did, my birthday date ended up in the backseat of our van in the parking lot instead of in the restaurant. We normally wouldn't have taken the risk, but it happened and neither of us regret it.

Me: I dunno. Will I end up in the backseat of the car again?

Bryan: That depends. How late do you want to show up?

My insides ache, like they want to be filled with him and only him. I'm on fire again. No other man has ever made me feel the way he does. I didn't have many boyfriends prior, and sex with them felt like something we *had* to do, but with Bryan, I desire it.

Me: Well, we could probably sneak some in before we go. I can drop Hunter at my mom's early.

Bryan: ...Woman, I have to work and now I have a hard-on.

My lips turn up as I dip my head. I'm warm to the core. I guess my toys are going to be used tonight.

Me: Oops.

Bryan: I have to get some rest before I go in. Think about me tonight. K?

I miss this. The flirting, the lust, the passion, that warmth I get whenever I think about him. Maybe this won't be so bad after all.

CHAPTER 29

Ellie: Hey, see you at 8. Are we still good to hop in the van with you? Really excited for our date, bestie!

Me: Me too. And yes, it's perfect. Bryan isn't drinking since he has work tomorrow, so he doesn't mind driving. He's on his way over now.

It's only five, but between taking up shifts at Sheer Threads and Bryan working, we haven't seen each other all week.

It hasn't stopped us from texting or sometimes sexting. Why did our marriage slowly sink into a sexless void? We barely touched each other or kissed for the longest time. He'd come home tired and grouchy, and I'd be passed out cold, or not in the mood for anything.

But now that we're taking a step back and exploring each other again, it all feels brand new and like we can do this. We can have this if we just try harder.

The doorbell rings and my desire for him grows significantly.

My body responds to him ten times more than it used to. Maybe time apart really is good for the soul. My muscles tighten and everything feels raw and open.

I'm trying my hardest to make this work, to never regret a single moment with him. If something were to happen to Bryan, I'd never forgive myself for not giving this another shot. It's not only for me, but Hunter. He deserves to have a family all under one roof.

I'm wearing the dress, even though we aren't leaving for a few hours, but underneath are my favorite silky black panties with the vibrator clipped in place. I turn it on with my phone, which I slip into the front of the tight red dress. The vibrator buzzes to life, and I can't help but smirk as I open the door.

The buzz is loud and seeing Bryan standing there in a light gray button-down and black vest gets me close to letting go. Grinning, he presses his body against mine pushing me into the house. The door slams shut as his mouth devours mine.

"Give me the phone," he growls.

"Go get it," I say, in a sultry voice, tugging at the fabric of my dress right where my cleavage pops.

His erection is hard against my leg. His fingers tickle along my skin as he caresses my breast. The vibrator is at medium speed. It's almost not fast enough, but perfect if I want a light buzzed feeling.

"Oh. It's not enough, is it?"

I love it when he reads my expressions. I've missed this so much. Should I cave and tell him to move back? Do we really need time to make this work? We do. I can't mess this up. He's my endgame, I know he is. Taking it slow is for the best. Although sex isn't really taking it slow, now, is it?

"It won't be enough until you're inside me."

"Char, I've waited so long for my dirty girl to come back."

"She's been right here. She just needed some time to heal."

"I love both versions of you, but this… God, Char." He takes a small step back, enough so the pressure of his hard-on leaves my leg. I don't mind though because while there's a sliver of space between us, the way his eyes trail over my body, makes me shiver. The spark is there, and it does me in.

I try to reach down for my phone, but he grabs my hand away and takes it.

"What do you say, you draw us a nice hot bath, so while we're fucking and getting dirty, I can clean you too."

I retreat towards the stairs, walking backwards. He narrows his eyes as I slowly creep away from him.

"I'll race you," I say.

I haven't smiled this much in over a year.

Somehow even though he's the runner, the guy who hits the gym with his fellow officers to stay in shape for his job, I make it up the stairs first.

After we moved in, we redid the bathroom. We wanted a Jacuzzi tub. It's small enough to fit the spot against the wall, but enough for us to sit inside together. It's also got sliding glass doors so we can shower too.

I stand in the doorway of the bathroom, and in one swift movement his hand grabs hold of my jawline. He pushes me back into the bathroom and up against the wall near the tub. I hiss as his free hand swoops into my dress and pulls out the phone. Blue eyes find mine, and I can't look away; he's got me in a hold, and I don't ever want him to let me go.

Controlling the buzz, he turns up the speed, and within seconds I'm coming undone. My body jerks with the force of an orgasm.

Shutting the vibrator app, he places the phone on the floor. On his way up, he pushes the fabric of the dress out of the way and slides my underwear off, vibrator and all.

With fumbling hands, I undo the belt of his dress pants and they fall to the floor. He kicks them off and they land over my underwear.

His fingers dance along my upper thigh as he pulls up the tight fabric of the dress and presses his mouth to my center, igniting the woman who has lain dormant for all these months. Unleashing a scream, I let go of another orgasm. We're alone, unlike at the cabin, so I'm not holding back. I never did when it came to him.

Getting to his feet, he slips his underwear off, throwing it into the pile with my own. When his hand is on my neck again, I cry out with pleasure, nearly coming from the embrace. My back is flush against the cool tile wall, as he helps position my leg so he can slide inside.

I lean back and moan. His lips gently graze over my neck. The sensation makes me so wet. I put my hand over my center to relieve the pressure, even though he's inside me.

"I love watching you help yourself. All these months did you think of me while you orgasmed in bed?"

"Ya-yes." My body hums with electricity as I continue to run my fingers in a fast circle, while he thrusts in and out. Every swirl of my finger, I tighten around him, and he hisses my name.

"Let me fill the tub."

I slip away, wetness dripping down my leg as he tugs himself out. I start the Jacuzzi and while we wait, we kiss. His lips trail over my entire body and the second my dress is off, his mouth covers my hard, aching nipples, taking them in between his teeth.

We step inside the heated water. Lowering himself he sits, and I follow, allowing myself to fully take him inside me. Rocking back and forth I throw my head back and release a low guttural moan. Molten waves of pressure course through me as we match each other's rhythm.

"Come here, Char. I need to kiss you," he whispers, his tone no longer rough; it's more mellow and filled with longing.

Leaning forward I taste his lips. I hadn't realized before he must have had some hot chocolate before coming here. The sweetness is still in his mouth, and I lick his lips to savor the rest.

"Keep going, baby, just like that."

He rolls his hips along with me and I moan out his name. "Bryan! I wanna come, please."

"I'll take care of you, Char," he whispers, his breath hot in my ear. "I got you."

His words send a surge of emotion mixed with pleasure and it causes a tear to slip down my cheek. I moan loud, screaming out his name as I orgasm. He's not there yet, but I can feel him tense.

I slip off him and turn around, then lower myself back down. I hold onto the edge of the tub. From behind he plants kisses down my back, and bites down gently as he goes. It doesn't take him long to get to the point where I know he's almost ready.

We get to our feet, and I bend over allowing him full access from behind. He thrusts back inside, and my hands slip against the tile, but I somehow hold steady.

"I'm close, Char."

"Me too," I moan. "I'm there, Bry. I'm there. Come, now, please." My words are broken up and my heart stutters at the same time as we both release.

Upon his release he thrusts, making me shudder several times. It takes me a full thirty seconds before I stop and relax against his body. I pull away, turn, and rest my head against his chest. Bryan pulls me into him and presses soft kisses to my head.

"You still feel amazing. I'll never get tired of the way you look when you're about to come for me," he whispers.

I snuggle into him more, unable to speak. My lungs are still trying to catch up with the rest of my body. When I don't answer him, he nudges me. Glancing up he becomes a blur.

"Hey, none of that. We're here together. Okay? We're going to focus on fixing whatever went wrong. We'll go slow, with our number one goal of being the best parents for Hunter. We got this, Char."

"I know," I whisper.

Pressing another kiss to his lips gets me all hot and bothered again.

"I'm glad we're trying," I whisper.

"Me too."

He's quiet for a few seconds. His breathing slowly comes down to a normal pace. Mine too.

"So, how much time do we have?" He grins.

"Clearly not enough, because I could do it a hundred times over and not get tired of it."

He chuckles, pulling me into his chest. "How about we relax, clean off, refill the tub, let the bubbles work their magic, then in a little while we'll go again, and get ready for the night."

"Sounds absolutely perfect."

CHAPTER 30

"Where are you guys? The door is open, anyone can just walk in ya know!" Ellie's voice is close as the stairs creak under her weight.

"Shit!" Bryan lowers me from my position against the wall.

We scramble to get our clothes on, laughing in the process. I slide my underwear up and on. He nearly jumps into his pants and tumbles over in a fit of laughter on the floor.

I reach down for him, my hand not even in line with where he is. My stomach aches from the laughter and my entire body shakes. Every time he tries to grab my hand he misses. My stomach hurts from laughing, and I have to get down on the floor with him. Our giggles are loud enough for Ellie to hear.

"Be down in a minute!" I yell. "The zipper on my dress was stuck!"

"Yeah. Sure, it was!" Her teasing voice echoes down the hallway towards us.

We stand up together and finish putting our clothes on. As I adjust the skirt of my dress, Bryan grabs hold of my neck again. I gasp in response. My attention snaps to him, and my muscles tighten like they are ready for more. His vest and shirt are still not fully buttoned. My eyes are glued to him, from the way his body tenses under his shirt, to his soft blue caring eyes.

"Do you want more later?" he asks with a devilish grin on his lips.

"Mmmm…"

After getting everything on we quickly make our way down. I'm sure my hair is a disaster. Being with each other again after all this time resulted in a long conversation, lots of cuddles, and more sex than we have ever had in one sitting. Maybe they are right, being apart does make the heart grow fonder.

Logan has an overprotective brother look on his face. His arms are crossed at his chest, and he clears his throat, but behind his taut lips is a smirk. Ellie comes to my rescue. She runs to me and attempts to straighten out the curls that have gone haywire. "There, that's a little better; but the flush on your cheeks… I can't help you there."

"Oh my God! Let's go!" I smack her arm, playfully.

Logan and Bryan give a friendly nod. Before everything happened, the two of them had been getting closer. Hopefully they can get to a good place again.

"Lily called. She got us a table, but the pub is really crowded tonight, so we need to leave now," Ellie says.

"Here, give me the keys, Char."

I search through my bag, then throw Bryan the keys to my van. As we reach the car something clunky in my underwear catches my attention. Shit! The vibrator is still attached. I got so flustered when Ellie showed up, I forgot all about it.

"Guys, I have to—"

"Oh, no, Char, we have to go like now or we might not get in."

Shit. Well, it's not like it's on, I can deal with a little lump in my panties. "Okay, let's go."

Lily and Jett have luckily secured our table. The pub is loud and there's a band playing up in the front. Even though smoking isn't allowed, the room is hazy and sweltering. There's very low lighting and it's hard to see. Over our table a hanging light gives off a low yellow gleam.

We scream our hellos and give each other hugs. Lily has redone the pink in her hair; it's brighter. Jett stands beside her and shakes Bryan's and Logan's hands. He's tall and gives off a emo-punk-rocker vibe. He and Lily are a perfect match.

"We didn't order yet, but they brought us menus," Lily yells over the music.

Our table is across the restaurant from the band. It's a little less noisy over here, but still hard to hear everyone.

"So good to see you again, Bryan. How was your holiday?" Lily asks.

"It's nice to see you too. It was absolutely amazing. I got to share it with the woman I love, so it was perfect." Bryan kisses my hair and I lean into him.

Either it's insanely hot in here or Bryan's tight squeeze has me all hot and bothered. We never finished our last round. He holds me closer, and only pulls away as the appetizers are placed on the table.

From across the way Ellie and I lock eyes, sharing a happy glow. Logan's looking at her suspiciously, but she ignores him.

"Oh, Charlotte. I was telling Lily about your honeymoon. She and Jett were looking for a good vacation spot. Do you still have any of the pics on your phone?"

"Oh, yeah of course." I reach down under the table and grab my bag.

It takes me a few minutes to search through my Facebook app. I freeze for a few seconds at the photo chosen to be the cover of the album. There's not a hint of sadness on either of our faces, two young newlyweds enjoying life without realizing what the responsibilities of the future would do to us. Instead of the overwhelming urge to cry, there's a sense of joy building in my heart as I scan through the first few. They are of Bryan and me on our first day. We're sitting on the beach watching the sunset, using our newly purchased selfie stick. While it looked ridiculous, I grew to love it by the end of our vacation.

"Oh wow, that sunset is beautiful." Lily touches her lips with her free hand. Her eyes are glued to my phone.

"The sunsets were like heaven, and don't get me started on the sunrises. Bryan, being the early riser that he is, literally didn't let me miss a single one."

"Hey, don't fuss. You would have regretted not seeing them," Bryan says, butting into the conversation.

After some more chatter, Jett and Logan head to the bar to get some more drinks. Bryan stays behind to hang out and chat more about our trip to Hawaii.

"That's true, but I was exhausted from our late nights." I bump my hip into his and he places a small kiss on my head. Leaning on him like this isn't enough, I want to get closer, but there's almost zero space between us as is.

"I'm all for early mornings, that is if I can get a nap in too," Lily says, giggling.

"If you're going to Hawaii, get in your nap like the week before. There's so much to see, and you won't want to miss a minute."

Lily scans through some more photos. There's a longing in her dark eyes, like she's already made up her mind on where she wants to go on vacation. When she gets to the last photo, she hands me the phone. "Do you think you would ever go back?"

"Oh absolute—"

"Yeah definit—"

Bryan and I both speak at the same time. The soft smile on his lips makes me grin. He throws his arm over the back of my chair as I go to stuff the phone back into my bag under the table. But I drop the phone and it lands in my bag with a thunk. Without warning my vibrator comes back to life.

What in the world? My cheeks warm as it vibrates on full force. Of course, it's the setting with the teasing pulsing throb that gets me off every time.

Holy shit! I grip the sides of my chair. My first thought is *Oh my God they can hear the buzz,* but it's so loud in here and the bass from the music is creating its own surge. I doubt anyone can hear it. My second thought is: I'm about to orgasm in public and it's totally frowned upon. I'm frozen and wish I could move to reach down and grab my bag. But I'm too stunned.

Bryan wraps his arm over my shoulder, and I stiffen at his touch. I press my legs together so I can hold in the build-up that's fighting to be released. I want to cry, but at the same time laughter tickles my throat. This has got to be the most embarrassing yet hilarious thing to ever happen to me.

I'm not sure what kind of look I'm giving him, but by the way he's searching my face with his narrowed gaze it's probably more concerning than anything.

I gasp lightly, and he leans in, his breath tickling my ears. This is so not helping. A small flicker of an orgasm leaks out, but I clench to try and stop it.

"Are you okay?"

I'm about to answer, but squeezing my legs together makes the vibrations more intense. Before I can answer, I suck in a breath, and grab hold of the table instead of the chair.

"I didn't—" My voice goes up a notch, and I grip the table tighter. "I didn't get a... oh shit. I didn't get a chance to remove the vi-bra-tor. It's going off, right now!" I squeak on the last word.

He leans forward watching me with amusement. Glancing down he chuckles at the sight of my legs pressed together. "Sure, that's what you want me to think," he teases.

Bryan snorts so loud Ellie and Lily stare at us with curious eyes. My body is lava, literally, and I'm about ready to explode.

"Not funny, dude, I'm about to have an orgasm at the table!" I whisper, maybe too loud, because Ellie's brows perk up at the word orgasm.

Bryan's laughter can definitely be heard over the ruckus in the bar. "You're making a scene."

I try to sound serious, but my chest bubbles with a deep laughter, and possible scream that I'm trying so desperately to hold back.

"Char, you okay over there?" Ellie asks.

I shake my head, but it's hard to control my smile, because I can't believe out of all my dumb luck I'd accidentally turn it on while returning my phone to the purse.

The jolt gets me, and I lean into Bryan to stop myself from twitching. To avoid her stare and now Lily's, and... shit Logan's coming back. Ugh! I'm finally able to reach under the table for my bag. Another one is building as Bryan sets his hand on my back.

The Facebook app and the vibrator app are right next to each other. I must have hit it while I closed the other one out.

With the pub's dim lighting under the table is even darker. I blindly search for my bag, and even as my hand dips into it, it's like the never-ending bag of junk, and I'm pulling out everything but my phone. *Where are you, phone?*

Finally! I struggle to get the thing to shut off and almost get to the completion of another orgasm, but it powers down. I clench the phone in my hand, and for a few long lingering seconds I breathe heavily, only to be calmed by Bryan's hand now rubbing along my back.

Dropping the phone back into the bag I attempt to sit up, between being flustered and turned on I forget how close the table is and bang my head on the underside.

"Are you okay?" Bryan asks, leaning down with me.

The impact of the situation, and the shock of hitting my head, has me laughing so hard I'm crying.

When I finally have my laughter under control everyone at the table is staring at us.

"I need to go to the restroom," I say, biting on my lip trying to control my grin.

"Maybe I should come too?"

"No!" I say to Bryan, pushing a hand against his chest. "No, not here."

He shakes his head.

"I think your presence has done enough."

His deep bellowing laugh echoes in the small space between us.

"I'm going with you," Ellie says, pushing her chair back. "I have to know what that was all about."

"Oh, you don't."

"I've got to pee anyway," she says, raising her brow at me.

She'd find out sooner or later anyway.

Before I get up, I turn to Bryan. He grabs my face in his hands and presses a kiss to my lips.

"I can't believe that happened," he whispers, as he pulls away.

"I'm never going to live this down, am I?"

"Nope."

Ellie and I hurry to the bathroom. I can feel her glare at the back of my head as I walk ahead of her. I check the stalls to make sure no one is here. It's much brighter than out in the main restaurant. The door slams shut with a bang, and I jump.

"What were you two cackling about, huh?" Ellie's watching me with almost a knowing smile. She crosses her arms at her chest, while she waits for me to explain.

"I am so embarrassed. So, remember the website we ordered those vibrators from?"

Ellie and I had gone to a few of those sex toy parties together and she had signed up for updates on new items coming out.

"The underwear ones, right?" she asks.

I nod. "I was kind of using it earlier and I put my underwear on in a rush and well... it kind of got switched on full force."

Ellie's mouth falls open. "Char, oh my God, that is—" She pauses to giggle. "That's hilarious." Her laughter echoes around the empty bathroom, and I can't help it, I start laughing too.

"Thanks a lot," I say, pushing her arm.

"What? It is funny, and clearly Bryan thought so too. No wonder he was giving you those sultry looks and offered to come to the bathroom with you! Good thing it's loud in here, huh?" she asks.

Again, my cheeks warm. "I'm still in awe." I lower my head and cover my face in my hands. "Did that really happen?"

"You're giving me ideas," she says, grinning. "You should leave it on."

I glare at her and cross my arms. My cheeks hurt from smiling.

She chuckles. "What? It could be fun."

"No. And what has my brother done to you? Sweet innocent Ellie who now goes to sex toy parties and sends her best friend news on the latest toys." I laugh.

"You don't want me to answer that."

"No, probably not." I chuckle.

"So, you're going to leave it on? Right?" She wiggles her brows.

I growl and push her out of the bathroom. "Tell them I'll be back in a minute."

"Hey, wait, I'm the one who actually has to pee." She goes into the stall to do her business.

I take a little extra time and tell her to go ahead without me. Setting the phone and device back inside my bag. I check my underwear and low and behold there's a small wet spot. Great, now I'm stuck wearing this underwear for the rest of the night. I sigh and put my brave face on.

When I walk out, both Ellie and Bryan are staring at me, attempting to cover their laughter. I shoot them both the finger. Thankfully, Logan, Lily, and Jett are occupied by something on Logan's phone. I don't need everyone at the table knowing what happened.

"Feeling better?" Bryan asks, as I settle back down into my seat.

I growl at him. The music drowns out most of his laughter, but it's loud enough everyone at our table hears him.

The evening is fun. More than I've had in a while. We eat, dance, chat, and there's not an ounce of doubt in my mind that Bryan and I are headed down a good path. I like taking it slow, testing the waters, and having some fun. Slowly relieving the stress in our life that caused our initial separation might be the key to our marriage. Everything feels perfect: spending time with the man I love and my friends. Nothing beats that.

CHAPTER 31

Ellie leans on my kitchen counter, a smug little smile on her face.

"What? Why are you looking at me like that?" I ask.

She chuckles. "You're happy. Oh, and I'm still amused by the vibrator. I can't get over it."

"Not funny, El." I toss a freshly baked sugar cookie at her.

It's been two weeks since the vibrator incident and I'm afraid to say it, but Bryan and I have been good. Really good. We haven't fought and the bad thoughts of our past have mostly stayed away.

Even so there's a lingering doubt in my mind. I am waiting for the next time I don't hear from him, or I pick the wrong moment to ask him where his head is at. Some days I want to drop this act of living apart and dive in headfirst, but then there's this voice in the back of my head wondering if we're both mature enough to handle it all again.

"So, what's happening between you two? I mean clearly, you're both still in love with each other."

Hunter is building a city on my kitchen table with his blocks, while munching on his snacks. In the end Hunter will be the most affected by what happens between Bryan and me. He will have to go between homes. And I fear it could put him in a situation where he'll feel obligated to choose sides. It's a lot to think about.

"Like ninety-eight percent of the time I'm convinced this marriage is going to work, then there's two percent that puts the doubt in my mind, and no matter how much I try the percentage will never go away. I don't know, maybe I'm the one who needs counseling. I feel like we are at the point where I could tell him to move back in, because we are in a good place, but then I panic again and I'm afraid that we won't get along. It's stupid really."

"It's not stupid, Char. I think taking things slow is a really good idea. I understand about the two percent doubt. Even I have them. Well, more when we first started dating the doubts were always there, but they still linger every once in a while." Ellie examines her hands, then peers up, like she's about to make a huge confession.

"What did my brother do?"

"It's not entirely the same situation, but when we first got together as you know with his history of not settling for one girl, I had well over the two percent doubt our relationship would go up in flames too. I think every relationship has its doubts. I never told anyone this but a few weeks after we got together, I found out Logan was talking to that girl again."

"You what?" My jaw hangs open and I stare at her. My first instinct is to go find my brother and kick him in the nuts, but at this point Ellie doesn't seem too fazed by it.

"She kept texting him because she didn't understand why he didn't want to see her anymore. He kept explaining it to her and eventually she got the hint and stopped. Your brother is awesome though, because he didn't hide it from me, but it also made me feel uncomfortable, and it was rocky there for a while."

I reach across the counter and cover her hand with mine.

She smiles. "I'm fine. It was forever ago. But what I'm trying to say is it still sits in the back of my mind. If I had listened to that voice, self-doubt would have destroyed us."

"Why didn't you tell me?" I ask.

"Because if I said it out loud the two percent would feel like a hell of a lot more."

I nod in understanding. Maybe I'm overreacting.

"You should always have the vibrator in your underwear ready to go, that will loosen things up for you. Give him the app on his phone and…"

"Oh my God." I wave my hand at her. "I'm never going to live it down."

"Nope," she says, popping a cheese Goldfish in her mouth with a cheesy grin.

"You know those are Hunter's, right?"

"I buy them for Logan all the time. Seriously, why do they make kids snacks so addictive, like they have to know parents are going to attack."

I snort. "Of course, Logan still eats those. Does he make you buy Gogurt too? He was obsessed as a kid."

"Yes," she says, rolling her eyes. "My fridge is stocked like we actually have a kid."

The front door creaks open. "Hey, Char. I'm back," Bryan says. "In the kitchen."

Ellie smirks. "Has he been spending the night?" she whispers.

"Mhmm." I don't know why, but my face warms. He's my husband, it's not like we're two teenagers sneaking around hiding from our parents. We're adults, yet the thought of him spending the night makes it feel like a dirty secret.

"Oh. Hey, Ellie," Bryan says, walking over to the fridge.

I can't help my wandering eyes. He's wearing his running gear, sweat pooling at his hairline. Wiping his forehead, he pulls out his black earbuds. For a second, I almost forget Ellie's in the kitchen, because I'm so focused on how much I've missed the sight of Bryan after a run invading the kitchen for food.

"Bryan." There's a slight teasing tone in her voice.

I throw her a playful scowl, as Bryan closes in on me and leans down for a kiss.

"Ew, you need a shower." I chuckle, touching his wet shirt.

"I do." He wiggles his brows playfully.

"On that note, I'll let you two have your shower sex. In fact…" Ellie checks the invisible watch on her arm. "Logan and I have plans with our bed tonight, or maybe the counter. Who knows, so you two kids have fun tonight."

"And those plans probably mean you'll be out cold by 9pm, while Logan plays video games on his phone."

Ellie purses her lips. "Yeah, that sounds about right actually. It's like we're married already."

I walk Ellie to the door, leaving Bryan and Hunter in the kitchen. Upon returning, I freeze at Hunter's giggles echoing through the house. I stand out of sight, watching them interact. Bryan is sitting beside Hunter, taking his food, and putting it into the dump truck. He's counting, showing Hunter, and then dumping the food out, and each time the food falls back onto the table his laughter bubbles over filling the whole house with his giggles.

Seeing them together again back in our kitchen makes me feel whole again. In my head I'm remembering the look on his face when he found out he was going to be a father. It was pure joy and excitement, and it wasn't because I'd been forced into wearing a sexy cop outfit. I wasn't terrified then. My relationship brought me nothing but happiness. He and I were in a good place.

The panic starts to seep in. There's no stopping it, but then I'm pulled out by a voice.

"Char… Charlotte."

I blink several times. His hand is pressed against my cheek, eyes scanning my face.

"Hey, baby, are you okay?" he asks unsteadily.

"I'm… yeah. I just… sorry. I zoned out."

"Are you tired? I could take Hunter off your hands, maybe back to Connor's with me."

"No, no. I'm okay. I was just remembering something."

"Yeah, and what's that?" He gently pushes a curl behind my ear.

"When I told you about being pregnant, and the whole cop car thing."

He chuckles, then leans in, pressing his forehead to mine. Our gazes meet and my stomach flips.

"That was a good day. You looked… so sexy. I wanted to ravish you right there against the police car."

"Ravish?" I giggle. I love when we can be ourselves around each other. There's not an ounce of tension other than the sexual kind.

"Well, maybe tonight you can put the cop uniform back on." His voice rings deep with passion.

"So, you can ravish me?" I tease.

"Mmmm," he moans, kissing me.

"That sounds—"

Bryan's phone goes off, and he pauses. Pulling it out he checks. "It's Mom."

"Perfect timing." I chuckle. "I'm going to give Hunter a bath. Tonight, you, me, and handcuffs?"

"We're doing this then?" he asks.

"Oh, we so are."

Bryan stands in the doorway of Hunter's room, leaning against the door jamb.

"Hey, what did your mom want?" I ask.

"Oh, she's uh, she wanted to confirm her and Dad's visit on February fourth on their way down to Florida."

I help Hunter into his new clothes. While Bryan was on the phone, I attempted to have him go to the bathroom but nothing came out. Thank God for pull-ups because two minutes after we got off the pot, he went.

"Oh. Yeah, that's fine. Um, what are we telling her?"

Hunter jets to the small wooden bookshelf where a ton of books are already piled on the floor from earlier. I'd meant to pick them up but didn't get that far.

"What do you mean?" he asks, crossing the room.

"About us. A lot of your stuff is still missing, she'll know—"

"We don't have to tell her anything. Just because she's a psychologist doesn't mean she can butt into everyone's problems." He takes several deep breaths before saying any more. "Plus, we're good now, right? Slowly getting towards living under one roof again?"

I nod as his hands slip into mine. "Well yeah, but…"

"Char." He squeezes my hands. "We are good, right?"

"Better than good. I—your mom knows everything…"

"We can figure it out without her help. Okay?"

My chest tightens as his tone changes.

He sighs and closes his eyes. "I love you and I want to be a family under one roof again. You're my everything, but I'm not going to push you and when you're ready I'll move back."

My nose itches, and the dreaded tears make my vision blur. Bryan doesn't allow a tear to fall. His finger is already catching them before they drop.

"I'm not mad, Char." He lowers his tone. It's softer, but there's still a hint of frustration behind it. "I wish you'd give us another chance."

"I will, I promise. I need…"

Why can't I commit to this? We are married and he spends every night when he's not working here. It's like he's already back in. So, what is my issue?

"Let's not fight about it, okay?"

"Yeah."

He leans in for a kiss as his phone goes off again. "Shit, it's work."

Our eyes meet, and I'm already fighting the urge to make him stay. Instead, I let him go.

In the doorway, he pauses and turns. "Don't forget, later, handcuffs, and cop outfit," he says, grinning, trying to bring light to the situation.

I take a seat beside Hunter, attempting to put away some of the discarded books that he's no longer reading. The door is left open, so I can hear every word Bryan is saying, and it seems as if our night is not going to happen, because they need him.

Everything in me says not to be upset. I take deep calming breaths hoping some endorphins will kick in and help. Maybe it is time for me to take charge and see someone myself, because if I don't get these soul-crushing thoughts out of my head, I'll never overcome it, and then he'll walk out of my life for good.

CHAPTER 32

Since it's winter and there wasn't much we could do outside of driving around, the three of us took a trip out to the east end of Long Island. We drove out to Montauk and took in the scenery.

Bundled up, we allowed Hunter to play along the rocky shoreline. Our cheeks were red and our fingertips frozen but seeing the smile on his face while we were there was incredible.

Now as we drive home in the early winter sunset, I feel this weight has lifted and it's easier to breathe. Hunter is in the backseat babbling about the beach and the pizza we ate. He's come such a long way recently and I love listening to him babble. While some of it is hard to understand, it's much better than where he was a year ago.

"You seem really happy today, Char."

For a second Bryan covers my hand before returning his hand to the steering wheel. We're on the expressway and there's traffic as usual.

"Today was wonderful. We needed a family adventure, free of fighting and drama and we got that."

"Do you want me to stay again tonight?" he asks.

"Yeah. I think you should. I also wanted to tell you something..."

My mind keeps slipping and I needed someone to talk to. I went to my mom's while Bryan was at work and she and I had a long chat about my situation and feelings. She made me feel better, and although she might have said it because she's my mom, she told me my feelings were valid. Fearing opening up again is not ridiculous.

Then she suggested I speak to Melissa, the therapist I saw when Dad died. I saw her weekly for the first year, then a bit less before I stopped completely. She taught me how to cope with the loss and with the disappearance of my brother. I had stepped up to be Mom's rock when he didn't, and it took a toll on me. But a simple phone call led to a good therapy session with Melissa. It was the best thing I'd ever done for myself.

Even in the pitch blackness of the car Bryan's smile lights it up. "I love being in our bed together every night." His voice is low and dark.

"Did you bring your handcuffs?" I whisper, in hopes Hunter's tiny ears don't pick up on our conversation.

I'm trying to build up the nerve to tell him about Melissa.

"You bet. Now what is it you have to tell me?"

Taking a deep breath, I give myself time to conjure up the words. "Two days ago, I went back to the therapist I saw after Dad passed. I want to get my life on track. It all came crashing down on me when you were called away the other night. I had the urge to fight you and tell you not to go, but I held back. I realized..." I swallow hard because this isn't easy to admit. "I should have understood and respected your position as an officer a little more. So, as for moving in, I think we need to wait because I want all the terrifying thoughts to not be so loud. They are so damn loud."

He's gone quiet, and it almost feels as if I've ruined everything. We had such a great day, and I went all serious on him with therapy. Knowing it's a trigger for him, I nearly hate myself for bringing it up.

"I understand if you don't want to stay tonight, if I've ruined it."

His hand touches mine again. "You didn't ruin anything, baby. You do what helps you."

While it feels like he's okay with my decision to get help, there's a stillness in the air that envelopes the carefree feeling of the day.

Once we get home Hunter is out cold. I'm glad he's a good sleeper. He doesn't even stir from the jostling as I place him into his bed. Pressing a single kiss to his head I stand and hit Bryan's rock-solid body. My hand lands on his chest, right over his beating heart.

"Don't take this the wrong way," I say. "Can we spend the night cuddling and watching TV. Like we used to? I'm not really in the—"

He cuts me off with his lips, but only for a split second before pulling back to look at me. "I'd like that a lot. You still have kettle corn?"

I nod.

"Okay. I'll make some, while you get into your pajamas and wait for me. We can catch up on some of our favorite shows. I haven't watched any since..."

"Me neither."

Our DVR is almost full of shows I've recorded over the last six months. I couldn't bear to watch them without Bryan. From silly sitcoms to baking shows and everything in between. On nights when work didn't consume him or my anxiety didn't get the best of us, we ate snacks in bed and binged all night long. After things went south, I didn't touch the TV much. Maybe I always hoped we would be able to have these moments again.

"K. I'll be right up."

He starts to walk away, but before he turns completely, he's

REGINA BROWNELL

back in front of me. "Charlotte. I'm sorry I didn't acknowledge you in the car much earlier. When you told me you went to therapy I…" He shakes his head, like he had something to say, but can't. "I'm proud of you for being strong about all of this and for taking the steps you need to get us back on track. I know I'm asking a lot to move back, and try again, and I know you need time, but I can't not tell you that I love you. I never stopped."

"I love you too," I say, my voice breaking, but no tears fall. "That's why I'm trying. I want to fix me. I'm broken—"

"You are not broken." He takes my face in his hands and holds me there. "Don't you dare think for one second you are. We aren't the only couple with marital issues. We both are at fault for how things went down. Don't blame yourself. I have faith we'll get there. I have to hang on to the hope that you'll see it too."

I wrap my arms around him and hold on for a few seconds. He pulls away and kisses me softly. "You look exhausted, baby. I'll go make the kettle corn and bring some sodas. We'll binge watch, eat snacks, and fall asleep in each other's arms."

"Don't take too long down there," I say.

"Wouldn't dream of it."

CHAPTER 33

It's a little after one and Bryan's parents will be stopping in a few hours. I pull up into the driveway and can't help the way my heart flips when I see Bryan's car there. I've just come home from a shift at Sheer Threads followed by my second therapy session with Melissa. We've set it up so I'm seeing her twice a week.

I'm already feeling like I know what I have to do to keep myself going. It's going to be a long road for me to open my heart back up, but I can't continue to miss out on opportunities with the man I love.

I'm going to tell him later after his parents have gone home and we're alone. I want him to move back in. No regrets. I wouldn't be able to live with myself if something were to happen to Bryan and we missed out on any more time together as a family.

Inside, the smell of the mac and cheese recipe Gayle shared with us permeates the air. The spices in the breadcrumbs make my stomach rumble.

"Hello?"

The stairs creak and I turn to find Bryan. "Hunter is out cold.

We went outside and kicked around a soccer ball. The kid has some skills. Have you ever thought of enrolling him in a sport or maybe even karate? You know I did read karate can help children on the spectrum and other..."

He pauses, staring at me. My heart is so full right now. The fact that he's taken it upon himself to learn these things and really try to understand why I did what I did, means a lot.

I wipe the ridiculous tear building at the corner of my eye and close the gap between us, dropping my bag. "I think it's a wonderful idea," I say, smiling up at him.

"Great. I know a guy who owns a karate studio," he says.

"Okay. Let me know the details and we can go together to sign him up."

Bryan's eyes glisten. "Really?"

"Really."

Rushing around the kitchen, I'm prepping for Gayle and Jack's arrival. It's now a little after three and the pressure of their visit is sitting heavy on our shoulders. I'm wiping down the surfaces when from behind me Bryan spins me, then lifts me onto the counter.

He slides his hand up my thigh. I'm not wearing much after my shower, only an old navy-blue T-shirt from one of the many events at the precinct. I've stolen so many of his shirts and sweaters and it never fazed him. In fact, his eyes are wandering all over my body, from my dangling legs back up to my eyes.

"Were you planning on answering the door like this when my parents showed up?" he asks, a crooked smile on his face.

I swat him away and giggle. "No, I didn't have time to put pants on, but I left them on the stool for easy access. I wanted to get some things done before their arrival."

His body slips between my legs, and I reach out, grabbing at him through his boxers.

"Mmm," he hums. "Are you sure that's all? Because it seems as if you're ready for something else."

I take his full length in my hands and pump slowly at first, then a little faster. He grabs hold of my hips and tugs me forward.

"We have a lot of time to make up for, so maybe."

I'm trying to ignore the nagging part of me that doesn't want to lie to Gayle anymore. Melissa seems to think, while it's truly our burden to deal with, it's not a bad idea to confess. My mom is in the loop and the guilt of lying to Gayle while we were in her home doesn't sit well with me.

I'm pulled back into the moment with Bryan as his fingers graze along my wet center. My heart and head are torn between two different places, but ultimately lands right here, caught up in what we're doing. We still have time. Hunter is fast asleep, according to the monitor, so I'm not worried about that at least.

"Charlotte, baby, look at me." With his free hand he cups my cheeks and lifts my face to meet his stare. I don't know how I ever doubted his love for me.

"Don't get lost in your head right now. I need you here with me. Okay?"

I nod as he releases my cheek and uses the hand to lift the T-shirt slightly to see my wet panties and his fingers pressing against my center inside the plain white underwear. I scoot enough to lift my bum slightly as a finger slides into me.

"I'm here, Bry."

"Good. I'm going to make you feel so many things right now." He lets go of a trembling breath and never allows his eyes to stray from mine. Even as he lowers himself and kisses my inner thigh, he's always watching. The pleasure is so great I have to tilt my head back. I grip the edge of the counter and keep my lips pressed tight to stifle the moan tickling my throat.

"You know how many times I've wanted to take you here on

this counter," he growls. "A thousand of my fantasies could never live up to this moment."

His words make my body ache for him and I want to cry at the same time. "So, you've had fantasies?" My voice grows low and raspy, like I've been sleeping and just woken up.

He straightens and stands for a moment, pressing his head against mine. "They never stopped, Char. You are fucking perfect." He kisses me. It's both passionate and lustful. "These plump lips are a dream." He slowly makes his way down so that he's staring up at me through hooded eyes between my legs. "And so are these lips," he says, as his fingers enter me.

I bite back a moan and hum with pleasure that vibrates through my entire body. Since we've gotten back together, the sex has been different. Not in a bad way, but it's like we had all this pent-up frustration and it's dirtier, but at the same time the love mixed in feels ten times stronger.

"Make me scream your name," I say, as his tongue enters me.

A sly smirk slides across his face, as he buries himself in me. I bite my arm.

"Bryan—oh—my—Bryan!" I yell out his name as I'd promised.

He stands up straight and adjusts me so it's easier to slide in, and when he does my entire body shakes from the intensity. He lifts me up and off the counter, I yelp and mistakenly knock some mail off and onto the floor. We both laugh and ignore it as he presses me to the wall only a few steps away from where we had been. When he thrusts himself into me, I whimper.

We move in such a way it makes me feel like we're in sync. I lower myself seconds later, kneel, and get a taste of myself on him. It makes him harder and turns me on more. He watches with wide eyes as I use my hands to help get me off while I lick him clean of me.

I get to my feet and when I do, with a strong steady grip he lifts me back up onto the counter. I wrap my arms around his neck as we meet each other's slow steady thrusts. His gaze is locked on mine.

There's not an ounce of dirty talk. It's more than that. The hands he has on my hips gently make their ascent up my sides. I shudder as the light touch has me locked into place. Then his hands are on my cheeks, slowly drawing a line down my jaw. He still hasn't stopped looking at me and I don't want him to.

"Charlotte, baby, I love you."

"I love you, Bryan."

His slow jabbing thrusts have me crying out his name several times until we're both close, and when we're on the verge, we release together. I quiver under his touch. When we both stop twitching, he wraps his arms around me, and I bury my face into his shoulder. I'm having a hard time getting my breathing under control, but with each beat of his heart under my ear I find myself coming down easier with each breath.

"I should check on the mac and cheese," he whispers, after what feels like a lifetime.

He helps me off the counter, then holds me again. His inhalation is again shaky and the grip he has on me is enough to make me feel like he doesn't want to let go.

"Yeah. I should finish cleaning up, especially the counter." I grin.

He chuckles, but the amusement dies on his lips only seconds after. Heaviness fills the air. What happened moments ago has faded into tension.

"Everything okay?" I ask.

He sighs. "I'm just not looking forward to Mom snooping."

Not all his stuff is gone, but there's a huge change in the atmosphere of the house, even with only a few of his things missing. It's as if he took everything with him when he left.

"Oh." I bite my lip. "Right."

There's a storm brewing. It makes my bones ache.

"Maybe we tell her we're struggling, but we're on the right track."

I lean against the kitchen counter as he pulls out his mac and cheese from the oven. His demeanor has changed drastically. We went from making love on our kitchen counter, to him holding me, and now... there's this coldness radiating off him. One I've feared for so long, the piece that could destroy everything.

"I don't even think we need to tell her now."

"My therapist thinks—"

"Your therapist?" He laughs. "Come on, Char. You're talking about that with her too?"

I cross my arms. "Of course I am, Bryan, what else would I talk to her about?"

"We're just getting our life back, Char. Why can't we let it go? See where this goes and then—"

"Bryan, she deserves to know we're struggling. Your mom has an inkling something is off. If she ever finds out that we've lied—"

"She won't! And Mom will suggest couple's therapy. That's her thing. I don't want to do couple's therapy!" he snaps.

And now we're back to this. I try to take deep breaths to calm myself. Fighting didn't get us anywhere good before and it won't now. This fight is no longer about his job; it's about us and what I think we need to do to move forward. How we can make this work.

"That's what you're afraid of? Couple's therapy? There is nothing wrong with asking for help, Bryan, or receiving it. At least I know what you really think of me getting therapy."

I don't want to bring it up, but I feel like it needs to be addressed.

"Your mom told me about when you were younger."

"That has nothing to do with this!"

"Bryan, there's nothing to be ashamed of."

"I'm not, okay?" His voice wavers and there's a hoarseness to his tone. "Just stop!"

I step away from the counter, my hands raised in the air. "Fine. I'm stopping. It's just, I can't lie. It's not in me to lie. It was so hard to be there over Christmas with all of them and have this secret hanging over me. I love your family and I want this to work between us, but what if it doesn't?"

"What are you saying?" he asks, removing his gloves, and throwing them onto the counter. "What do you mean what if it doesn't?"

My pulse is throbbing hard against the skin of my neck. I lift my hand to cover the spot, wondering if it's visible or if it's my imagination.

He takes a step closer, enough so I feel the heat of his anger radiating off his skin. His cheeks glow red and his entire body tenses making the muscles on his arm pop.

"So, what has this been? What have we been doing? Is it just the sex, Charlotte? Is that all it is to you? You are clinging on just for that."

"How dare you!" I spat, throwing my arms in the air. "How dare you say sex is the only reason we're together right now! You know me better. I'm scared to fall into a pattern again. One where you work, come home, and the stress of your job on your shoulders gets to you, and me being home all day pushes me back into a dark hole..."

He narrows his eyes, a scowl darkening his features. "Isn't that why you went out and got yourself a job? So you could stop nagging me about mine?"

I'm taken aback by the venom in his tone. How did we get here? Can we rewind? While he and I were making love a few minutes ago, it made me feel like we were making strides; but now we're back to square one.

"This—what's between us—is more than sex. I love you so

goddamn much it hurts! Loving you was never the problem. I still do, always will."

Deep breaths, Charlotte. Don't mess this up. I take a few seconds to collect myself.

"We both pulled away. Both of us are at fault. Too tired to have a real conversation, too tired to make love, too tired to say I love you. It became all too much. All I wanted was for us to cuddle on the couch and watch our favorite shows together, to maybe have one date night a month to be ourselves, and to maybe say I love you a little bit more. It felt like you weren't in this at all," I say, tears pressing behind my eyes. *Not now, emotions, not now.*

"Charlotte, I'm all in. I've always been all in. That was never a question I had to ask myself. The question I have is why didn't you fight for us?"

My mouth falls open. How could he even think I didn't want to fight? He walked out on me. I only sent him away, because what he did hurt me, it made me feel like I wasn't good enough, and at the time, I'd lost myself enough to believe it.

I take a deep breath to push the knot in my throat down. My hand lifts to my collarbone. Staring at his chest is the easiest for me, because if I look him in the eye, I'll break.

"Because..." I say, barely above a whisper. "Because you walked out." The sob builds and I'm finding it hard to finish my sentence. I grip the counter beside me for support. His icy eyes releasing tears does me in.

"You walked out, and-and-and you didn't—" *Fuck this is so hard.* "You didn't look back." I swallow so hard it hurts.

Bryan rarely cries, but I've hit a nerve. He's wiping hard at his face like he's angry for crying.

My own tears fall and my lip trembles so hard it's like I'm shivering from a deep freeze. He says my name, but it comes out as nothing, a failed attempt.

"I came back, and you sent me away again," he says.

I focus on the pile of papers we knocked over. The divorce papers are uncovered. I'd hidden them between the junk pile and now staring back at me in black ink was Bryan's signature. The paper must have slid out of the envelope.

"You—you signed it?" I'm trembling from head to toe. Blinking does not help the tears.

"Charlotte, that was before..."

Biting down on my lip a sob escapes. "I was going to ask you to move back—" I shake my head.

"I-I t-thought." He swallows hard. "I thought that's what you wanted. Wait! You what?"

"I... never mind." I lower myself to the ground, grabbing for the papers and shuffling them back. It's hard to do it with the tremors coursing through me. As he kneels beside me the doorbell rings.

"Fuck, they're early," he groans.

I wipe my face with the back of my hand. Compiling everything into my arms, I get to my feet and set it all back on the counter, then turn away.

His sniffles behind me grow loud as I try to regain my composure to answer the door. It's my turn to walk away. I can't do this anymore. I square my shoulders, wipe my tears, grab my pants, and prepare myself for what's waiting for me on the other side of the door.

CHAPTER 34

Taking several deep breaths, I open the door. Gayle and Jack are standing there beaming.

"I'm so glad you made it," I say.

"I'm sorry we're early, I hope that's not an issue."

"Actually, the food is done already."

Gayle's brows rise as she observes my face and posture. I straighten my shoulders and stand a little taller. I step aside and allow them both to come through. Their eyes dart around. They saw the place when it was first bought so it was empty then. No kid toys scattered about, not a single speck of dust. Now it's lived in with both the love and downfall of two people. So many things happened here in the short time that we've had it.

"Thank you for letting us drop by before we drive down to Florida."

"Of course," I say. "Bryan, your parents are here."

Bryan comes bouncing in from the kitchen as if he hadn't been crying seconds earlier. There's redness stained on the whites of his eyes though.

The scent of four cheeses topped with a savory breadcrumb wafts through the house. Gayle sniffs around. "Smells amazing."

"Thanks. It's your recipe," Bryan says, giving a half smile.

"Here let me take your coats."

They shrug them off and I head to the closet under the stairs. Gayle follows and as I open the door, I realize none of Bryan's things are in the closet anymore. He took most of his clothes and jackets with him, and only left a few things that wouldn't fit in the room he was staying in at Connor's.

Shutting the door, I turn to find Gayle's curious eyes scanning over everything. I put the pictures back up, and—*shit*. The wedding photo I'd turned over is still facing downward. I sneak around her and lift it.

"Hunter is always knocking down my pictures," I say, chuckling under my breath.

"Well, lunch is ready," Bryan says.

"Great, I'm starving." Jack rubs his hands together and follows him into the kitchen.

Behind me Gayle is still walking around slowly, taking in everything.

"Are you okay?" I ask.

"Just fine, dear," she says, as she follows me into the kitchen.

We should have come clean. There's tension, not only in my own body, but around the room. We all slip into our seats as Bryan brings over the hot dish.

"So, is Hunter napping?"

"Yeah, but he should be awake soon."

"Oh, about that," Gayle mutters. "Your father decided to not tell me the hotel we booked in Jersey for tonight had a massive flood and our room was one of the ones that got the worst. So, we were wondering…"

"Oh, you want to stay here?" Bryan asks with his guard up.

"If that's not a problem. I mean I know the couch isn't ideal, but—"

"It's fine," I say.

Bryan is too caught up in stabbing his pasta to say anything.

He swirls it around allowing the breadcrumbs to fall and the cheese to mix. "Yeah, Mom, it's cool." His voice is clipped when he speaks. A tone he should know his mom knows.

The idea of us ending has been on my mind for months, but now that we've been trying, knowing it's probably over makes it even harder. Giving ourselves a second chance was the worst thing we could have done. It's only going to make me miss him more when he's gone.

"This food hits the spot. You really made this, Bry?" Jack asks. He's watching us carefully, like he knows we're treading on thin ice.

Bryan looks to his mom for approval. "Yeah. Hope I did okay." His cheeks still have the stain of tears left behind. Guilt piles over me. An itch tickles my nose and I try to cover it up by shoveling food in my mouth.

"It's wonderful, sweetheart. I think it's ready to pass down to your kids."

She adds the S, and it makes us shift in our seats. I check on him again. He hasn't taken a single bite, and is still swirling the food around, like a toddler refusing to eat.

"Have you tried it yet, Bryan?" she asks.

His shimmering eyes unveil every hidden secret we've been hiding. "Yeah." He fights to get out. "I had a bit to taste test it. I'm just... we had a big breakfast."

We had cereal out of the box before I left for work. There was nothing big about breakfast. The image causes me to wince. Everything okay a few short hours ago. How can it now feel like the end?

"Are you two going to tell me what's going on, or do I have to pry it out?" Gayle shakes her fork at us.

Jack chokes a little on his food. "Gayle, they're fine," he says in a low, warning tone.

"Jack, clearly they haven't been since Christmas, maybe even earlier."

Bryan drops his fork, and it echoes through the room, ringing harshly in my ears. "We're not together anymore. Is that what you want to hear, Mom? Does that make it all better?" He raises his voice, but the sound wavers.

His eyes water again, breaking my already crumbling heart. It's all my fault: I should have never let it get as far as it did. My lips quiver and I bite down to stop them, but it's not working. With a tight chest I close my eyes and try to count backwards in my head, but the murmurs around me are not helping.

I open my eyes and yell, "We're getting a divorce."

Saying the words out loud kills me. Bryan lowers his gaze and grabs the table.

I push down the lump in my throat, but it's stubborn. Standing, I face Gayle. She doesn't appear hurt, but there's a sad glimmer there like she's trying to figure out how she can fix it, how to put us back together, like a puzzle that just won't go.

"You guys are more than welcome to stay," I tell them. "Bryan, I think you should stay here with your parents and Hunter. He'll be so happy to see them again. I won't take away your time with him. I'll get an overnight bag and go stay with my mom. I'm sorry, Gayle, I didn't mean to lie."

My entire body shakes. With all the strength I can muster, it's my turn to walk away, but unlike when Bryan did it, I glance back over my shoulder. Piercing blue glassy eyes find mine. Releasing an agitated breath, I swallow the bile rising in my throat. If I hold his stare any longer, I'll never leave.

"Have a safe trip."

I hit the stairs at full speed and slam the bedroom door. I hope I didn't wake Hunter. Sliding down to the floor I pull my knees to my chest and tug my phone from my jean pocket. Mom doesn't answer. Ellie is next. It rings, and rings, and when I think she won't answer my brother's voice picks up on the other end.

"Hey, Char," he says. "Sorry, Ellie is currently taking a shi—"

"Are you answering my phone?" Her voice is muffled in the background.

Their laughter would be contagious if my heart didn't feel as if it were breaking into a million tiny bits.

"Char? Hey, did you butt dial—"

A sob louder than I expected comes tumbling from my lips.

"Char, Char, where are you? Tell me what's wrong?" Big brother mode has kicked in. His voice is tight with worry.

"Home. Can I stay with you? Please, just for tonight. Please."

He's quick to reply. "Of course, you can. Do you need a ride?"

"No, no. I'm okay. I-I need to get my stuff packed up."

There's commotion on the other end, but I need time to pack, so I hang up and get myself together. I gather an overnight bag, plus some extra essentials, and check on Hunter who's still out cold. Then I head back to my room to calm myself a little before driving to Ellie and Logan's.

I think about Hunter. My heart hurts. He won't get the family I imagined for him. A little sister or a brother, a mom and a dad together under one roof. If I hadn't messed everything up, we would have still been a happy family.

Gayle is in the living room sitting on the couch when I come down the stairs. She stands, crosses the room, and wraps me in her arms. Her warmth radiates like Bryan's, and it makes everything even worse. Her hand runs over my hair, smoothing it out to relax me. It's working, a little.

"I thought we'd be okay. That I could make it work again. I want it to work."

"I think what you both need is some time away—"

"We did, for six months. Apparently, it's over. I'm not ready for—"

"I know, sweetheart. I know. You'll figure it out, and if not, you'll love again."

"I don't want to. There's no one else I want to love." My knees give out and somehow, she's holding me up, keeping me on my feet.

"I got it from here." My brother's familiar voice pulls me from the darkness. What is he doing here? Standing up straight I get a view of him. With every bit of energy I have left I run into his arms.

"I told you I'd drive over myself," I say, hitting him, a bit of playfulness seeping through.

"And I'd never forgive myself if something happened to you on the way over. Plus, when Ellie heard me talking to you, and ran out of the bathroom with her pants halfway down her legs, she insisted we come, even though she wasn't finished in the bathroom."

Ellie throws Logan the finger. "Way to plant a visual in everyone's head."

Despite the situation, I chuckle.

"You know I always have your back," Ellie says.

"You could have finished." I laugh while wiping my tears.

"I'm okay."

I search the room for Bryan and the pain returns when he's not here. Images of his tear-stained face play through my head, along with everything that was said tonight. *Why didn't you fight for us?* he had asked. Hadn't I though? Maybe not enough, because now it's over, and sure I'll be okay eventually, but right now, as dramatic as it sounds, it feels as if my world is somehow ending.

My tears build again, releasing in a cascading waterfall down my already wet cheeks. They sting as they fall. My gaze meets Gayle's, and she points upstairs.

"He's with Hunter. We'll take care of them. Okay? Don't you worry. Go get some rest. I'll call you to check in."

"No, I'm not. I'm right here."

I whirl to Bryan's tense voice coming from the top of the stairs. In his hands is a manilla folder. The entire room falls silent, sans Bryan's heavy footsteps headed towards me. Only inches from me he stops. His shoulders rise and fall dramatically with each breath.

"This, Charlotte. This is why I worked all those long hours. Why I always said I was doing it to give you something better. I wanted you to have what you missed out on. This was only the first of many I was going to give you. I finally felt we were in a good place, and I had enough money to splurge and not go into debt at the same time."

His red rimmed eyes nearly make me take back everything I've said.

"Take Ellie and Logan." He nods towards them. "I'm sure it will mean as much to Logan as it does you."

He holds out the folder. My attention falls on his trembling hands and the shaking of the papers inside. One flutters to the floor face up. Our eyes are trained on it. It's three tickets for a two-week trip. First to the Pacific Northwest and then Alaska— to the place my dad and I always meant to go. The trip we were supposed to take the summer I graduated.

My words fail me as I'm greeted by the back of Bryan's head as he walks away.

"Charlotte, do you want to stay?" Logan asks.

I shake my head, not trusting my voice. Logan bends and picks up the lost paper, shoveling it back into the folder settled tight in my grip. He sets his arms around me, and Ellie takes the bag I've dropped onto the floor.

The car ride to their house is silent. Ellie sits in the back holding me and allowing me to be numb, while Logan drives, gripping the wheel. Big brother bear has come out and his claws are ready to fight. The divorce is my fault: my fault for being too emotional, too needy.

Logan helps me to their guest room, and I bury myself in the comforter. The fresh scent of detergent hits my nose. They sit with me. Neither of them says a word and that's okay because I'm not ready to talk, not yet anyway. I've lost Bryan for a second time, and my heart hurts even more than before. Getting over it the first time was hard, but the second time is soul crushing enough to make me believe I'll never be whole again.

CHAPTER 35

There's a soft tap on the door, bringing me to the present. "Char, I have some food for you. Are you awake?"

It's Logan.

Their guest room is still being worked on. It's a cross between what might become an office and what could become a kid's bedroom. It's cluttered with a desk, shelves, and books piled in the corner. The bed I'm using is Ellie's from her childhood home. She brought it here to have an extra one if anyone needed a place to stay.

"Come in," I say in a rasp. I cough to clear my throat. It hurts from crying; my entire body does.

It's been several hours since Logan and Ellie rescued me, and I hate that I broke down to the point of needing help. I'm the one who is supposed to be put together. I always was. Now I'm nothing but a sad shell of that woman.

Logan steps inside the room, a bag of my favorite barbeque chips in his hand. "Ellie went out and got them. I'm just the delivery boy."

I laugh, but it's half-assed and sounds nothing like me. I knew going into this having my heart broken a second time would kill me, and it truly did.

He takes a seat on the bed, and I crawl out of the covers and attempt to be less of a mess. He hands me the bag and as much as I'd love to devour it, I put it to the side.

"I'll make you some real food soon. You are hungry, right? I'm grilling tonight."

"Grilling? It's frostbite weather out there. And yes, I am. I never got to finish my dinner."

"It's never too cold for a nice meal on the grill. Burnt burger for you?"

I smile. "Yeah. Of course. Everything must be burnt."

He bounces his shoulder into me. I turn away from him. "Go ahead, say it. I set myself up for disappointment."

"I didn't say anything."

"What am I going to do now?" I ask. Maybe it's to him, or maybe I'm asking out loud to see if the universe will shout the answer back at me.

"You're going to do what Charlotte Fields would do." He emphasizes my maiden name, because I guess it's who I am again.

"And what's that?" I ask, picking at the lavender comforter on the bed.

"She'd pick herself back up. Charlotte Fields took problems head on. When Dad died you were the strong one."

"No, I wasn't. I just waited until no one was watching before I broke. When the crowd eventually died down, and the house was silent, after you disappeared, was when I fell."

"But you are strong. You were the one who stood up at the funeral and gave a whole speech without losing it. You helped mom get everything ready, even went with her to make arrangements, and me? I ran away. I was a scared little boy who didn't want to deal with anything. See, you're more durable than you give yourself credit for. You'll be okay, Charlotte."

"It's Hunter I'm worried about."

"He's got his mom's spirit. Always fighting. I mean look at how far he's come. You're doing amazing things with him. I'm not saying it will be easy, but I know my sister, and I know that nothing gets her down."

"What would you do if Ellie left you for good?"

A flash of pain shimmers in his eyes. He almost lost her once when he hid his feelings. He gave her space until he couldn't anymore. He had been in love for years; losing her was never an option. "I wouldn't let her. I'd fight. I'd fight till the very end. Until I turned blue."

I sniffle. I can't face my brother. My lips tremble as I try to speak. "Am I worth fighting for?" And all over again I'm done.

"Char, of course you're worth it."

I bury myself under the covers again and pull them up over my head. My entire body shakes. What is wrong with me? Logan places his arm around me, and a few seconds later the bed dips, and my best friend's vanilla shampoo fills my nose. Her familiar scent and touch calms me.

"I'm sorry I'm burdening you both."

Ellie's arm tightens. "You were there for me when I needed you, even though it had to do with your dorky brother. I'm here for you, always. Both of us. Don't be afraid to reach out. We love you."

"Ellie's right. Don't be sorry, and don't feel bad," he says. "I'll leave you two for some girl-talk. Love you, little sis," he whispers.

"I love you too, you big doof." I smile through my tears.

He chuckles and kisses the top of my head before walking out the door and leaving Ellie and me alone.

"So, does this call for a marathon of Jonas the TV series or the 3D concert experience?" She tugs on the covers, pulling them down to see my face. She's lying beside me on the tiny twin bed. We spent many sleepovers on it, but now it suddenly seems way too small.

"Both."

"It's that serious, huh?"

I nod.

She leans forward and kisses my forehead. "Let me go get my old DVDs. K?"

"K," I whisper.

"Charlotte, we meant what we said. We are here for you. Anything you need. A babysitter, a shoulder to cry on, a girls' night sleepover. Just call me. Okay?"

I know I have the world. Even though my love life is crumbling before my eyes, I have my son, my best friend, my brother, my mom, Ellie's mom. There are so many people in my and Hunter's life who can help get us over this hurdle. It's going to take me time to heal, but my brother does have a point. I am strong and I'll come out on the other side stronger. No matter how much it hurts. Life is only going to move forward from here and I have to either roll with it, or I'll get caught in the undertow.

The house is eerily quiet. I hate it.

When Ellie dropped me off early this morning, Bryan had gone to work, and Gayle and Jack were here with Hunter. They left a few minutes ago, and Hunter is napping on the couch. I held myself together well while I said goodbye, and she told me to keep in touch. She was also pretty confident things would get better.

I keep myself busy. I've already thrown on a load of laundry, mostly my overnight stuff and some things I didn't get to while Bryan and I were busy playing house. It was all pretend.

My stomach growls, and while I don't feel hungry, I know I am. I pass by the kitchen counter and my eyes land on Bryan's signature. Scanning the papers, I find it to be a standard contract. Agreeing to things that are all reasonable. We aren't fighting for anything, and Bryan wants me to have the house, the van, and a big portion of his money. I'm confused. What husband wanting a divorce gives their wife everything? Why is he being so easy about this?

As I stuff the contract back in, it wrinkles a little. Instead of dwelling I get myself to stomach a bowl of instant ramen, and then spend the rest of the day with my son. We play and cuddle, watch his favorite shows, while I slowly attempt to heal.

It's going to be a long road. If it was a divorce without something anchoring us, it would be easy, but there's still a tiny human who loves us both and deserves to have parents who are civil with one another. Co-parenting with the man who broke my heart is going to be the hardest part of this. If he moves on, I'm not sure what I'll do. I'll have to take it day by day.

CHAPTER 36

The front door opens, reeling me from my thoughts. I'm leaning over the kitchen counter staring down at the signature, and his name under it. I wipe away the tears and quickly cover the page with the other mail scattered about.

It's been over two weeks since the fight with Bryan. Work and therapy have both been helping to keep my mind from fraying. I've been opening up a lot more in therapy and I'm slowly starting to understand where things went wrong. It's now about me allowing myself to heal and how I can overcome my wrongdoings.

"Charlotte?" Bryan peeks into the kitchen.

"Oh, hey. Sorry I got caught up in reading some mail."

For a second his eyes narrow in concern, like he wants to say something, because it's clear as day I've been crying. There's no way the tears have dried that fast. I can still feel the wetness on my cheeks. I sniffle.

"Okay," he says. There's a stone-cold edge to his voice, but his eyes hold a different story. He's still observing me from afar, but I don't think he's going to press me for answers.

He clears his throat. "Um... is Hunter ready? Connor and I are going to take him to the indoor kids place with the trampolines."

"I'll pack his ear defenders, in case. He's been having more issues with loud noise. I took him to the park the other day and he stood there with his hands over his ears while the kids were running around him."

Bryan nods. "Is there anything else I can do to help him?" he asks sincerely.

"Well, the best course of action would be preparing him for the environment. Talking or even a social story. So maybe next time let me know in advance so I can prepare him better."

When Bryan steps forward towards me as I come around the counter, I almost expect him to reach out and touch me, but his hand is at his side balled in a fist. "Maybe I should take him somewhere a little quieter."

"I mean you already made plans..."

"No, it's okay. We can figure out something more appropriate. I don't want to stress him out."

"I have a few things that could help." I walk past him but pause briefly as his hand rubs against mine. The butterflies flutter around in my stomach. I pretend I don't feel it, because it's probably all in my imagination, and make my way into the living room.

Hunter is on the couch watching his favorite episode of *Blue's Clues* for the hundredth time today.

Bryan follows and I grab a few fidget toys off the table. A pop-it, a tiny bean bag doggy he can squeeze, and a few others. "These work well, I'll stuff them in the bag."

Our movements around each other are stiff. I lift the bag, place the items in, then hand it to him in a robotic way. Everything feels off and I hate it so much, like things are final, like everything is over.

I kneel in front of Hunter. "Hey, Hunter." I attempt to get his attention. His eyes are on me, but really, they are focused behind me.

"Look, Mama, a clue!"

"Yes, baby, you're watching *Blue*, but Daddy is here. You want to go play with Daddy?"

He nods, and his body rocks. Bryan kneels beside me. Hunter flaps his hands. Bryan picks him up hugging him tight. He stands with him in his arms. I get to my feet and I'm only inches from Bryan. His lip quivers slightly, but he clears his throat once more, and any signs of him feeling remotely anything, vanishes.

"I'll come up with something calm for him to do. It's a beautiful day, maybe I'll break out the bike and take a ride with him."

"I think he'd like that," I say.

"Okay. I should go."

"Okay."

"Okay," he repeats but doesn't make an effort to move. His hooded eyes fall heavy. Exhaustion is weighing him down. He's been working non-stop, and this is his first day off.

"I'll drop him back off on Thursday."

"Okay."

I'm working for the next few days. I took some extra hours to fill the void of the empty house. Bryan offered to take Hunter and I'm not saying no to it. While our relationship might be over, I would never not allow him to see his son.

"Hunter, say goodbye to Mommy." Bryan's nose twitches and he sniffles. I peek up again and notice the hazy look in his eyes.

He leans Hunter towards me and when I go to kiss his cheek, Bryan's eyes linger on mine. I'm so close, his hot breath dances on my face. We meet each other's stares again, sorrow and want floating between us, but it's overshadowed by Hunter squealing.

"Bye, sweetheart," I say, placing another kiss on Hunter's cheek.

As he walks away, I wait for it. Wait for the moment when

Bryan turns back to look over his shoulder at me, like this is all some big misunderstanding. But he doesn't.

With tight rigid shoulders he straps Hunter into the car seat. The only time he stares at the house is when he sits in the driver's seat. But he never looks towards the front door. It is several long minutes before he pulls away.

I know what needs to be done. He hasn't mentioned the papers, but it's clear this is over.

> Me: Can you come over after work?

Seconds later my phone is ringing. Ellie's name on the screen. I lift the phone to my ear but can't form the words.

"Char, what is it?"

"I just need my best friend," I whisper, suppressing the urge to cry.

"Don't move, okay? Let me just... I'll be there in fifteen minutes."

"But you're at work—"

"I'm doing paperwork. I'll be there. Even though we ripped up those stupid rules, number nineteen still stands; If it's possible, drop everything when your best friend needs you. If not, reassure them and get there when you can."

I push out a laugh. "That list was..."

"I don't care. That rule will always be number one in my rulebook. Hang tight. Okay?"

I nod, even though she can't see me.

Twenty minutes later my front door bursts open and footsteps rush through the house. I'm at the kitchen table, my head in my hands with the divorce papers in front of me. Ellie nearly slides across the floor in her socks. She barrels into me and wraps me in her love.

I've cried so much the past few months, but this cry is an end-of-the-world one. It's got snot, ugly faces, loud noises that don't sound like me, and lots and lots of salty tears. I'm strong, I know I am, but my heart is in a fragile state right now.

Once the hiccups end and my body has stopped shaking, Ellie pulls up a seat beside me. She focuses on the papers.

"Are you going to do it?"

"I don't know what else to do. There are hints of regret on his face, but when he stares at me it's like I'm a random person he never loved." The words are blurring. Tear-drop stains are scattered over the document.

"Have you asked him?"

"No. But maybe it's what I need. Closure is better than limbo. Right?"

Ellie looks at me with sad eyes and I know she's struggling to tell me her opinion. She's trying to protect me from what I already know. If I got closure with the divorce I could move on and find a new life to live. I'm not the only person in the world going through this, and there are bigger problems out there, poverty, people fighting for their lives, losing their livelihoods, and here I am crying over a stupid broken heart. But then why does it feel as if the world is on fire?

"Honestly, Char. Maybe it's for the best. Going back and forth isn't good for anyone. Whatever you decide, I'm here, and I'm not going anywhere."

I lift the pen and let it linger over the line. Signing these papers doesn't mean my life is over. I have to channel the old Charlotte, the one who could take on the world in leather pants, like Charlie's Angels.

The pen hits the paper, a small dot forming. While I do this the hand covering the corner of the paper is wrapped up by Ellie's warm grasp. She holds on to it for dear life, as I would do for her if—God forbid—she and Logan split.

I press harder on the paper and slowly my name forms in black ink and my heart breaks for the millionth time, but I have no tears left to cry.

CHAPTER 37

"Hello, is this Mrs. Holmes?"

I cringe. I'm still not sure what I'll do with my last name. "Yeah, this is she."

"Hi. My name is Reginald Quinn. I work over at the Pee Wee Academy. You interviewed with us last week?"

It's nearly mid-March. I've pulled some of myself back together and went on two more interviews. While I love working at the store, it's not what I want to do. I want to get back into what I love.

"Yes."

"Well, if you are interested, we would like to offer you the full-time position in our 12:1:1 preschool room as a lead teacher. It currently only has eight students. Is that something you would be interested in taking on?"

I've worked in many different sized classrooms before, and a 12:1:1 consists of twelve students, a teacher, and an assistant. I can't help smiling. Not only is it the perfect class size, but Hunter's school is two blocks away. From the interview I learned the hours are similar, but it was the best option because my mom offered to do drop-off and pick-up.

"Yes. Yes of course. I would love to. I have to give my current job two weeks' notice; is that okay?"

"Of course, Mrs. Holmes."

We set up a time for me to come in to fill out the paperwork and give them background check information. When I hang up I immediately text Mom, Ellie, and Logan. Things are finally falling into place, even if there's one thing I still haven't done. I'm waiting to build up the nerve before I hand over the piece of paper that ends my marriage for good.

Feeling good, I head to Connor's house to pick up Hunter. It's a small two-bedroom California ranch a few towns over. He's a bachelor so Bryan is staying in the guest room.

The door opens and I'm greeted by Connor. He's tall, well over six foot. He and Bryan went to high school together and he was also the best man at our wedding. He shakes his brown hair from his eyes. "Hey, Charlotte. Looking lovely as usual."

Leggings and a gray sweater dress doesn't really qualify as dressing up too much, but maybe he's talking about the glow I feel from the phone call about the job.

"Thank you. It's nice to see you."

I step inside the living room. Hunter is playing with some toy trucks. He's lying down observing the wheels, unaware of my presence. I'm about to call his name when Bryan walks in, his hair wet and messy like he's just come from the shower. My pulse skips several beats. Seeing him with his freshly clean scent wafting through the room makes this so much harder. I try to ignore how handsome he truly is, but I'm drawn to his unbuttoned work uniform, and unable to pull my attention away.

"Hi," I whisper.

His eyes start at mine, before wandering down, taking me in. It's a slow descent, as he takes in my entire body before he meets my eyes again. The butterflies aren't dead. They are more aggressive today. I try to forget them.

"Hey, Char. He's all ready to go. Um… he cried when we took

him to dinner last night. I'm not sure if maybe he's not feeling well, or if it was too much, but we took a to-go doggy bag, came home and he ate here. His teacher said he was okay today, but I'd just keep an eye on him."

"Oh. Okay. Thanks for letting me know."

He nods.

"Well, I'll let you two do your thing. It was good seeing you, Charlotte," Connor says. He waves at me as he walks back towards the bedrooms.

"Other than that, everything went well. You look nice today. Going somewhere?" he asks.

"No. I just… I'm having a good day, that's all."

He takes another step forward, closing in the distance between us. Watching me, he closes the buttons of his shirt. My eyes wander to his hands and memories flash of me buttoning his shirts after we had a long night together and he'd be off to work.

"Ah. Okay. I'm working a lot the next few days, but I'll text."

"Are you working more over-time?"

He shrugs. "I have nothing else happening, so…" He lowers his head, and for a brief second closes his eyes, and when they flutter open, they swing back up to me.

Silence lingers between us, and when he goes to take another step, I expect it to be in my direction, but he goes to the left and scoops Hunter up off the floor. I can't take my eyes off him as he hugs his son like he'll never see him again.

"Oh, I um… so I got a full-time position. It's at the Pee Wee school. It's close by and on days when you can't, Mom said she'd drop off and pick up Hunter. I start in two weeks."

"Charlotte, I still want to provide…"

I hold up my hand, turning away, so I can't see him. "I know, and part-time was nice, but I need this. I feel like I've been home for so long I don't even know who I am anymore." I want to tell him that's where everything went wrong, but I hold back. I'm trying to heal and rehashing it with him is not moving forward only back.

"When you have him in your care, I have nothing. I want to feel human again."

"Okay. I understand, I... never mind," he sighs.

I don't allow the conversation to continue, no matter how curious I am to find out what he was going to say.

Bryan walks with Hunter hand in hand to the car. I stand behind him as he buckles him into the car seat. When he's done, he turns, jumps a little, and places a hand over his chest. "Sorry. I uh, let me know when I can see him again."

"You can take him whenever you want, Bry. I'd never come between you and your son."

"I know," he whispers.

A soft wind ruffles my hair. Bryan reaches up out of habit to replace the flying hair behind my ear. A silent gasp escapes my lips.

When our eyes meet, he pulls back and shoves his hands in his pocket. "Bye, Char." With his head down he walks away, and for a moment I almost think he's about to turn back, but he doesn't quite make it all the way. I shut the van door and hop into the driver's side. By the time I glance up Bryan's already inside the house.

CHAPTER 38

March is flying by. Spring is in the air, and I'm loving the beautiful sunshine. Some days it's been nice enough to open the windows. Spring is a time for new beginnings, and I think I'm well on the path to this new normal.

I love my job. My students are sensational, and my co-teacher has been amazing in showing me how things work. Ellie and Lily were a bit sad that I'll no longer be working at Sheer Threads, but I did offer to work during the holidays if they need part-time workers for the weekends.

Things have been okay between Bryan and me. I've already seen him twice this week and haven't felt the urge to break down. It's a good thing, or so I've been told, but it still doesn't feel good.

Keys jiggle in the front door, and it opens. "Char?"

"In the kitchen!" I'm on my back under the sink trying to figure out why my pipe is leaking. I'm not good at home repair, but if I can figure out the exact location maybe I can get a better idea of what's happening. A droplet hits me square on the bridge of my nose. I growl at no one. I'm already struggling to hold the flashlight upright, by placing it under my armpit and shining it up.

"Everything okay under there?" Bryan asks.

I lift my head, although I expected him to walk in, I'm not prepared for how close his voice is. My head meets the pipe, not hard, but enough to disorient me. "Fuck, ow," I groan.

Bryan chuckles. "Hitting your head again to get my attention?"

"Funny." I smirk and rub the spot on my forehead.

"Come out of there before you hurt yourself further." He holds his hand out. His face is shadowed by the darkness of the cabinet.

I can't read his expression. Grabbing hold of his hand, I try not to act like it still feels like home. I slide out and his fingers immediately go to my forehead to examine my clumsy bump.

"A little red, nothing too crazy." His hand lingers there. My eyes roll up as his fingers dance across the spot.

"Glad to hear."

He grabs an ice pack from the freezer and a towel, then presses it to my head. I reach up to take over and my hand touches his. My lips part. A soft gasp tumbles out of both our mouths in unison. He pulls away quickly as I keep the cold pack to my head.

"So, what's going on down there?" He pulls away but doesn't hide the hesitation in his retreat.

I place the pack of ice on the counter. "There's a drip and I don't know where it's coming from."

He sighs. "I'll take a look." Bryan rolls up the sleeve of his uniform. He just got out of work and is taking Hunter out for dinner but will be bringing him back later because he has to work in the morning.

"I can call a plumber…"

"Char, it's fine. Anything you need, I'll take care of you." He pauses. "Of it. Whatever it is."

Every time he tells me this, it doesn't get any easier to let go.

He slides under in the same position I was in and reaches out for the light. I hand it to him. My brain needs a switch to shut off the emotional side when I need it to stop yelling at me. Seeing him under there, comfortable, like this was still his home, is enough to make me want to cross the room and tear up the papers I signed. But this time there's no going back. If he wanted to talk, I'm sure he would have already.

"I'll be right back. My toolbox is still in the basement?" he asks.

"Yeah. I never moved it."

"Perfect." He slides himself out, wipes his hands and then heads downstairs. While he's down there I send a text to Ellie.

> Me: He's here. He's fixing the sink. How can I give him the papers now?

It's been weeks, but I think if I don't do it soon I never will.

Come on, Ellie. Answer your phone, please. I lean over the counter and tap a beat on the surface with an impatient finger.

> Ellie: Has he asked about it?

> Me: No. That's the strange part. I mean doesn't he want to move on?

Ellie is taking forever to type, and I have no idea what's taking Bryan so long to find his toolbox. I didn't move it.

> Ellie: Maybe he doesn't. What if you brought it up that you signed it, or ask him if he wants the papers? Gauge his response. I hate to say it, but are you sure this is what he wants?

With Bryan, I'm never sure. He acts as if everything is done, but his eyes are always telling a different story.

> Me: If he wanted us to work wouldn't he have tried already?

> Ellie: Not necessarily. Men are stubborn. Do you need me to come over later?

> Me: I'm scared.

> Ellie: Is that a yes?

> Me: I think I'll be okay. I'll let you know.

It's been over ten minutes since he went down there. I'm about to make my way to the basement steps when Bryan walks into the room. He refuses to meet my eye at first, but when he does, his are rimmed with redness like he'd been crying.

"Everything okay? Thought you got lost down there."

"Yeah. G-good. Everything i-is… everything is okay. Can you get me a dish rag?"

I hand him one from the closet then excuse myself to go check on Hunter in the living room. I left him sitting in front of the TV while I was figuring out the sink debacle. He rocks back and forth as Steve is trying to find a clue he keeps staring at. I roll my eyes. *Come on, Steve, it's right there in front of your eyes.*

"Momma, Steve got letter," he says, flapping with excitement.

"That's awesome. What did it say?"

"It's a secret."

It's amazing how far along he's come in such a short time. From not talking, to babbling, then one word, and now two-, three-, even four-word sentences. This little boy is going places.

Instead of going back in to check on Bryan I sit beside Hunter. He doesn't notice me but being here with him is better than watching my ex fix things around the house.

"Just had to tighten the packing nut." Bryan's abrupt voice startles me.

I glance over my shoulder at him. "The who, what?"

Bryan laughs; it's held back, and doesn't sound like him.

I stand and turn in his direction. "Thank you for helping me. I'm sorry it cut into your dinner with Hunter…"

"It's okay. Anything you guys need. Like I said, before you call a professional, call me."

"Because you know more than them?"

He grins, but his laughter has died out. "No, because it will save you money if it's an easy fix."

I tap my lip. "Let me guess: you saw it on YouTube."

He allows himself to laugh again, the sound brittle and broken. Why does he seem so sad? I know it can't be about us.

"Hey, remember the time I had to take apart your laptop to add memory? That was all YouTube."

I roll my eyes. The movement is playful, but the feeling doesn't last. My hollow chuckle dies out with the knowledge of what I have to do.

"I'll put these back down—"

"I signed the papers." I hold my arms down at my sides and clench my hands into fists. "I uh, I signed them."

He winces. His eyes stare off behind me, a distant look clouding them. My chin trembles, but I bite down to suppress the emotion.

"Oh. The papers." A shadow falls over his sullen face. "You signed them?"

This is weird. I thought he wanted me to. He had them drawn up and sent to the house, and even signed them. We haven't talked about them since he said they were getting done, but now he doesn't seem ready. Or maybe it's my imagination.

"Yeah," I whisper. "Let me get them."

"You can give them to me when I drop him off."

"Okay. Yeah. Yeah, I'll do that then."

"You ready, Hunter?" His voice raises an octave.

When the two of them leave and the house is calm and quiet, I take the toolbox Bryan left behind and bring it downstairs. I shove it back onto one of the large wooden shelves. The basement is old, not the nicest room in the house. There's not much down here and it's cold. A chill surges through me and I hold myself together with my arms crossed at my chest.

I'm about to go upstairs when something catches my attention. On the floor to the left of the stairs beside an old folding table there is a photo. I cross the room and bend, flipping the picture over. I cover my mouth as the image shocks me. I land on my ass on the hard floor. Our favorite wedding photo is staring back at me.

I lift myself up by grasping the table. A book lies on it: our wedding album. Biting my top lip, I dig in so hard I expect to taste blood. My eyes flicker back over to the shelf where I'd put his tools. Above the toolbox is another shelf and a green storage box. It's partially opened and it's the same one I had the wedding album in.

His reddened eyes and change in demeanor were because of this. *No, Charlotte*, I tell myself, *it's over. It's better this way, and you're just setting yourself up for more disappointment.*

I slip the picture back into the empty space inside the album. Out of all the pictures, he chose my favorite one. We took pictures outside the venue where they had this fancy pool. The photographer had him dip me to make it look like he was going to toss me into the pool, and while I almost went tumbling in, there's nothing but pure love in Bryan's stare.

Slamming the book shut, I try to put it away, but as I grab the box it comes crashing down and all the photos and our glass candle centerpieces come crashing to the ground with it. Glass shards scatter everywhere.

Will this ever get easier?

"He's out cold," Bryan says, jogging down the stairs.

I won't mention the wedding album or ask why he was looking at it. Maybe it was his closure.

"Great. Thank you. I'm sure he had a great time." In my hands against my chest is the envelope with the papers. If I don't do it now, I never will.

I thrust it away from me like it's on fire. "Here," I say. I keep my eyes down at an angle and stare off to the left instead.

"Oh. Right. The papers. So, they're signed?"

I nod. "I thought you wanted me to…"

"Yeah. Okay. I'll g-get it to my lawyer soon." Bryan goes still, and I make the mistake of looking up, and when I do, he's blinking away the moisture pooled in his eyes.

My heart is screaming at me to reach out, to take those papers from his hands and tear them up, but I don't.

"Have a good night," I whisper.

"You too, Char." As he reaches the door, I expect him to leave without acknowledging me, but when his hand touches the knob in the porch, he glances back. His piercing glassy eyes stare right at me. For a minute I think he's going to backtrack, but instead he turns and walks out the door, again.

I don't cry, maybe I've done it enough.

> Me: It's done. He turned back, he looked at me, and then he was gone.

> Ellie: Leave your door open, I'll be there in ten!

> Me: It's a weeknight, don't you have work tomorrow?

> Ellie: You do too. *Cough, cough* Oh darn. I think I've come down with the flu.

> Me: I hope it's not a man cold.

Ellie: LOL! Definitely not. The doctor says some wine and a healthy dosing of Camp Rock One and Two will do.

Out of everyone in my life Ellie is my person. I wish you could marry your best friend, because she is the only one who has never disappointed me. Even when she kept her and Logan's relationship a secret, she never once broke my heart. If I can help it, I never want to feel this kind of pain again. It hurts to breathe.

Ellie: OMW. Don't start without me!

Me: Wouldn't dream of it. 🩶🩶🩶

CHAPTER 39

Life has moved forward. Bryan and I haven't discussed the papers. I wait anxiously for the day when it becomes official, but it's already April and I still haven't heard a thing. Spring is here for sure, in full force too. Today is a pleasant day, no jacket or sweatshirt needed. The sun is shining and I'm out on the playground with my class.

While there is still a gaping hole in my heart, I'm almost myself again. Therapy has been a huge asset and this job even more so. While some days are hard, I'm managing so much better than I did those first six months. Bryan seems happier too and our co-parenting skills are better than I imagined.

"Oh, no. Billy, we can't bring the rock back to class. It lives out here."

Billy, who is one of the sweetest kids I've ever known, likes to collect rocks. His mom warned us how when they go to the playground she ends up with rocks in her washer. I've been trying to get him to leave them in a certain spot, so he can come back and play with them at recess.

Billy's wide green eyes stare up at me. I smile, and take the rock, put it with the others, then redirect him back towards the school building. It's time for lunch anyway.

"Boys and girls, let's all line up behind Billy."

My co-teacher, May, helps me gather the kids to form a line. She pushes her strawberry blonde hair up into a high pony, like she's ready to take on a huge task.

We start for the school when a very serious Hannah Taylor, principal of the Pee Wee school comes strutting towards us. Her black heels click along the pavement. "Mrs. Holmes. Can I steal you away for a moment?" Hannah asks. Her cheeks are flushed, and her eyes tell a story of concern.

"Yeah, sure. May will take the kids back inside. Are you good with that?"

"Yeah. No problem."

"Your son's school called." Hannah doesn't waste a beat. "He went missing on the playground. They have called the precinct and are searching. The school has gone into a soft lockdown. They said they couldn't get in touch with your husband, though."

My heart stops and if I wasn't still breathing, I'd think I was dead. Those words are not anything a mother wants to hear. I have noticed Hunter becoming more distracted lately and wandering a bit more frequently, but he has never eloped.

"Is my classroom covered?"

"Yeah, you don't worry about a thing, we've got the substitute on her way now."

"Thank you." I hurry to gather my things and attempt to stay calm. It's harder than it seems, but so far, I'm holding it together. I'm trying to get out without my kids being too aware of the change. Some of them have a hard time when their routine gets jumbled. Charlene, one of the young girls, cries out for me as I leave, but thankfully May is there to hug her.

The second I'm in the car I dial Bryan's number. Turning the key in the ignition I back out.

"Hello this is Bryan."

Straight to voicemail.

"Fuck, Bryan. Where are you?"

My hands tremble as I pull out of the school parking lot. I'm so glad Hunter's school is close. I'm not sure I could handle a longer drive than this. The build-up of tears sits heavy in my eyes but I have to push them back, because, while I'm terrified, I have to be strong. I've come so far, the last few weeks and I know I can think logically when I'm calm.

"Bryan, where are you? Our son is missing from school. Please call me when you get this. I'm begging you, Bry."

Hanging up again, I call Connor, but he doesn't answer either. I hit the steering wheel as I come to a stop at a red light. When I arrive, I don't bother to pull into the lot. It's on the other side of the building and I'm not waiting another second. My parking job is terrible. The ass end of the van is sticking out into the street, but I ignore it.

I dial Bryan again. *Where the fuck is he?* When he doesn't answer for a third time, I want to revert to the weak Charlotte who got angry at him, but instead a wave of concern rushes over me. Maybe he knows already? And is here? Someone at the precinct must have told him.

As I step foot on the grassy knoll in front of the school, I call Mom. "Mom?" My voice wavers, but I'm still keeping the tears at bay. "It's Hunter, he's gone missing from school. I'm here now."

My body seems to be stuck in slow motion, or it's my mind. I can't get to the main entrance quick enough.

"Oh, honey, do you need me to come down and help search?"

"No, yes, I don't know. Can you try and call Bryan? He's not answering."

"Yes of course."

A white and blue police car comes zooming up the circular driveway in front of me. I immediately recognize the man inside. It's Keith. He steps out and sees me crossing the grass. I hurry to him as Vivian, his partner steps out, her hair pulled back into a tight bun under her blue hat.

"Charlotte." She's around the squad car in a heartbeat.

Coming out of the bright red doors of the school is Principal Mullens and Hunter's teacher Mrs. Grey. A little pressure subsides as I see them diligently doing everything in their power to find Hunter.

"Is Bryan in today? He's not answering his phone."

Vivian touches my arm and squeezes it lightly.

"I'll radio him," Keith says. "I think he's close by. Give me a minute. Vivian, go with Char, will you?"

"Of course."

She wraps her arms around me. She has a daughter around Hunter's age, so I know she's putting herself in my shoes. Keith walks back to the car and sits half in and out, the static of the radio bleeding out of the opened door.

"I am so terribly sorry, Mrs. Holmes."

I understand Mrs. Grey's dismay. Not only as a mom, but as a teacher, losing a kid is one of my biggest fears. Whether they are yours or not it is terrifying, especially on your watch.

Worry lines crease her forehead, her eyes glisten like I'm sure mine are. She's plagued with the guilt of losing him.

"We were on the playground, and he was so interested in the daffodils. We talked about them for a few minutes, and then one of the other students fell so I raced to them. When I looked back the gate was wide open, and Hunter was gone. I searched the perimeter, but I don't know what happened." She's sniffling and using a tissue to wipe her nose.

"I'm so sorry, Mrs. Holmes," Principal Mullins says, greeting me with a warm yet firm smile. "Should we go talk inside?"

A hard lump forms in my throat as the burning sensation in my eyes becomes more and more harsh. I keep trying to tell myself it will all be okay. "Can I search for him? He shouldn't be too far."

"I'll go with you," Vivian offers.

While Mrs. Grey escorts us to the back playground, Keith hangs back with Mrs. Mullins to take a report, and hopefully get in touch with Bryan.

My eyes frantically dart around as we walk to the right side of the building. The school sits in front of an open green field. Behind it is a wooded area, and my heart sinks. It's not deep woods. There are horse riding trails and hiking trails.

"Did anyone check back there?" I ask.

She opens her mouth to respond when screeching tires along the street catches our attention.

Bryan jumps out of the passenger side almost before the car has stopped.

"Bryan!" I yell for him, but it comes out sounding like a blood-curdling scream as reality comes crashing down.

When he hears me and races across the field to where we are, my eyes can't hold the tears back anymore. They race down my cheeks as fast as he's running. He hops the black chain-link fence separating the fields from the street and is to me in seconds. I suck in a breath as his body collides with mine without hesitation.

"What happened?" he asks, taking my face in his hands.

He's ignoring Vivian and Mrs. Grey. His full attention is on me falling apart in his arms.

My body is trembling so much I can hardly get my words out. It's all hit me so hard. "Hunter walked out of the p-playground." My chest is heaving with heavy sobs. I've become complete mush in Bryan's arms.

"Mr. Holmes," Mrs. Grey says.

He doesn't let go of me but turns to her.

"Your son was playing on the playground collecting flowers. I turned to help another child and when I looked back the gate was open, and he was gone. I am so, so sorry. We are doing everything we can to find him."

"I know. Thank you for calling the station right away. I was out on a call, which is why I didn't know at first."

His attention is back on me. "Char. Look at me." His voice is soft, yet trembles with worry.

I take several calming breaths and meet his gaze for truly the first time in what feels like forever. There's not a single hint of hostility in his eyes.

"It's going to be okay. I will find our son." He plants a warm comforting kiss to my forehead. He holds it only seconds, but it feels like hours, then pulls away and starts for the wooded area. I compose myself because crying isn't going to get me anywhere.

I turn to Mrs. Grey. "You said he was picking the daffodils, right?" I ask.

"Yeah."

A thought hits me so I scan the field. There's a line of white daffodils at the edge of the wooded area. Without another word to her or Vivian I head off that way. The white flowers are peeking through the grass. It's nice to see new life in the world after the emptiness of winter.

I take note of how there are clearly some missing from the clusters. A flash of blue running through the trees to my right catches me off guard.

"Bryan." I point to the flowers. He slows when he approaches. "He was picking daffodils; there's some missing that way."

His eyes follow where I'm pointing. We run on opposite sides. Him along the beaten path of the woods, and me along the green grass of the field.

"Charlotte, I think I see something, quick over here." He steps towards me and holds out his hand. I make my way through the blossoming branches of bushes and trees and onto the path with him. We let go of each other and he takes off ahead of me. I'm only a few paces behind.

His feet pound on the dirt as he runs. I waver through some of the leftover fallen leaves from autumn, and through some sharp sticks of newly budded bushes and trees. I fall in line beside him as I catch up. My chest heaves from running, I'm not very athletic and will be feeling it later, but the adrenaline coursing through me is no match for my out of shape body.

Something moves in the short distance and stands. A small figure with an armful of flowers.

"Hunter!" We yell at the same time.

He doesn't hear us at first, and while I'm gasping for air, Bryan's tall lean body lunges forward. When Bryan calls his name again, Hunter turns, and a smile lights up his face. He had no idea he was lost or that we were worried, he was happily picking a whole bouquet of flowers.

Bryan skids to a stop beside him, scuffing up his shoes and dirtying his blue uniform. I get there only seconds later and kneel to wrap Hunter in my arms. I'm sobbing, gripping him, allowing all my emotions to flood out. Bryan sniffles. There's pure panic in his shimmering blue eyes.

I free one hand from Hunter and pull Bryan against me. He leans in, kissing the top of my head. All the fears running through me somehow subside from the simple touch of his kiss. I inhale and hold my breath, needing a moment to remember what it felt like when we were one unit.

"Mama, Dada, flowers. Mama, you have flowers. Dada says dat Mama are sad, give flowers. White flowers, New Years. We give white flowers. Mama no sad no more."

He's quiet for a few seconds, then says, "Mama, Dada, together? Please together?" he asks.

"Oh, Hunter." I'm sobbing all over again.

He's smarter than we think sometimes. I've always known he was a bright kid, but he pays more attention to what's happening around him than we think.

Bryan places a steady hand on my back. "Let me radio Keith to let them know they can call off the search."

"The flowers are beautiful, Hunter, but you can't leave school.

You had Mommy and Daddy so worried. You have to stay with Mrs. Grey. No matter how pretty the flowers are, okay, buddy."

"I'm sorry, Mama. Don't be sad."

I grab a tighter hold of him, squishing the flowers between us. Bryan's light touch on my shoulder causes me to jump. I gasp. My lips won't stop trembling. With a knowing sigh, he kneels beside me, cupping my cheeks in his hands. He holds me there without saying a word, but through the silence his words are louder than anything.

"Come on. Let's get you two home."

He helps get me to my feet.

"Hunter, why don't you put the flowers down—"

"No. No. No." His eyes well with tears as he clenches them to his chest, shaking his head.

"Okay, okay." I lift him and the flowers in my arms.

"Want me to take him?"

I shake my head. "I'm okay."

CHAPTER 40

Mrs. Grey's shoulder's fall when we come out of the woods, and it nearly brings me to my knees. I know she didn't mean for it to happen.

"I am so relieved you found him," she says, taking a few steps closer as we enter the playground.

Keith and Vivian are standing with her, talking to Principal Mullins. The panic on her face subsides too.

We stop walking and Bryan grabs my hand, making me turn to him. I'm met by the eyes of the man who came to my rescue. Not once, not twice, but so many times. I've made such a huge mistake letting him go. I didn't mean to lose myself or fight with him over trivial things. I hate that it took therapy for me to realize all the wrongs I need to make right. What if it's too late to fix what I broke?

"I'm going to take care of a few things with Keith and Vivian, and I'll come back to the house when I'm done. Will you be okay?"

Keith clears his throat. "Bryan?"

We both turn to him.

"I was told to let you go home with Charlotte and Hunter when we're done. We can handle the rest."

Bryan gives his friend a swift nod. His attention is back on me as the group retreats towards the building. "Charlotte, would it be okay if I came home with you?"

My chest trembles, and my jaw clenches as I nod. I don't try and hide the tears. There are so many things I need to say to Bryan. I have so much to apologize for.

"Daddy, come home and stay," Hunter says.

My lips part and I'm about to tell him I don't think it's possible, but then I'm torn away from Hunter's reaction to Bryan's. He gives one of those half smiles and shrugs. We are both thinking the same thing. We'd underestimated how much this affected our son. I'd like to try again for his sake and for ours too, but it's up to Bryan. And as the thought pops into my head, Bryan speaks.

"That's up to Mommy," Bryan says.

"I'm open for discussion."

As I say the words Bryan's shoulder's fall and his smile becomes watery. "Let's go finish up with everything and then we'll head home. Okay, buddy?"

Bryan messes up Hunter's hair and our beautiful boy giggles. "K, Daddy."

My body aches all over from how tense it's been, not only from today, but from the last year. Standing over Hunter, I watch his back rising and falling in slow motions. The build-up of tears is starting again. I can't help them. They have been happening on and off since we got home.

When we got back, Bryan helped me bathe him, ran out in the van to go get Hunter's favorite fast food, then we watched hours of *Blue's Clues* and *Blippi* until Hunter dozed off a few minutes ago. It's close to nine but feels much later. This day has taken a toll on us.

Arms snake around me, and I fall back into Bryan. He holds my weight as I nearly crumble. Tears slowly stream down my face. We didn't have a chance to talk when our son was awake. Hunter has already dealt with so much and has seen far too much between us. So we mutually agreed to wait until he went to sleep to talk.

"Come on, Char. Let's not wake him. Okay?"

I nod because my voice is blocked by the large knot in my throat. Out in the hallway Bryan closes the bedroom door, but not all the way. Without thinking I wrap my arms around him. He teeters a bit and chuckles lightly into my hair. "You almost took me out there."

When I don't laugh, he presses me closer, using one hand to gently stroke my hair. "I'm so sorry I didn't pick up, Char. I'm so sorry." His tears wet my temples. I almost pull away, but instead I take his face into my hands and run my thumb along his cheek.

"I was wrong, Charlotte."

I cock my brow. "Wrong?" The word somehow slips through the knot.

He waits while soft sobs rattle his chest. "Wrong for not telling you why I worked all those hours. Wrong for not understanding your side of things. Trying to hold you back, telling you it's better to stay home, and for not believing Hunter needed help. All of it, Charlotte. I am so sorry."

I lift on my toes and pull him down so our heads meet.

"I sta-sta-started to see a therapist too. She made me see everything I was doing wrong in our relationship and helped me figure out how to work on myself. I wish I would have realized sooner, because then I wouldn't have lost you."

He presses his eyes closed tight, allowing for more tears. The sobs build in my own chest, releasing a fresh set of tears.

"Have you been sad? Was Hunter telling the truth?"

I nod. Sure, things were heading in the right direction, but still, nothing felt right without Bryan.

"I-I've been getting better. Feeling like myself again. This job has given me a life. My therapist says I'm making huge strides and I think I'm in a good place. But yes." I breathe out slowly. "I still cry. The other day I was cleaning out the closet and a photo frame fell out. It was the picture of us on our honeymoon, the one on the beach. Hunter found me sitting in front of it crying."

"I don't want to make you cry anymore, Char. I want to make things right between us. I'm sorry I never told you I had therapy. I was ashamed and embarrassed. You have such a big heart, Charlotte. You would have seen past it, seen past all the dark moments I had with it. You would have loved me either way."

"I'm also sorry. The depression of being a stay-at-home mom took the woman you met and turned her into someone who I didn't like. I never meant to push your buttons. We both were at fault. I don't blame you, we both lost a bit of ourselves when Hunter was born, and it happens. We aren't alone."

He sighs, pressing further into me and I'm basking in it. His warmth, the way he's holding on.

"I don't want to do this anymore. I don't want to be without you. Hunter needs you. I need you. We should be a family. No regrets, Bry. I don't want any. I can't lose you the way my mom lost my dad."

My chest heaves with long sad sobs, and my hand slips from his face. He wraps me into him with an embrace so tight I can barely breathe, but I'm happy there.

"Baby, I don't want to be without you either."

"But the papers," I say, glancing back up. "We signed them already."

"What papers?" He narrows his eyes down at me with his glassy gaze.

My lip twitches.

"I never sent them in," he confesses. "I was hoping you'd come back to me. I wanted it so bad, and I was waiting."

"You waited for me?" I ask, leaning into his touch.

"Of course I did. You're my whole world. Without you it was like I stopped living. I was going through the motions, but nothing felt right. Not without you by my side. I want to be with you and Hunter. I never want to be apart from either of you again. I know we're going to fight; every couple fights. But I want it to work."

"Really?" I love the sincerity in his words.

"I told you, Char. I'm all in. I've always been all in. I was worried I wasn't good enough."

"You're so much more than enough."

"I have faith we're going to make this work. For our son, mostly, and for us. Because I know nothing in this world is worth living for if I'm not living it with both of you. I'd like to try couple's therapy with you, because you're the only woman I want in my life, and if we need a little help to get things back to the way they were, I'll do it. I'll do anything, Charlotte. Anything."

I reach up and brush away the tears from the corner of his eyes, then wipe away the few that have grazed his lip. We don't make it to the bedroom before our lips crash into each other, hungry for what we've both been missing.

Pushing my hand against his chest, our lips never part as he walks towards our room. Our. Gosh that sounds nice. He's taking small steps backwards as I guide him with my hand. When the door shuts, trapping us both inside, a new one opens with opportunities for our family. While I know our relationship isn't perfect, Bryan and I will make it through till the end.

EPILOGUE

8 MONTHS LATER

"Am I really doing this?" Ellie asks.

Her face is pale, a hint of green shining through. She glances down at the sparkling ring on her finger, then up at me.

It's here. Ellie and Logan's wedding day. They are getting married in their backyard, inside a heated tent, with fifty of their friends and family. It's small and intimate and is the perfect sized wedding for them. They don't like over the top fancy, and everything is perfect, like a fairy tale.

"You are," I say, grabbing hold of her face.

She blinks, tears sticking to her long dark lashes.

"Why are you crying?" I ask.

"I can't believe I broke our rule." She chuckles, through her tears.

"I can't believe you're marrying my dorky brother."

She swallows hard. I reach down and take her trembling hands in mine. "But I am so happy you are, and I get to call you my sister, for real now. I mean, we were sisters well before this, but now it's kind of more official."

"It is, isn't it?" She takes a few deep breaths. "It feels like yesterday I was watching you get married. And now, you've got one beautiful kid and another on the way," she says, touching my round growing belly.

I smile so wide it hurts my cheeks. "It's been a long journey, but here we are, and I've never been happier than I am now. Sure, things aren't one hundred percent perfect, but nothing feels like the end of the world. This all feels like the beginning."

"Yeah. It does."

"Ellie, it's time," her mom says, as she slides in next to her. She's the one walking Ellie down the aisle today as her father is out of the picture, and she and her brother don't get along.

"You got this. I love you," I say.

"I love you too."

I lean in for a hug and she wraps me in her arms, holding me like she never wants to let go. Ellie and I have always been destined to be sisters; there's not one single person I'd want to share these moments with other than her.

A few minutes later, I'm standing at the altar waiting for her to appear. My eyes are glued to the back of the tent where Ellie is about to walk through. Logan stands a few feet away from me in front of a large wooden arch, like the one Bryan and I had at our wedding. His body sways back and forth while he waits for the woman he loves, my best friend, to walk down the aisle towards him. He fidgets with his jacket and clears his throat.

Logan's dark eyes shimmer in the twinkling lights hung all around us. Our eyes meet and I place my hand over my heart. He nods in understanding. Logan has always loved Ellie, loved her more than anyone I know. His nerves are getting the best of him. He reaches up and wipes at the corner of his eye.

I close the distance between us and set a hand on his shoulder. "Hey, don't look so nervous. She's loved you almost our whole lives; nothing will ever change that."

I find my own husband watching me with a glimmer of love in his shining blue eyes. A year ago, I imagined this might have been a little bit different. The man I love wouldn't be standing beside Logan as one of his groomsmen. Our love almost slipped away, and lingering in Logan's eyes I see the same fear I felt all those months ago. I know he's scared, afraid he'll mess up, because he has in the past.

"I trust you with her heart, Logan. More than anyone else."

As I say this, the guests stand. Down the end of the aisle is Ellie with her mom.

"Dad would be proud of you. You know that, right?" I whisper.

Logan stares at me briefly, and nods. I reach up, and plant a soft kiss to his cheek, then step away. My eyes land back on Ellie and the tears start almost immediately. My best friend is the most beautiful woman in the world. I love the simplicity of her white knee-length dress. We were sold on it when she twirled around, and it lifted in the air as she spun. Underneath, the tule made it a little fluffy, it was simple yet elegant. It goes perfectly with Logan's midnight blue tuxedo.

The hairs on my neck stand she walks towards my brother. His eyes are solely planted on her and no one else. Mine drift. They wander over to my person. The man who, despite everything, gave us a second chance and a new life as a soon-to-be family of four.

He's already watching me, and I don't think I'll ever get over how my entire body tingles and comes to life when he looks at me. It's ten times stronger than it was before our separation.

Ellie steps between us; a tear rolls down her cheek. As MOH I reach behind me on a small bench for my pack of tissues, and hand one each to Ellie and Logan. They thank me, as a soft chuckle echoes through the guests.

As Ellie and Logan stand before one another, Some of my attention is still across the way, on Bryan. Beside him stands our son. He's all dressed in a shiny black tuxedo and stands stiff as a board holding on to the small white pillow. He has taken his duty as ring bearer very seriously.

When the priest asks for the rings, Hunter squares his little shoulders and Bryan has to give him a nudge to walk forward. Ellie smiles at me. Her hair is swirling in beautiful ringlets over the lace at the top of the dress.

There's a few soft giggles and we turn our attention to Hunter and Logan. He whispers something to him, and Logan chuckles, then gives his nephew a kiss on the head. He stands, and returns to Ellie, ring in hand.

"Ellie Garner," Logan says, blinking back tears. "I've known I was in love with you since we were eight. I'd give little hints, but I was icky back then, probably even had cooties."

Even from here with her head turned from me, I know she's rolling her eyes at him.

"My biggest grand gesture, the famous ice cream melting incident, was when it became clearer to me. You were the one, but how could I tell you without my sister killing me?"

There's a chorus of laughter at his words.

"The night we almost kissed I was not in a good place, and maybe me vanishing for a while is what brought us to the pivotal moment at Charlotte's wedding when you caught sight of me from across the room and made a face. I knew then you'd forgiven me for leaving you all behind."

Logan's eyes bubble over with tears, and Ellie reaches up to wipe them away, her own shoulders shaking with light sobs.

"My dad always loved you, El. He knew I did too. In fact, I never told you or anyone this, but he told me I shouldn't give up on you, to wait until the time was right, and although it felt like it took a lifetime, I'm so glad life brought me back to you. I know I'll never live up to Charlotte, and your obsession with the Jonas Brothers."

Now I'm bawling like a baby. No one could ever love my best friend as much as I do, but I think Logan comes in a close second.

"But I do know I can't wait to start this new journey together.

Ellie Garner, I, Logan Fields will love you forever—or as long as you'll put up with me." Logan chuckles, and Ellie does too.

He slips the ring on her finger, and then it's Ellie's turn. She cries through most of her words, but Logan doesn't care, he's too busy falling in love over and over.

When the ceremony ends, I rejoin Bryan and Hunter in the center to walk down the aisle. He takes my arm in his. His eyes beaming with love for me.

"I love you," he whispers in my ear.

"Love you, for always," I say.

Bryan's eyes light up with a smile as the three of us head down the aisle together, a whole unit once again.

Today might be perfect, and even if tomorrow is not, I'm okay with it. And if I've learned anything, it's that I need to live here in the now, take in everything I can, because any of us could leave this earth, like my dad. I never want to regret a single moment with anyone I love, and I'm grateful for every experience good or bad because it led me back here, where I belong.

THE END

ALSO BY REGINA BROWNELL

The Two Week Promise

One Lucky Christmas

Capturing His Heart

A NOTE FROM THE PUBLISHER

Thank you for reading this book. If you enjoyed it please do consider leaving a review on Amazon to help others find it too.

We hate typos. All of our books have been rigorously edited and proofread, but sometimes mistakes do slip through. If you have spotted a typo, please do let us know and we can get it amended within hours.

info@bloodhoundbooks.com